A SHORTCUT TO MURDER

The Dr Adam Bascom Mysteries

WILLIAM SAVAGE

Published October 2016

ISBN 978-1-520321509

Ridge&Bourne
PUBLICATIONS

For Jenn

A SHORTCUT TO MURDER

One

The Hunt Begins

"HOW DID YOU DO IT?" DR ADAM BASCOM ASKED. The young man was looking self-conscious without his coat and shirt. "You've succeeded in hurting yourself badly. These bruises are as severe as any I've seen in a good few years." His patient was about to reply, Adam's touch on the side of his chest caused him to gasp instead.

"Did that hurt?"

"Indeed it did, sir," the patient said. "Like the very devil."

"Hmm," Adam said. "Thought it might."

"Might I be allowed to ask why you did it then?"

"Had to be sure. Very well, you may put your shirt and coat on, Mr Scudamore. Pray excuse me a moment while you do that."

Adam returned to his desk, sat down, took up pen and paper and wrote a short note. When he had finished, he sanded the note carefully, blew away the excess, folded the paper and rang a small bell that stood convenient to his hand.

"The bruising you knew about, Mr Scudamore," he said. "It's severe, as I told you, and will cause you a good deal of pain until it heals.

1

The four ribs you've broken on your left side will hurt for longer. To avoid greater discomfort, avoid any kind of exercise that will cause you to breathe deeply. Ah, Hannah." This to the maidservant who had entered in response to the ringing of the bell. "Take this note at once to Mr Lassimer and bring back whatever he gives you. If he adds any instructions to our patient here, ask him to write them down. Memories are fallible things. Quick as you can, girl."

Charles Scudamore's puzzled expression was sufficient to provoke an explanation.

"I have sent Hannah, my housemaid, with a note to Mr Lassimer, the apothecary whose shop is just a little way from here. I've asked him to prescribe you something to ease your pain while healing takes place."

"An apothecary? I thought physicians and apothecaries despised one another."

"Not in this case, sir. Mr Lassimer is most skilled in his profession and knows far better than I what particular formulation and dosage will be best. He also happens to be one of my oldest friends."

Mr Scudamore blushed. "I did not mean to imply any criticism …"

"Of course not," Adam said. "You repeated what you've been told. I dare say it's true in some cases. Let me put it this way. I, as a physician, understand the causes of your pain and what will be best to bring you a cure. In this case, nothing but complete rest. However, I would not leave you without any means of alleviating the pain you surely feel. To do that, I am consulting a learned colleague whose knowledge is greater in that area than my own."

"You are truly a most unusual physician, sir," Mr Scudamore said. "My aunt, Lady Alice, told me as much."

"She is well, I trust?" Adam asked. "I've hesitated to intrude upon her grief at her husband's death, but I hope she may be willing to receive me again soon."

"I am sure of it," Mr Scudamore said. "When she sent me here, she told me to indicate as much to you."

Adam smiled. "So," he said, "you are her nephew. You must be more or less the same age as your aunt. Take a seat, sir. It will be a few minutes before Hannah can return."

Mr Scudamore perched on the edge of the chair Adam indicated to him. Bruised and broken ribs can be a fine aid to good posture.

"My father is her eldest brother," he said. "The siblings arrived over many years and he married at a young age. Lady Alice is the baby of the family."

"I see," Adam said. He imagined he could discern some family resemblance between aunt and nephew. Both were fine-boned and slim, though this young man must be taller than his aunt by a head at least. "I'm glad she has company at this time."

"Our two families have always been very close. My father dotes on his little sister. Unfortunately, his business keeps him in London. He sent my sister and I in his place."

"Your sister, you say?"

"My twin sister, Ruth. She wished to come with me today, but I forbade it. It is enough for you to meet one of us at a time. Besides, she is better occupied in keeping my aunt company than watching over me like a broody hen—and doubtless questioning your every word or action."

"Is she so very protective of you?"

"Sadly, she is. But her heart is good, I assure you. Once she has learned to trust you, she will only question one half of your words."

Adam shook his head. Lady Alice Fouchard, this Mr Scudamore's aunt, had a special place in his life. They had been brought together by a shared grief over her husband's death and a determination to ease the pain of his passing in whatever way they could. It was a bond neither wished to see broken. Now the remembrance of that time threatened to shake his composure and Adam hurried to change the subject.

"I applaud your decision to come alone, sir," he said. "You were about to tell me how you sustained your injuries."

"By falling from my horse," Mr Scudamore said. "At least, through being thrown by the wretched beast. It took fright at a mere nothing, the flapping coat of a scarecrow, and promptly heaved me headlong onto the ground. Damned stony ground it was too. It was a good time before I could get up again. When I did—"

"Your ribs hurt like the very devil."

"By God, they did! Yet I would not have come to you, only first my sister and then Lady Alice set about me. No man could endure that. One would have been bad enough, both of them … unbearable! Well, nothing would content them but that I seek medical advice, nothing would content Lady Alice but that I come to you. So here I am."

"They were wise to insist you came, Mr Scudamore," Adam said. "In the event, your injuries are not too severe, but a bad fall like that has been known to end in death. Only a few weeks ago, a neighbouring farmer, returning homewards much in drink on market day, fell from his horse and broke several ribs. However, in his case, one of them at least pierced his lung, so he sickened and died within the week."

"I declare you're as cheerful as all physicians," Mr Scudamore replied. "The members of your profession delight in tales of death and disaster. Perhaps it's to prevent any questions about your fees."

Adam laughed. There was a good deal of truth in this. Physicians charged the highest fees of any of the medical professions and were always being chafed about it.

"Fear not, Mr Scudamore," he said. "I would not dream of charging any of Lady Alice's household."

Mr Scudamore protested. "But you must. I did not mean … I am quite able to pay my way … Oh Lord, when will I learn to watch my tongue?"

"Let us speak no more of it," Adam said. "Now, my instructions to you are simple. Rest! You must not stir from your bed until I tell you that you may. After that, you may rise for part of the day and sit quietly on a chair or undertake short walks in the fresh air along level ground. No riding or travelling by carriage until I allow it. I want to be sure your ribs heal in the correct position. If they do not, you may suffer lifelong problems with your breathing."

"Could you not shoot me instead, sir? That would be kinder, I assure you. To be at home and unoccupied for so long … I swear I shall run mad."

"Have you nothing to occupy your mind?"

"My father thought my aunt might need assistance in running her estate. I am, sir, an attorney by training and well used to legal matters relating to property and leases. However, her steward has all well in hand, for Sir Daniel had been a most careful and diligent landlord. There is little for me to do beyond approve what he is doing already."

Mr Scudamore rose and walked over to the window which looked out onto the street. "In which direction does the apothecary's shop lie, doctor?"

"To your left. I assure you Hannah will not dawdle. She has become immune to Lassimer's foolish blandishments. She's seen too many servants have their hopes dashed that way."

"Mr Lassimer is—"

"A confirmed philanderer, Mr Scudamore, yet a most kind-hearted one. He cannot resist praising a pretty face or a fine figure, yet rarely goes further—especially if the lady concerned has her mind set on tempting him into marriage. A good many widows in this area have discovered that. Only if they are content to remain unmarried, is he willing—eager even—to share their beds."

"I thought London was the repository of every vice. Yet it seems your little town is not immune either."

"Hardly vice, sir. A little naughtiness, perhaps. No more."

"What is your girl doing? Should she not have returned by now? Perhaps I will walk that way and meet her."

"No, Mr Scudamore. Be seated again. Rest I said, sir! Do as I tell you. Would you have me report to Lady Alice that you are ignoring my advice?"

"A foul blow below the belt! She and my sister would make my life a misery. Anything would be better than that. Very well, I promise I will carry out your instructions to the letter. Only, for pity's sake, do not set those womenfolk on me. Are you married, doctor?"

"I am not."

"Nor am I, nor likely to be if the wedded state is anything like I am experiencing at Mossterton Hall."

Adam looked long at his patient, unable to decide how much of what he said was truly felt and how much sprang from a mischievous disposition. Before he could reach a decision on the matter, he heard Hannah return. She brought a package from Peter.

"Mr Lassimer says he has written down the instructions as you asked, master. He also told me to tell you this first supply is set at a strong level of relief. As the injuries heal, he suggests you may wish to reduce the dosage. He fears—"

But what Peter Lassimer feared they were never to know, for at that moment the doorbell rang. Whoever was outside beat with the knocker as well. Hannah rushed from the room, eager to get to the door before the visitor caused a general tumult.

She returned with another young man, this one breathing hard and red in the face. The liberal dusting of sandy dirt showed he had been riding hard.

"Your brother's footman, master. He says he was sent in great haste, but I told him that's no excuse for beating on the door as if he would throw it down. If I had my way—"

"Thank you, Hannah," Adam said quietly. "Let me hear my brother's message, since this young man has flown here to deliver it."

"My master asks ... that you do come to Trundon Hall ... as quick as you can, sir," the footman gasped. "He has ... great need of you. This morning, Sir Jackman Wennard has been killed ... out with the fox hunt. Thrown by his horse, 'tis said. Coroner planned to hold his inquest tomorrow ... but his doctor isn't satisfied what caused the death. My master wants you ... to give a second opinion. The coroner can only wait another day before convening his jury. The weather is warm ... and the dead man's son, Sir Robert as is now, be making a most fearful fuss."

"Very well," Adam said. "Return to your master and tell him I will set out within the hour. Hannah, give this poor lad a drink of some good ale to wash the dust from his throat. Then send him on his way." He turned to his patient. "Our time is cut short, Mr Scudamore, but you have all you need. I will visit you in two or three days to check on your progress. Please inform Lady Alice that I will venture to call upon her at the same time, should it be convenient."

Charles Scudamore ignored all of this. "Sir Jackman Wennard," he said. "Isn't that the ugly, pompous brute who lives at Upper Cley Hall? Dead, by God! From what I've heard, his tenants will hold a grand party to celebrate."

"You have the advantage of me," Adam said. "I do not believe I ever encountered the man, though he must be a near neighbour to my brother. I do recall, as a child, there was a Sir Henry Wennard. An old man, much addicted to hunting and fishing."

"Sir Jackman's grandfather. The next baronet was, I believe, an uncle who died childless. Drank himself to death in the family tradition. Sir Jackman inherited a few years ago."

"Interesting," Adam said. "Now, sir, I must make ready and you must return to Mossterton Hall."

"You may come in the carriage with me, doctor. I will ask my cousin's coachman to make the detour and hurry …"

Adam interrupted. "I myself will tell Lady Alice's coachman to bear you straight home as quietly and gently as he is able, Mr Scudamore. There you will go to bed, as I instructed. At once, if you please!"

"But, doctor, it will be so much more expedient if—"

"Maybe I will give the coachman a note for Lady Alice," Adam mused. "It might be best in the circumstances."

"I declare I cannot understand why my aunt regards you so highly, doctor," Mr Scudamore said, "for you show a nature of exceptional cruelty. I am not a curious man—"

"By those words you declare yourself to be a liar," Adam said with a laugh. "Go, sir! If it will ease your pain a little more, I promise to bring you word of this sad event when I see you next. Until then, you must be patient. Hannah!" No bell this time, but Adam's habitual bellow for the maid. "Show Mr Scudamore to the door and send the coachman to speak with me before he leaves. I must make sure he understands that this gentleman is to return home directly; and that any deviation from my instructions in the matter will be at the risk of his continued employment by her ladyship."

Adam's elder brother, Giles, failed to offer more than a perfunctory welcome and a vague apology for asking Adam to come to Trundon Hall at such short notice. Instead he turned at once to what was uppermost in his thoughts.

"A stupid death! Just when I'm near overwhelmed with the business of this war. Recruits to swear in for the militia. Returns to be made. Nonsensical demands from this and that commander to report on the state of our maritime defences. By God, brother, I wish I had never assumed the duties of a magistrate. Nothing but business and trouble!"

"The dead man was Sir Jackman Wennard, I believe," Adam said.

"Damned blustering fool! Never liked him. Now I'm supposed to clear up the mess." Giles had started pacing up and down, forcing Adam to keep turning his head to face him.

"Why you?"

"Dead man was a neighbour, brother. In my area. That puts me, as magistrate, in charge of investigating his death. I wouldn't have thought anything worth investigating, had not our coroner come to me. At the start, he accepted the account given to him by the son, Robert—I suppose I should say 'Sir Robert' now. A simple riding accident, caused by too much enthusiasm while following the hunt. Sir Robert is sticking to that explanation, I should warn you. You know the routine. Body has to be examined by a competent medical practitioner before the coroner's court is held. That's when the problem started."

"Before you go into that," Adam said, "tell me about the coroner. I believe the previous one retired a little while ago. What's the new one like?"

"People will tell you he's a fussy little attorney with a practice in Holt. Very precise. Very careful. Many of the landowners around here use him, because he's so reliable. I've done it myself."

"And as a coroner?"

"The same. He knows his law, and will make sure that everything is done in the approved manner. He's already postponed the coroner's inquest for twenty-four hours, so we can clear up the doubts his medical examiner is raising."

"Who's the medical examiner?"

"A middle-aged barber-surgeon called Michael Virgo. I don't know him."

"I've heard of him," Adam said. "Spent a number of years as surgeon aboard several of His Majesty's ships. He may be a member of the humblest part of the medical profession, but everyone agrees he knows his job. He will also have seen more violent deaths than almost anybody else in the neighbourhood."

"Well, he claims that Sir Jackman didn't fall from his horse by accident. Some trap was set to throw him off."

"If that's so, it's murder," Adam said. "Or manslaughter, I suppose. Either way, a bad business. Tell me more about Sir Jackman Wennard. I do remember the man's grandfather."

"The grandfather lived to a good age," Giles said, "which was surprising, considering his wild lifestyle when he was young. The estate then passed to his only son, who didn't survive long to enjoy it. Drank himself to death. Since he had no children, the inheritance next went to the dead man's nephew, Sir Jackman. I suppose he's been in possession no more than three or four years. He, in turn, has one son, Robert, who's as unpleasant and arrogant as his father."

"Sir Jackman was not liked, then," Adam said.

"If you start looking for enemies, you'll have to include most of the county on your list. Certainly all his tenants. I'd also add all his neighbours, any tradesmen who ever had to deal with him and all the villagers round about."

"Why was that?"

"Mean with money and greedy for more. The man lacked any pretence of culture or politeness. Arrogant and rude towards all he met. He had only two interests in his life: breeding racehorses and hunting foxes. He was also ferocious in his application of the Game Laws. He took delight in seeing poachers imprisoned, hanged or transported. It's rumoured his gamekeepers were rewarded for every person who was maimed by the man-traps and swivel-guns set on his lands."

"If he was murdered," Adam said, "it's likely we won't find much help in bringing the killer to justice. From what you say, people would rather give whoever it was a substantial reward."

"You're right," Giles said. "However, as magistrate I have no choice in the matter. I must be seen to set an investigation underway. But enough of this. Tomorrow you'll meet our coroner and Mr Virgo. We'll all go to Upper Cley Hall, where the body was taken. Just don't expect a warm welcome."

"I've been trying to recall the place," Adam said. "By the river, isn't it? On the side of that valley which runs down from the ridge to the sea. I wouldn't like to live there. The ferocious gales we get from the German Ocean must make it a truly desolate spot in winter."

"That's right. Owner and property were well matched. Both full of bluster and cold as ice."

"It's not for me to judge whether he was murdered or not," Michael Virgo said, "that's for the coroner's jury. What I do believe is that he neither fell from his horse by chance, nor was he killed by falling. But I'll say no more, Dr Bascom. You examine the body and tell me what you think."

The two of them were standing just inside the door of a small, poorly furnished bedroom at Upper Cley Hall. Adam doubted this was the bedroom Sir Jackman had used in life. It seemed too mean. Sir Robert, the son, must have already appropriated the best room for his own use. Adam looked around him. The house struck him as gloomy, old-fashioned and much less well-appointed than he had expected, a dwelling that had received a minimum of attention or expenditure for a good many years past. The only touch of grandeur came from the stables,

11

which must have been of recent construction. They were worthy of a duke's palace and so large they near dwarfed the house.

The body of the late Sir Jackman Wennard lay on the bed in this meagre room, covered with a single sheet for the sake of decency. Adam was no surgeon, used to cutting and slicing. It was with reluctance that he pulled the sheet back and began his examination. He saw before him a man of middle age and average height, somewhat running to corpulence. Remembering what Giles had said about the fuss any finding other than accidental death would cause, Adam worked slowly and carefully. He began with the feet and moved upwards, double-checking everything relevant. At length, he straightened up, and beckoned Mr Virgo to join him.

"Well," he said, "it was certainly a broken neck which caused his death. The head is attached to the body only by the soft tissue and flops about horribly if you lift it in your hand. I suspect the windpipe has also been ruptured. The question is, how did he do this? There's severe bruising under his chin and down the upper part of the front of his throat. To me, that suggests that he collided at high speed with some object—perhaps a rope or a thin rod of metal, a stick would break—which forced his head back violently, snapping his neck bones and windpipe at the same time. If I'm right, and I believe I am, he was dead before he fell from the horse's back. Does that accord with your findings?"

"In every detail, sir," Michael Virgo said. "If his neck had been broken in the fall, most likely his head would've been forced forwards by the weight of his body. In such a case, I would have expected to see injuries to the top of his head as well. There are none. It looks to me as if, when he fell, his body was so limp already that he sustained few bruises or injuries on striking the ground. I've seen many a poor sailor who was shot and killed high up in the masts, then fell to the deck maybe fifty feet below. They looked like this. Some bruises from the fall, of course, but nothing like the ones you get when someone stiffens as they sense the deck approaching them."

"There are no signs either to suggest that the man stretched out his arms or raised his hands to protect himself as he fell," Adam said. "I've fallen off a horse myself. You try to protect your face and head from contact with the ground. It's quite involuntary. Yet there are no signs on the man's palms of scratching or bruising. Not even dirt, let alone cuts or scrapes. The other marks and bruises on his body seem to indicate he hit the ground face uppermost. That's extremely odd, wouldn't you say?"

"I've never seen anything like it in my experience," Mr Virgo said.

"Quite so," Adam said. "Well, Mr Virgo, we are at one in our analysis of the way in which this man died. That is what I will tell the coroner and my brother."

"I thank you, sir. Your reputation as a physician has reached even to my ears, so I am delighted to find that you approve of the way in which I have undertaken this examination."

Adam's brother Giles, however, was far from delighted with this finding. All the while Adam was making his examination, Giles and the coroner waited downstairs in the Great Hall of the house. Its new owner, Sir Robert Wennard, had not condescended to make an appearance in person, sending his steward instead to represent him. That poor fellow was so unsettled by his employer's behaviour he quickly made the excuse of pressing business and left them alone.

When Adam explained his findings, his brother and the coroner listened intently, their faces growing gloomier by the moment. "Oh Lord," Giles said. "This will cause me a great deal of bother, not to say the perpetual enmity of Sir Robert. Still, it cannot be helped. If the man was murdered, the law must take its course."

"No one is above the law, Mr Bascom," the little coroner added. "Not even the squire of Upper Cley Hall." He turned to Adam and Mr Virgo. "The inquest will take place tomorrow morning at ten o'clock precisely. I regret that I must ask you both to give evidence. It is clear Sir Robert will be greatly angered by your findings. I would not be surprised if he tries to make a complaint against the proceedings. The opinion of one medical examiner would doubtless be dismissed as simply mistaken. If you both give evidence, I am sure the jury will accept this is not the case."

"We will enjoy your company for another night then, brother," Giles said. "Amelia and the children will be delighted. Now, gentlemen, I suggest we leave this house straight away. The atmosphere of anger and hatred is almost beyond bearing. I don't doubt that Sir Robert is here, even though he saw fit to ignore our arrival. To be honest, if he ignores our departure as well, I will be relieved."

Next morning, the inquest began exactly at the time appointed. The members of the jury had all declined to inspect the body personally, doubtless aware of the welcome that would have met them at Upper Cley Hall. The coroner therefore proceeded to take evidence of identity from the dead man's son. Sir Robert had first tried to refuse any part in what he termed "these pointless proceedings". Eventually, advised by his lawyer in muttered undertones that this was not an advisable line to take, he acknowledged the dead man was his father, and went on to give a bare-bones version of the events leading up to the man's death.

His father had become separated from the rest of the hunt and was hurrying to catch up. His death was but a simple accident due to haste. He, Sir Robert, was the first to come upon the body, so he should know. No, he did not recall where his father had been during the time he was absent from the hunt. Why did it matter? Sir Jackman had been taking a well-known shortcut and his horse must have stumbled and thrown him. That was all there was to it. No need for all this legal paraphernalia.

When he was at last allowed to stand down, having given the tersest of answers to every question, Sir Robert returned to a seat near the back of the room alongside his legal adviser. From there he glowered at anyone foolish enough to catch his eye.

Few local people had bothered to attend the inquest, expecting it would be a simple formality. Now there was an audible gasp of surprise as Mr Virgo gave his evidence from the examination of the body. Sir Robert jumped to his feet at once and shouted in a loud voice, "Rubbish! The man's an incompetent fool!" It took the little coroner some time, and much hammering of his gavel, to restore order. Then he spoke to the jury.

"Gentlemen. Mr Virgo informed me of his findings immediately after he had made his examination. Anticipating the surprise that this might cause, I decided to seek a second opinion. I now call Dr Adam Bascom to give evidence. Dr Bascom is probably known to many of you as a distinguished physician with a practice in the town of Aylsham. He examined the body late yesterday morning."

Adam was called forward and gave his evidence. Again, there was a ripple of surprise throughout the audience. Sir Robert's adviser tried to restrain him, but the man was beside himself with fury.

"Another nincompoop!" he shouted, leaping to his feet. "Doubtless as big a fool as his brother at Trundon! For God's sake, it was an accident, I tell you! I was there!"

The coroner stayed silent for a few moments, waiting for the noise to subside. When he did speak, his precise, quiet voice contained a greater power than any shouting could have done.

"Such behaviour ill becomes a gentleman, sir," he said to Sir Robert. "You will remain silent and seated, or I will have you removed, by force if necessary. You must also take a care with your words. When you gave your evidence, it was under oath. You stated that you had first come across your father's body already on the ground and his horse some distance away. If you now say that you were present at the time he fell from his horse, and thus able to state with certainty how that happened, your earlier evidence was perjured. I am sure that I need not remind a person of your education that the penalties for perjury are most severe."

If Robert now remained seated, it was in large part because his lawyer was actually holding him down. However, his words were clearly audible to everyone in the room. "Pompous ass!" he said. "Jumped up little nobody who thinks he can lord it over his betters! Whole affair here is complete nonsense! A group of ignorant bumpkins playing at being a court of law."

This was too much for the coroner.

"Your remarks are offensive in the extreme," he said, "both to myself and to this court. As you will find, this is indeed a court of law, whether you like it or not. I find you in contempt of court, sir, and sentence you to pay a fine of five guineas within two days or be placed in the common prison for a month. Constables! Remove this man!"

It was, perhaps, a measure of the general popularity of the new squire of Upper Cley Hall that a number of members of the public attempted to applaud as he was dragged away. Only furious glares from the coroner, accompanied by much banging of his gavel, prevented them from doing so.

"Silence!" he thundered. "If members of the public cannot behave with proper decorum, I will have the court cleared."

From then on, the rest of the proceedings continued more calmly. The coroner summed up the evidence, the jury whispered amongst themselves, indicated that they did not wish to retire and were ready to give their decision. Finally, the foreman of the jury stood up and pronounced the verdict.

"We find that Sir Jackman Wennard was murdered," he said. "Murdered by person or persons unknown."

The coroner recorded the verdict, thanked the jury and dismissed them. It was all over.

As they left to return to Trundon Hall, Adam had a grin on his face. "I find I like your coroner enormously," he said to his brother. "His handling of that oaf of a son was little short of perfection. What says 'the fool at Trundon' to today's proceedings?"

"Oaf is correct, brother. Sir Jackman was unpleasant, but never such a churlish, ignorant and loud-mouthed clown as his son has proved himself to be. But to business—"

"I feared this was coming," Adam said. His brother ignored him.

"I doubt very much that Sir Robert will take any action to investigate his father's death," Giles said. "In such a case, I could, I suppose, avoid further unpleasantness by stating that I have no reason to get involved until someone is brought before me and charged with a crime. However, I have the firm belief that no man in this realm should suffer an assault on his person, let alone be murdered, without a proper investigation being made under the law so the guilty may be brought to justice. If the son will not act as he should, I see no reason why I, as magistrate, should be bound by his inaction."

"Quite right," Adam said. "Let me be the first to wish you good luck in your endeavours."

Giles looked at him in a pained way.

"Don't try to make fun of me, brother," he said. "You know I have neither the capacity, nor the curiosity—and especially not the time—to carry out a proper investigation."

"Whereas I, your poor brother, do nothing all day?"

"Less of the 'poor', sir. Aside from the exorbitant fees you doubtless charge for your professional advice, you have that pension from the king. That alone would make you a wealthy man. Now, I understand, the late Sir Daniel Fouchard made a handsome bequest to you in his Will. Since he was a rich man, I doubt it was merely a few pounds."

"If I could restore him to life, I would forego a bequest of any size. I only knew him for a short time, but I will mourn his passing for the rest of my days. His generosity to me was typical of the man. I did try to ask his widow to take the money back for her own use, but she refused, saying it would be wrong to frustrate her husband's wishes in such a way. His attorney also told me bluntly that it was the duty of the executors to fulfil the last wishes of the deceased, not to either comment upon them or decline to carry them out, unless there were insufficient funds available."

"Which there would not have been."

"No, that is so."

"So what did he leave you?"

"I thought you lacked curiosity, brother," Adam said severely.

He knew this must come one day. Giles, as the elder, had inherited what remained of the Bascom lands after their profligate father had done his best to ruin the family. By hard work, frugality and a natural ability for estate management, he had restored his fortunes to a great degree. Yet it is one thing to have a younger brother earning his way in the world, and another to wonder whether he has somehow overtaken you in wealth and income.

"Very well," Adam said. Better to be honest and get it over with. "He left me the sum of ten thousand pounds."

Giles quite jumped at the figure and opened his mouth to comment. The stern look on Adam's face caused him to bite back his words. Both knew a frontier had been crossed.

"At present, those monies are invested in the funds, where they bring me a significant income. In time, however, I shall consider a more suitable way of providing a memorial to a great and generous benefactor."

Giles was far from being the quickest in the matter of calculations, but even he could see that this 'significant income' must be some three or four hundred pounds annually—a greater amount in itself than a good many gentlemen could obtain from their estates. Add in his other sources of income …

There was a lengthy pause as Giles reassessed his little brother. Then, eager to change the subject, he tried to lighten their conversation.

"Have you thought of marriage?" Giles said. His wealthy younger brother would surely draw the attention of every mother of good family in the county possessed of an eligible daughter.

Adam burst out laughing, as much in relief as from amusement. "Now you sound like our mother," he said. "I am sure she is already drawing up a fine list of young women to parade before me. You are both wasting your time. I have absolutely no thought of marriage at present. When—and if—such a notion does occur to me, I will, I assure you, make my own choice of lady to propose to without any resort to motherly—or brotherly—intervention. Now, let us return to Trundon. If I am to do your job for you and investigate this murder—note I say 'if'—it is high time I was on my way. I do have patients needing my help, whatever you imagine to the contrary."

A SHORTCUT TO MURDER

Two

Suspects

"SO YOU'VE GOT YOURSELF INVOLVED IN ANOTHER MURDER," Peter Lassimer said. "You seem to be as attracted to them as moths are to a candle flame."

Three days had passed since the inquest, days Adam had devoted to his medical duties to make up for the time that he had been away at Trundon Hall. Now it was time to honour his promise to his brother to look into the matter of Sir Jackman Wennard's death.

Adam made his way early to sit with Peter in the apothecary's compounding room. He found the sharp scents of the herbs and spices stimulating and valued the opportunity to discuss whatever was in his mind. Peter was sharp and alert—critical in the best sense as well, for he was ruthless in exposing faulty reasoning while never implying any fault in the reasoner. He could also be trusted to keep his mouth shut and his ears open to useful gossip.

"You do exaggerate, Lassimer," Adam said to his friend. "I was not attracted to this killing, as you suggest. My brother asked me to give a second opinion on a purely medical matter."

"So now you are going to walk away and forget about it?" Peter replied. "Really, Bascom! I know you're the scholar, but at least you should credit me with the brains I was born with."

"I suppose I might ask one or two questions, just to help my brother out," Adam replied. "Nothing more than that. That's not really investigating, is it?"

"Of course not," Peter said with heavy sarcasm. "Nothing like it. So you won't want to hear any of the news that has already reached me on this matter."

"Well," Adam said. "I suppose—"

"I suppose that you are the most shameful of liars, Dr Bascom. You're more curious than any cat I have ever come across. Admit it! You're on the hunt yet again." He put down the pestle and mortar he had been using and turned to face his visitor. "Do you want to hear what I have to tell you or not?"

"Yes, I do," Adam replied, "provided it's not some fairy story dreamed up by one of your amorous widows."

"You keep away from my amorous widows," Peter said. "Find your own! By the way, while we're on the subject of such delightful encounters, I gather that you have been paying a suspicious number of visits to London of late."

"Ye gods!" Adam cried. "Can I do nothing in this town without it being reported to you?"

"Not a thing," Peter said. "I assure you, the activities of the town's most famous physician are observed by everybody, then discussed in depth in my shop. I know what you're up to almost as soon as you do it. So—tell me what you have been doing in London."

"If you must pry into my activities," Adam said, "I had various pieces of business to attend to there and listened to a number of learned lectures by physicians and natural scientists of high repute."

"By day, perhaps. But what did you do in the evenings?"

"Mind your own business! Now, are you going to tell me what you know about the death of Sir Jackman or not? I did not come here to talk about my private affairs—"

"Ah! A significant word perhaps."

"That is enough, Lassimer. Please return to the matter of Sir Jackman Wennard."

Peter grinned. "Since you are becoming so irritable, I had better leave off the subject of London—for the moment. Don't think that I have forgotten it. One way or another, I will have the truth out of you before long."

"Sir Jackman Wennard? Remember him?"

"Popular suspicion of his murderer is evenly divided between his son and one or more of his tenants. The son because he is much disliked, with good cause. He is, by all accounts, a worthless spendthrift, a gambler and an idle fool. The tenants had every reason to hate their landlord, who considered nothing beyond how large a rent he could extort and how little he could spend on repairs to their houses. You should also look at his land agent, whose life he made a misery. Amongst the villagers, there are many whom he treated harshly, not to mention those whose wives, sisters or daughters he debauched or made attempts upon. Add to that the families of the poachers he caused to be hanged or sentenced to be transported, as well as those killed or maimed by the various traps he ordered his keepers to set upon his land. May I bring you pen and paper to make notes? I would not wish you to forget anyone."

Adam glared, but remained silent.

"Now then," Peter mused. "Let's turn to the elder of his two surviving daughters—"

"Surely you do not suspect a woman of this crime." Adam could not help protesting at the very idea.

"Why not? To set a trap to bring a man off the back of his horse requires cunning, not physical strength. Have you ever known a woman to be lacking in cunning, when some matter concerns her closely? I was about to explain that I exclude his elder daughter because she was not hereabouts at the time. She has eloped. "

"What?" Adam cried. "Eloped? Eloped where? With whom?"

"If my information is correct," Peter said, "she eloped for the purpose of marrying a Mr Lancelot Pashley. I imagine they are married by now. She took advantage of the absence of her father and brother on that fox-hunt to slip away and head for Scotland, I imagine. Her father had set his face firmly against her chosen suitor."

"Why?"

"Three reasons. Sir Jackman wished her to marry Lord George Gossett, an especially ugly and ill-tempered widower of some sixty years of age, in return for a racehorse he coveted but could not afford. Next, the Pashley family is in trade. Mr Pashley's father is a tea merchant. Gossett is an aristocrat. Finally, the Pashleys are Quakers."

"How old is the girl?"

"Twenty or twenty-one."

"What did her brother think of this plan?" Adam asked.

"Agreed with their father, I expect. Both men are—rather were, in one case—as proud as Lucifer. Besides, nothing would please Robert more than to cause his sister pain. That's the kind of fellow he is."

Adam shook his head. "No wonder my brother suggested a good many people in this part of the county would rather see Sir Jackman's killer rewarded than punished. I don't think I've ever encountered a man with so many potential enemies."

"Indeed," Peter said. "Now, amongst the less likely murderers—"

"Stop!" Adam cried. "My head is reeling. Enough of the gossip that swirls around in your shop! What I need are facts."

"Gossip makes a business pay," Peter said sternly. "Without the lure of gossip, ladies will send their servants to make purchases for them, which has ruined more businesses than you can imagine. A servant comes under instruction to place specific orders, those and no others. If the mistress—better still, the mistress and one or more of her daughters—enters the shop, her eye may be caught by other items placed for that purpose. Indeed, the enterprising shopkeeper will make sure to let drop that several of the lady's neighbours have already made purchases of the same objects. In a trice, they become things she knows she is quite unable to do without and they are added to her order. The same happens with any daughters, whose acquaintances are sure to laugh at those unfortunates who do not wear their hair, or adorn their faces, or perfume their skin with whatever is fashionable and in the latest mode."

Adam burst out laughing. "I see I am also to be sold gossip under the pretence that it is essential to my purpose in finding a killer. Fie upon you to treat your old friend so! I'll return home now and be your fool no more!"

But as he left the apothecary's shop, Adam's expression was one of intense concentration. A daughter who eloped on the day her father was murdered. A son whom everyone thought vicious and worthless. The neighbourhood united in its hatred. How would he find the murderer among such a host of suspects?

Back at his home, Adam went at once to his parlour and took up pen and paper. His notes from his meeting with Peter were long and detailed. The man might be something of a joker, but Adam had learned some time ago that all the news in the neighbourhood might be heard in that apothecary's shop. Nor was Peter as simple and straightforward as he might seem. He delighted to share the most important things he knew under the guise of jests and frivolous remarks.

At last, Adam put the pen down, rested his chin on his palm and tried to consider the situation using sound logic. There was no lack of suspects for the crime, yet that would not serve to move the investigation forward on its own. It would take weeks to question all the people mentioned, even if they were willing to speak to him. What he needed was a way of narrowing the possibilities. Who had the strongest reason to wish Sir Jackman Wennard dead? Who had the best opportunity to bring his death about?

No, he thought, first he needed a way past the central problem, how any killer setting a trap could have known Sir Jackman would pass that way. Not just ride along the track, but do so at high speed. Whatever means had been used to catch the man in the throat, could not have done so much damage if he had not come into contact with it with extreme force. The killer must also have known that Sir Jackman would be alone. You cannot set up the means to catch one man in the midst of a host of others, any one of whom could have fallen into the trap first.

The more Adam thought about it, the firmer his conclusion became. He must set aside all question of suspects. Instead, he should concentrate on trying to discover precisely what had happened on that day, starting at the point where the hunt met in the yard outside the inn.

Now even that would have to wait. Lady Alice Fouchard had sent a response to his message via her nephew, saying she would be delighted to receive him the next morning at eleven o'clock.

"Damn!" Adam said aloud. "Another delay. I wish there was some way that I could put off going to see Lady Alice."

But even as the words left his mouth he knew the real reason for his reluctance to go to Mossterton Hall had nothing to do with pursuing the case of the murdered baronet. It was fear. Whilst Sir Daniel had been alive, Adam's visits had always been directed towards his care. The same had been true of his conversations with Lady Alice. Now that refuge had gone and he must deal directly with the woman herself.

He had no idea what to say to her. Would he enjoy her company, without the obvious source of empathy that her dying husband had offered? Would she enjoy his? He could not bear it if his fond memories of that household were replaced by the realisation that he would now only be accepted by virtue of his position under Sir Daniel's Will. Her late husband had made Adam promise to watch over his widow and help her move on with her life. At the time, Lady Alice had welcomed the idea. Would it still be as attractive now she was in charge of her own affairs?

Lady Alice came of a noble family. Adam's forebears were mere country squires. Might she look down on him? Might he find her stiff, formal and distant in her manner? Surely it would be better to allow the acquaintance to cease? Yet he could hardly do so, when Sir Daniel, on his deathbed, had enjoined him to be a friend to his widow. You do not break a promise made to a dying man, nor did he wish to. Thoughts of Lady Alice were lodged permanently in the back of his mind. To cut himself off from her would hurt as much as the amputation of a hand.

"Curse all women!" he cried, not realising he was speaking aloud. Since, by the merest chance, his housemaid, Hannah, had come into the library at that point, she assumed his remark was directed at her and fled. It took prolonged ringing of the bell, followed by equally lengthy assurances that he was not upset with her and she had done nothing wrong, to coax her back into the room. When finally she stopped crying, she could deliver the message that she had tried to bring before.

"A servant has come from your brother, master," she said. "He says as how his master would be greatly obliged if you could visit him again as soon as you may. He has information to give you."

"Great heavens!" Adam said. "How is a poor physician supposed to run his practice and still be at the beck and call of everyone else? No, Hannah, don't back away. I am not angry with you, only with the world in general. Very well. Tell my brother's servant that I am engaged tomorrow, but will make my way to Trundon Hall on the following day."

After the girl had left, Adam sighed extravagantly and settled down to an hour or so of pleasant self-pity. The fact that he didn't really need the money he earned as a physician, and that the previous two occasions when he had been forced almost to abandon his wealthy patients had resulted in more referrals, not less, would not be allowed to spoil it. Besides, it would serve to take his mind off the disturbing images of Lady Alice Fouchard filling his brain, and his anxiety at what tomorrow might bring.

Adam experienced this same conflicted mass of emotions as his chaise rumbled up the driveway to Mossterton Hall the next morning. His grief at the death of Sir Daniel Fouchard might be made sharp again, but he could not help experiencing a glow of pleasure at the recollection of the enjoyment he had taken from their talks about life and the world. Nor could he deny his excitement at the prospect of seeing Lady Alice. He strove as hard as he could to exclude her image and voice from his head, but he could not do so. Remembrances of her grace, of her large, soft eyes, of the infectious grin when she was amused and of the soothing quality of her voice plucked at his consciousness. The mingling of pleasure at seeing her again with fear at what a meeting might bring was almost more than he could bear.

To Adam's relief, the manservant who answered his knock at the door was under orders to take him directly to see Mr Charles Scudamore. As they climbed the sweeping stairs towards what had been Sir Daniel Fouchard's room, every step threatened to bring tears to Adam's eyes. He would never again speak with Sir Daniel—a man he had come to value like a father towards the end. Please God, don't let Mr Scudamore by accommodated in the room which Sir Daniel had used.

Happily, that we not to be. The manservant turned in the opposite direction to the one Adam had taken in the past and they came swiftly to the door of Charles' room. There, the servant announced him and ushered him into a cheerful bedroom whose large windows looked out to the gardens towards the south. Charles Scudamore lay propped up on a fine bed with the covers arranged neatly about him. Only his face betrayed any annoyance at being there.

"Come in, come in, doctor! There, you see I have obeyed your every instruction and lie here like my master's dog, prone but inwardly mutinous at the orders I have been given. What new miseries have you come to visit upon me? Let me tell you, before you speak, that I am mending at high speed, as much to escape the cloying concerns of my sister and my aunt's severe strictures as from your treatment."

All this Adam ignored. He was well used to patients who delighted in complaining about what he prescribed, but would complain more loudly if he did nothing at all. Instead, he crossed to the bed, looked carefully into his patient's eyes, demanded that he open his mouth and push out his tongue, then allow his bruises to be inspected.

"Well?" Charles demanded. "Am I to die tomorrow?"

"That I cannot tell you," Adam replied calmly, "for I am no soothsayer. All I can assure you is that, if you do, it will be no fault of mine. Your hurts, as you said, are healing quickly. Much of that is due to you being young and healthy to begin with."

"What? No claims of miracles from your ministrations?" Charles said. "I am disappointed, doctor. I thought every physician learned at the start of their training that any improvement in a patient must be taken as a proof of their skill—and all deterioration laid at the door of the inescapable workings of a malign fate."

"Not this one, Mr Scudamore. My belief is that trust begets trust. If I want my patients to trust what I tell them, I cannot also gull them like the worst kind of mountebank. Your improvement has little to do with me, sir. However, I will not include my friend Mr Lassimer in my disclaimer. I suspect the drops he made up for you have been far more directly beneficial."

"Doctor, doctor!" Charles cried. "Enough! I cannot withstand so much modesty and regard for others at such an early hour. It is something any man needs to be prepared for slowly and with due regard to the pain he might suffer as his preconceptions are so rapidly destroyed."

"Well, sir?" Adam asked. He was striving to keep his face straight. "Am I correct?"

"Indeed you are. Thanks to those drops, I have been able to sleep at night when otherwise the pain of my bruises and broken ribs would surely have kept me awake."

"I am glad," Adam said. "So … what reward would be suitable to mark your improvement?"

"There is only one I wish for, doctor."

"Very well. You may leave your bed, Mr Scudamore, and betake yourself elsewhere. Nevertheless—mark me well—I forbid you absolutely to leave this house and its grounds. If the weather is fine, you may take one or two gentle walks in the garden, but nought else. To get upon a horse—even to ride in a carriage—is banned. I expect you will not find these restrictions too hard. You may imagine, lying there, that you are completely fit. Even one day out of your bed will convince you otherwise."

"Thank you, doctor," Charles said with becoming humility. "If I may, I will beg you to communicate these changes to my aunt and sister. I am ashamed to admit I am such a bad patient they will not believe I am allowed to rise until they hear it from your own lips. Now to more interesting matters. I gather you gave evidence at the inquest on the unfortunate baronet. Better still, you proved that he was murdered!"

"Better? Surely not."

"Well … not for him, I suppose, but certainly better from the point of exciting interest in this sadly quiet and dull corner of the kingdom. Are you on the track of his killer? My aunt assures me you are a most experienced and tireless investigator."

"Hardly that, Mr Scudamore. It so happens that—not by my seeking, I assure you—I have become involved in considering two puzzling cases of violent death. That hardly merits the epithets you give me."

"It is two more than most doctors, I am sure. But no matter. Tell me all, for I am dying for want of news. My sister would chide me, were she here, but she is not. I admit most freely that few cats will be able to match me in the matter of curiosity."

Adam hesitated, then decided to tell his tale, if for no other reason than it would delay further the meeting with Lady Alice. When he had finished, Charles lay back, pondering all he had heard.

"It all sounds very suspicious to me," he said. "Have you been to the place where it happened?"

"No," Adam said. This should have occurred to him well before now. Fool and idiot! "I have not had sufficient leisure." He walked across to the window and stood looking down into the garden. Already the briefer days of autumn were tinting leaves with red and gold.

"I really think you should, doctor. Until you have those kinds of details in your mind, some person may tell you of a significant matter, but you may not recognise what it means. For example, precisely how was the man's body arranged when it was found? If Sir Robert's statement of a simple riding accident is the right one, you would expect to find the horse had stumbled and thrown the rider forward, over its head. There would be nothing which might have caught on Sir Jackman's throat as he fell and inflicted the injuries you found. He must rather have struck the ground head first, bending his neck forward and breaking it by the momentum imparted by his body. Then his body might come to rest face up or down, but certainly well beyond whatever caused the horse to stumble. If your supposition of colliding with a rope or piece of wood or metal is correct, the rider would be thrown off his horse over the tail, landing behind somewhere. There would be little sign of any stumbling by the horse. Go there as soon as you may would be my advice. Rain and the passing of time will soon erase all useful signs. I would offer to come with you, but ..."

Adam grinned. "No, Mr Scudamore. That I cannot allow. Still, it is good advice and I will act upon it quickly."

"You will come back and tell me what you find?" Charles asked, anxious now. "I will be in such a fret of curiosity until you do that I am sure it will quite retard the healing process."

"You have my word," Adam said.

"Good. Now you really must hasten to see Lady Alice and my sister. The longer you spend with me, the more convinced both will be that you have found some serious malady. Then they will ignore your permission for me to rise from this bed and keep me prisoner for several more days. Never underestimate the power of loving women, doctor. Most males can break the bonds of instruction or coercion with ease, but the sight of a woman snuffling over your ingratitude will reduce almost all to helpless obedience."

Charles Scudamore's swift tug on the bell-pull by his bed had summoned a maidservant, ready to conduct Adam to the parlour where Lady Alice and Miss Scudamore awaited him. He went meekly enough, yet with more of the appearance of a condemned man walking towards the gallows than a welcome visitor on his way to greet the ladies of the house. When he entered the room and caught sight of Lady Alice, his breathing became tight and his heartbeats far more rapid than they should have been. Why should that be? He didn't know. Then, when she smiled kindly on him and offered him her hand, he found himself wholly uncertain whether to take it or run away. It was all far too puzzling for comfort!

She still wore the black bombazine of full mourning, for her husband had died a little less than six months ago. It was not the most becoming colour for her. Even so, something of her vitality still showed through the sombreness, while nothing could conceal the supple grace of her movement as she turned to face her visitor. She was undoubtedly beautiful, Adam decided afresh, but it was her eyes which drew you most. They seemed to look as much within you as on the surface. Oh Lord! Don't say he was developing an affection for her. He told himself to stop all such nonsensical ideas at once.

As he had seen her several times before, Lady Alice was seated near to the hearth with what was now a half-grown cat asleep upon her lap. Seeing the former kitten grown so much was a painful reminder to Adam of just how long it had been since he had paid her a visit. Beside her sat a young woman so strikingly alike to the man he had just left that, had he been told that man had swiftly run down the stairs and assumed women's clothes, he might have been half tempted to believe it.

"My dear Dr Bascom," Lady Alice said. "It has been far too long since we met. I have missed you sorely. Are you well? Good, I am glad to hear it. May I now present to you my niece, Miss Ruth Scudamore? As I am sure you know already, she is the twin of that reprobate upstairs who has made our lives a misery by his continual whining to be released from the sensible restrictions you have placed upon him."

"Good day to you, doctor," Miss Scudamore said. "I noticed you start when your eyes fell upon me. The resemblance is striking, is it not? Few twins are quite as alike in appearance as my brother and I. Yet there the likeness ends, I assure you."

"I am delighted to meet you, Miss Scudamore," Adam replied. "You have indeed found me out, for I was certainly surprised. I have encountered identical twins in the past, but they are always of the same gender, in my experience. To find a male and a female—"

"Fie, doctor," Miss Scudamore said, "I am not a specimen to be wondered over and pickled in a jar."

Adam was startled anew. He had not realised he was viewing her as a scientific wonder rather than a normal person, but there was a good deal of truth in her accusation.

"I do apologise, Miss Scudamore," he said at once. "I did not intend to give offence."

"I have taken none," Miss Scudamore said, "but my aunt was right when she said I should find you unlike the normal run of gentlemen."

To this Adam gave no reply, since it occurred to him at once that it might be taken in several ways. Did Lady Alice see him as special in some way, or did she count him as lacking in the normal civilities to be expected from a gentleman? Seeing his frown, Lady Alice hastened to clarify.

"Please take a seat, doctor. I have asked for coffee to be brought, since most gentlemen prefer that to tea at this time of day. What my niece means—though she expresses herself altogether too bluntly—is that I told her she should not expect to find someone interested only in flirtation, as so many young men are these days. Miss Scudamore tends to terrify such creatures. I have heard her called 'blue-stocking'—and several other names. Blue-stocking was the most flattering of them."

"Just because I have a brain and am determined to use it," Miss Scudamore said. "What think you, doctor? Do you agree that a woman may be as intelligent and capable as any man? Or are you also determined to put the so-called weaker sex on some kind of pedestal, where they can be admired, yet prevented from doing any harm?"

"Ruth!" Lady Alice said. "Now you have gone too far. I declare I am quite ashamed of you. Such impoliteness is unbecoming in any person, man or woman. Stop it this instant!"

Lady Alice might be soft and feminine in appearance, but she was not a person to cross. Miss Scudamore blushed and apologised.

"Indeed," Adam said, seeking to release the young woman from the baleful glare Lady Alice was directing towards her, "I am more than ready to acknowledge men and women are at a parity in matters of intelligence.

Please do not scold your niece further, my lady. I admire plain speaking. It is much to be preferred to fine words coming from dissembling hearts."

Lady Alice appeared to relent, but Adam suspected Miss Scudamore had not quite heard the last of the matter. In an attempt to turn the conversation into other channels, he began once again to express his immense gratitude to Sir Daniel for his most unexpected bequest. Lady Alice waved his words away, saying her husband had thought it a poor return for all Adam's help and friendship. In the circumstances, it was the best he could do.

"It is I who should be thanking you," she said. "Not just for your past kindnesses, but for the good care of my nephew, whom I suspect is a cantankerous and ungrateful patient. I do all I can to persuade him to follow your instructions, but I fear I have less control over him than he needs."

Her words at once recalled Adam to his promise to convey in person the lessening of the restrictions he had placed on Mr Scudamore. When he had finished, Lady Alice turned to another topic.

"I am sorry to hear you have been caught up once again in an unpleasant matter, doctor," she said. "It must be hard to run a practice when you are so often taken away to deal with non-medical matters. Yet somehow I have a sneaking belief that you find ordinary doctoring a little dull and relish a good mystery. Is that not so?"

Adam admitted it was and their conversation moved away into other matters. In the end, he took his leave with reluctance, altogether puzzled as to why he had ever felt anxiety at coming to Mossterton Hall. Throughout their meeting, Lady Alice had been both friendly and attentive, often startling him by her insight into his thoughts and concerns. He left elated by the evident kindness with which he had been welcomed, telling himself he must indeed return more often. On Miss Ruth Scudamore he bestowed little thought, which, had he known it, would have caused her severe disappointment. Quite what she had expected he could not have guessed. The notion that what she had found had stirred her interest to quite such an extent must have caused him great alarm.

Three

The Lie of the Land

THE PLACE WHERE SIR JACKMAN HAD MET HIS FATE WAS TOO FAR OFF TO REACH THAT DAY. However, if he left early in the morning, Adam reckoned he would have time to inspect the ground and still reach Trundon Hall at about the time he was expected. That assumed he could find the place easily; he had only the descriptions given at the inquest to guide him. He hadn't taken more than a passing interest at the time. Still, his memory was good and there might well be local people about to set him on the right path.

The day began cool and misty, the kind of morning that might promise a fine, autumn day to follow or might as easily turn into rain. Mists and fogs were common along the coasts of the German Ocean, especially when the cold water came up against land warmed by the sun of the day before. Adam was well used to such conditions, so he set out wearing the kind of clothing he often needed as a doctor to armour him against the cold dampness of autumn or winter. If the sun broke through later, he would be able to set aside his upper layers and enjoy any late-season warmth.

Much of the way Adam knew well; he travelled it often going to Trundon Hall. It was only when he turned aside from this path that he began to lose his bearings. Fortunately, despite being deep in the countryside—Holt, a small market town some three miles distant, was the nearest settlement of any size—there were a surprising number of travellers abroad. He came upon a brewer's dray bearing barrels to supply the inns in the area, several heavy wagons taking barley to the local maltings, as well as walkers, riders and drivers of carriages. It seemed as if all of north Norfolk must be on the road going somewhere, but where he could not imagine. Even after he had turned northwards towards the coast, along a narrow way that was more of a lane than a road, there were labourers walking to their work, a man driving a small herd of sheep—even a fellow with the sober, threadbare clothing of an itinerant preacher.

As he neared what he hoped would be his final destination, a weak sun broke through the mist, its rays making the water droplets into diamonds and decking the gorse and dying bracken with thick skeins of jewels—all by courtesy of innumerable spiders. Autumn at its best, he thought.

Adam had chosen to ride his horse, Fancy, rather than harness her as he usually did these days. That it was a wise decision was proved when he paused and asked an elderly man, lounging by the wall of a tumbledown cottage, if he could tell him the way.

"Ah, my boy," the veteran said, pausing first to consider who was asking him. Whether this was to satisfy him of the properness of Adam's request, or to weigh up the likely size of his reward, was unclear. "You'm be Squire Bascom's brother, I reckons. The one what's a doctor. Am I right?"

Adam nodded.

"Thought I was. Now, do you be wanting the spot where folks says the old squire was foully murdered? 'Tisn't far. You sees that track leading off leftwards by the oak tree? Take that and 'twill bring you direct to the place. You'll know it by the way the path goes into some good-sized trees, then runs down and crosses the river. All the folk round here knows and uses that pathway—aye, and 'as done since the world was made, so far as I knows, though old squire said 'twas 'is land and 'e didn't want no common folk traipsing across it. That did 'im no good though, did it? We all went on as we 'ad before and 'e 'ad to put up with it. Now, doctor, a word of advice. Keep you strictly to the path and don't go wandering either side, nor takin' no shortcuts. You'll be safe enough then, for all 'tis steepish in places. They says the old squire fair filled the wood and the rough heath with all kind of traps and guns to catch poachers. Don't want a fine young fellow like you getting' hurt. A doctor's no use to his patients if he be hurt hisself, is he? You stay on the path and you'll be in no danger. My poachin' days is long gone, but I had many a fine rabbit and pheasant from those woods when I was a young man!"

Adam duly handed the old man sixpence, which he regarded suspiciously, then tucked away when it was clear no more would follow it.

As Adam rode onwards, he heard the old man call out again. "Remember! Keep to the path. No traps there."

Adam knew many local landowners used these dreadful machines to keep poachers away, even going so far as to advertise their presence in the local newspapers. How far it was bluff and how far reality wasn't easy to tell. In this case, it must be a genuine hazard. Another reason for Sir Jackman Wennard to be hated.

As directed, once they reached the oak Adam urged Fancy onto an even narrower path leading to the left. Soon man and rider were heading steeply downhill. There were signs people passed this way on foot or on horseback, since the track was too narrow to allow any wheeled vehicle to use it. For generations, most of this part of the county had been near-barren heathland, fit only for rabbits and half-starved sheep. More recently, some of the landowners and their tenants had cleared the gorse and furze, then used marl and manure to make the land fit for the production of grain. None of that had taken place here. The squires of Upper Cley Hall drove their tenants hard, while denying them the extra capital expenditure needed to introduce modern farming methods, using the land much as it had always been used, for hunting and shooting. As a result, all kinds of wildlife abounded. Pigeons, crows and magpies could be heard all around. Several rabbits rushed across the path. Adam even glimpsed a deer, before it caught his scent and bounded off into a denser stretch of heath.

At length he found himself on more level ground, where the path made its way along the front of the ridge before turning to the right. There it would descend into the valley via a series of sharp bends designed to cope with an even steeper incline. Here the woodland began, protected by the lie of the land from the worst winter gales. Not a neat, planned plantation, as you might expect to find within a mile or so of some gentleman's house, but a tangled mass of trees, fallen trunks and bramble bushes. Once within, you could find yourself entirely lost, though the path was barely twenty yards distant. Once or twice, Adam thought he saw signs where someone had pushed a way through this thick mat of vegetation recently—fresh breaks on some of the fallen branches, some bramble tendrils still drooping where they had been broken or bent. However, bearing in mind the old man's warning, he kept firmly to the path. He knew what injury a man-trap or a swivel-gun could cause to horse or man.

After some few hundred more paces, he reached the foot of the hill and stood on the nearer side of the stream. This must be the place he sought. Before him, the River Glaven ran the last part of its course towards the sea. Save in severe floods, it was too small to be called a proper river, yet it was always too fast-flowing and too variable in depth and width to merit dismissal as a mere stream.

On the side where Adam sat on Fancy, the path came out from between the trees onto a small beach of flint pebbles. Cattle had been drinking here, widening the little river into a series of shallow pools. On the other side, the bank was higher, so they had worn two or three narrow paths down to the water. Though the water seemed easy enough to cross that day, Adam suspected heavy winter rains would turn it into an impassable flood. Much of the bank on the other side was crumbling and undercut. If you walked a horse across, as he intended to do when he had finished here, and used one of the paths up the bank worn by the cattle, it would be quite safe. But it you came upon it at speed—especially if you tried to jump over the water—he judged it would be very easy to come to grief.

Was this what had happened? Had Sir Jackman been in too great a hurry, tried to jump the stream and been thrown in the process? If so, his son was correct in calling it an accident. Their belief in murder would suffer a bad blow.

Adam got down from Fancy and went to tie her to one of the trees by the path. As he did so, his eye was caught by some marks higher up the trunk, too high up to be seen clearly from the ground. It looked as if something had been tied around this tree at a height of six feet or a little more. He looked around, but too many people had passed this way since the baronet's death. Any useful signs had been obliterated, muddled or smudged. He climbed again onto Fancy's back to take a better look at those marks on the trees. From this vantage point, all was clear. Something like a thin rope had been wrapped around the tree trunk and had cut into the bark deeply on one side. There was nothing there now, but the signs were plain enough once you had spotted them. There was also a deeper groove crossing the others, where someone must have used a knife to cut away the rope and gouged deep into the tree.

Adam rode swiftly to the other side of the path and peered into the trees there. Yes! There it was. A second thin area of wounds to the bark of a tree, the mirror image of the first. He was right! Somebody had tied a thin rope across the path, at about the height where it would catch an unwary rider; then returned later and removed the evidence.

Adam walked Fancy down to the water's edge, seeking any sign that someone had attempted to jump over the water. A jump must have left deep marks on this side where the horse's hind hooves had dug in to propel it upwards and forwards. Nothing. No, there was something there. Not a jump, though. He walked Fancy through the water and inspected the other bank. Had one prodigious leap been attempted and the horse fallen short of reaching the top of the bank, there would also have been deep hoof prints where the beast had landed and signs of the ground broken away. Nothing like that. All he could make out were places where an animal might have tried to struggle up the bank directly, without following the cattle-tracks.

He pondered what he had seen, trying to fit it into a sensible pattern. A horse could have come to the river, probably moving too fast to turn up or down to find a suitable path, then plunged through the water and scrambled up the bank. He looked back at the water. Ah! From here he could make out two deep indentations in the bed of the stream, as if a horse had reared up, then thrown itself forwards. Was this where its rider lost his grip and fell off backwards? Or was it where the horse felt the rider already falling, caught by the rope? It could well have reared up in fright as he fell, then plunged ahead and scrambled up the other side as best it could. Without a rider to direct it, the animal would probably have sought the most direct route away from the place, even if that might prove a struggle.

For a few more minutes, Adam urged Fancy round and round the immediate area to see if there was anything else to be learned. Then, having convinced himself there was not, and hearing voices approaching, he made off before he was discovered.

It was not until he was a mile or so further on his way towards Trundon Hall that he was struck by a disturbing thought. It was all very well theorising about the events at the ford, but none of that helped make clear what had caused Sir Jackman Wennard to be upon that track in the first place. The inn where the hunt had started out was a little to the west of where Adam was now, close to the parish church. Even if the hunt had moved off directly eastwards, which must have meant splashing its way across a boggy area, quite unsuited to chancing upon any fox, Sir Jackman, coming along behind, would have been facing in the opposite direction to the way Adam had just travelled. Turn through the points of the compass as he might, Adam could imagine no course of events starting at the inn yard that would have brought Sir Jackman onto that path to catch up with the hunt. That he had been there seemed certain enough. Why he had was a mystery, as was the reason he had been galloping like a madman—which must have been the case to inflict such damage to his throat. Until those matters were cleared up, all the rest was worthless.

When Adam reached Trundon Hall, Giles was waiting for him. Even with the first glance, he could see that his normally placid and cheerful brother was greatly agitated. He therefore decided to let his own news wait and allow Giles to start into his tale at once. It looked as if he might burst otherwise.

"That strutting buffoon Robert Wennard is the most arrogant, ignorant and obnoxious person it has ever been my misfortune to encounter!" Giles began. "I swear I came close to calling him out yesterday."

"A duel? Surely you are not serious, brother?"

"Deadly serious. He insulted me both as a man and a magistrate."

"But to fight a duel?" Adam still could not credit what his brother was saying.

"And why not, pray?" Giles said. "I am a fair shot and know how to handle a sword. It was only my sense of how any hurt to me would affect my family that held me back."

"And your good sense, I imagine. Now, brother, be calm and tell me what has transpired to make you so angry with that puppy."

"Aye, that's what he is!" Giles declared in a loud voice. "The yapping whelp of a mangy cur! A rabid dog that infects the very air around him! God! To have him as a neighbour will probably turn my hair white in a month!"

"Only if you let him annoy you," Adam said. "He isn't worth so much as a single thought. Now, please, please calm yourself and tell me what has transpired."

"Very well," his brother said reluctantly. "But one day ..."

"You have too much intelligence, Giles. Men like that always bring about their own downfall in time. From the little I have heard of the Wennard family, none of the owners of Upper Cley Hall have been good for anything. Blood will out!"

"True, true. His father and his grandfather were both ill-tempered men in their time, so it would be a miracle if he turned out any better. But to speak to me as he did!"

It took Adam a little while to coax his brother into telling his story. Even then, it was peppered with curses upon the whole Wennard family and Sir Robert in particular. Adam ignored these. It took a good deal to upset Giles' temper, but if something did, he was as slow to calm down as he had been to become roused.

As Giles told it, he had gone to Upper Cley Hall in his capacity as local magistrate. He thought he should ask the new baronet whether he intended to launch an investigation into the death of his father. If the response was negative, as he thought it would be, he would inform Sir Robert that, as the magistrate responsible for the King's Peace in the area, he felt it incumbent upon him to investigate for himself. Sir Jackman

Wennard had been a prominent man in the community. His murder should not be passed over without a full consideration of events.

All this Giles had explained, while Sir Robert stared at him with an attitude of cold indifference. When Giles added that he hoped he would receive the full co-operation of the Wennard family, Sir Robert had shaken his head.

"I have no intention of wasting any of my time on such a foolish procedure, Mr Bascom. My father's death was an accident, whatever that pompous little coroner and his jury of country bumpkins pronounced. That is an end of the matter, so far as all sensible people are concerned. If you wish to play the village-Hampden and pretend to an importance you do not have, I cannot prevent you, but I will certainly not lend credence to such a pointless endeavour. Now, good day to you, sir. Do not call again, for you will not be admitted."

By now, Adam was almost as angry as his brother had been. He stood up and began to wander around the room, stopping from time to time to stare at some ornament with unseeing eyes.

"Such effrontery!" he said. "Now I see why you wished to slap his face for him. The brazen arrogance of the man! Yet is it only that? Might he have some darker reason for wishing there to be no investigation into his father's death?"

Giles was a straightforward man, not given to conjectures. It took him several seconds to respond, while his mind grappled with what Adam had just suggested.

"Such a thought never crossed my mind, brother! Kill his own father? Could that snivelling little jackanapes be guilty of such a heinous crime? Surely not! He is all talk and bluster."

"Perhaps," Adam said, "perhaps. Yet I cannot believe he has no reason beyond the obvious one for trying to make this death out to be an accident."

"I fear I do not see even the obvious one," Giles said. "Were I in his position, I would shift heaven and earth to find the murderer and bring him to justice."

"Do you know anything of Sir Robert's financial position before his father's death?" Adam asked, changing the subject.

"Poor, I believe. The fellow has been an inveterate gambler almost since he was breeched. From what I hear, he is one of the worst kind of that sorry breed—a man who wagers too rashly, then seeks to recoup his losses by yet more wild play. His father had to bail him out many times to save the family name from being dragged through the mud. Though, now I recall it, I did hear that Sir Jackman had reached the end of his patience and was refusing to pay any more."

"Thus his untimely death must be the lifeline his son required. All that stands between him and enough money to set him up again is the process of probate."

"Indeed," Giles replied. "He could well be desperate for money. It's rumoured things are so bad he risks being blackballed from every gambling club in England, as well as ostracised by the young fools he likes to associate with. The executors of his father's estate will handle any immediate expenditure and advance him enough to live on, but it's unlikely they would hand over money to pay his gambling debts. At least, not without a full explanation and a good many promises of future good behaviour."

"Would he give those?"

"He might. He wouldn't be the first young wastrel who wished to make people forget all about his former life as he tries to win a rich wife. As it stands, few fathers will be willing to allow him to approach their daughters. Sir Jackman had a formidable reputation as a womaniser. Many will assume his son is likely to follow in his footsteps."

"Sadly," Adam said, "all this is mere conjecture. If we are to discover the killer, we need facts."

"I may supply a few," Giles said. "After I left Upper Cley Hall, I was even more determined to see justice done. I know I had already asked you to investigate, but it came to me that I could at least assist you by collecting information where I might. To that end, I made a small diversion and called on another neighbour. His name is Jasper Caxton. He's new to these parts since you lived here; a prosperous man, now somewhat past middle age but still active and healthy. I was almost sure he would have been amongst those out to catch a fox on that day."

"And was he?" Adam asked.

"Indeed he was. Even better, he said he had ridden up close on young Robert's heels. When he reached the fatal spot, Sir Robert was kneeling over the body of his father and looking distraught. Nothing had been moved, at least so far as Caxton could judge. The body was lying at the edge of the river on the far bank from where Caxton was standing. It appeared Sir Jackman had tried to take a shortcut through the trees, then attempted to jump the stream rather than slow down and allow his horse to wade through it. That was where he must have been thrown. His body was stretched out, full length on his back, with the head pointing back towards the way he had come."

"I went to the site of the murder on my way here," Adam said. "I am sure I could see signs where something—it could well have been a man on a horse—had pushed a way through the furze onto the pathway a few dozen yards from the place where the track crosses the little river. But why did he come that way? I thought the hunt set out from The Bull at Gressington. That's on the west of the valley, not the east."

"I don't know," Giles said. "Would it have been a shortcut?"

"By no means. It must have doubled or trebled the distance he would have to ride to catch up with the hunt—unless my belief in where the hunt had stopped is completely wrong. I must take pains to find out. Now, could Mr Caxton tell you anything of Sir Jasper's horse?"

"Why his horse? So far as I know, it was unhurt. At least, I recall Mr Caxton saying that he believed the horse had scrambled up the nearer bank and galloped off into the field beyond. When they caught it later, its sides were streaked with foam and it had clearly been ridden very hard. Aside from that, as I said, it was uninjured."

"Hmm," Adam muttered. "A most significant point."

"I do not follow you, brother," Giles said. "As always, your mind is too devious for mere mortals like me to comprehend."

"No matter," Adam said. "It may be nothing. Was this Mr Caxton able to add anything else?"

Giles shook his head.

"That's all."

"Yet it is a good deal and needs much reflection," Adam said. "Tomorrow I must return to Mossterton Hall to see how my patient fares—and satisfy at least some of his curiosity about this affair. If I do not, I fear he will drive the whole household insane with fretting to be allowed to seek me out."

Mention of Mossterton Hall at once diverted Giles' attention into seeking what Adam would tell him of Lady Alice and her visitors. It was, Adam reflected, typical of Giles to be more interested in the lives of his neighbours than in solving the mystery of Sir Jackman's death. Then, before he could leave for home, Adam had to endure further questioning on the same subject from Amelia, his brother's wife. When he proved unable to give full descriptions of what Lady Alice and Miss Scudamore had been wearing and how they arranged their hair, she was disgusted.

"You are hopeless, Brother Adam," she cried. "At least describe Miss Scudamore to me better than you have. Does she have a pleasing face? A good figure?"

"I imagine so," Adam said. "She certainly did not strike me as ill-favoured in any way. She is extraordinarily like her brother."

"Since I have not seen her brother," Amelia said in exasperation, "that means nothing to me. Can you say no more?"

"Well," Adam said, eager to be on his way to escape such an interrogation. "Mr Scudamore is tall—a little taller than I am—has a pleasing face and … his hair is light-coloured, I think."

"That is it? Oh, go home, sir!" Amelia cried. "I despair of you. You can describe the signs of disease in the finest detail, but set a woman before you and all you can recall is that she looked like her brother, who is tall and has—you think—light-coloured hair. How will you ever persuade a woman to marry you?"

"Fortunately," Adam said, "That problem—if it proves one—is many years away. I promise I will take notes next time I see Mr and Miss Scudamore, so that I may satisfy you on every point." And with that he pleaded pressure of business for staying at Trundon Hall no longer, kissed her on the cheek and left her staring after him.

"This is indeed a fine conundrum," Charles Scudamore said when Adam visited Mossterton Hall the next day. "I had begun to think Norfolk a very dull county. Now I must change my mind. Is Sir Jackman's son such a surly, ill-mannered and arrogant fellow by nature, or is he hiding the very darkest of secrets? What was his father up to on that last morning that he should ride along such an eccentric route? And—as you so rightly noted—how could any murderer have known—or caused—Sir Jackman to ride off alone, out of his way, then gallop headlong through trees and gorse bushes to meet his death in a trap prepared some time before? Oh, this is wonderful amusement!"

"I'm glad you find it so," Adam said drily.

"I do, I do!" Charles replied. "Ah … but your face says you find me flippant and superficial. So I am, at times. My sister tells me so again and again. Very well, I will assume the grave expression of a lawyer and assure you that your thoughts about the executors of Sir Jackman Wennard's Will are certainly correct. I do not believe any responsible executors would hand over a large amount of cash to pay the gambling debts of a son and heir without some very cogent reason—maybe not even then. No, they would delay as long as they could and offer a good many sober lectures on the need for improvement. Do you know who the executors are? No matter, I can easily find out. It also occurs to me that it would be sensible to look into the financial position of the estate as a whole."

"Surely that will not be known until the probate inventory is made?" Adam said. "Nor would it be easy to gain access to such documents without a good reason."

"What? Gain access? Nothing easier, my dear fellow. Leave that to me. All I need from you is permission to leave this estate for a few days …"

"No!" Adam said.

"But if you want …"

"I want your ribs to heal fully and your strength to return to normal," Adam said firmly. "Until then, you will remain here. I will not have Lady Alice tell me later that I should have treated you more firmly."

"But time …"

"Is of no great matter, sir. There are many other facts to be established before I let you go chasing rainbows amongst the diocesan archives."

"You are no fun," Mr Scudamore said bitterly. "I am the lawyer, and even I have more sense of adventure than you."

"Do you wish your physician to have a sense of adventure, as you put it? To abandon a sensible course of treatment and launch out into the unknown to see whether the patient survives or dies as a result? To abandon established practice and the remedies listed in the pharmacopeia medica in favour of the nostrums of 'The Great Professor Katterfelto' and his kind?"

"I suppose not," Giles said.

"Indeed not, sir. Let me proceed in my own way, dull though it may be. It will at least have logic and sound reasoning from the evidence on its side."

"But I can help you!"

"Why is it everyone wishes to help me?" Adam said. "Do I seem to be so plainly in need of assistance? During the last mystery I sought to unravel, Miss LaSalle, my mother's lady companion, appointed herself my deputy and lieutenant."

"A lady of mature years, I imagine."

"Not at all. Miss LaSalle is but four or five-and-twenty."

"Young enough then. Splendid! Is she pretty?" Giles asked at once. "There seems to be a sad dearth of pretty young women in this area."

"Tolerably pretty," Adam said warily. For some reason, the thought of Mr Scudamore paying court to Miss LaSalle seemed at that moment thoroughly unpleasant.

"Only tolerably. Alas! I had hoped …"

"My mother—and Miss LaSalle—live in Norwich, Mr Scudamore."

"But I am sure they visit you. Next time they do, you must invite my sister and I to meet them. I am not sure I trust your 'tolerably pretty'. You may be seeking to keep some treasure to yourself."

"Miss LaSalle and I have always behaved towards one another with the greatest propriety," Adam protested. That was true enough, though he had more than once entertained the most unbecoming thoughts about covering her neck with kisses, then proceeding to her breasts … Enough, he told himself. First Lady Alice, now Miss LaSalle.

"Then why are you blushing?" Giles asked.

"I am not blushing," Adam protested. "It is a little warm in here. Now, I am a busy man, Mr Scudamore, with no time for such nonsense.

Continue as I have instructed you and I may—may, I say—release you from your confinement when I see you next. Are Lady Alice and your sister at home, do you know? It would not be polite to leave without speaking to them."

"You are out of luck, doctor. They have gone shopping to Norwich. My aunt will soon be able to assume half-mourning, so she needs new clothes in the appropriate colour. My sister, being eager to seize any chance to view fine fabrics and other fripperies, has gone with her." Adam thought Mr Scudamore looked at him in a slightly odd way. "My sister will be most upset to have missed you. Ever since your last visit, she has quite pestered me with questions about you. I wonder ... well, no matter. You would not be the first."

As Adam took his leave and drove his chaise down the driveway from Mossterton Hall, he could not help wondering what that last remark might portend.

Four

The Bull Inn

BACK HOME AT LAST, ADAM WAS EAGER TO TALK THROUGH THE NEW EVIDENCE WITH HIS FRIEND, Peter, but it was too late to call that day. Had his news been sufficiently pressing he might still have done so, but it would be churlish to interrupt a man's dinner with little more than oddments and conjectures. The next morning would have to be soon enough.

In this too he found himself frustrated. William, Adam's groom, returned from the apothecary's shop with the news that Mr Lassimer had left very early to visit a number of patients in Blakeney and the surrounding area. He was not expected home until late. By rights, Adam too should have settled down to working through the various tasks from his practice that had begun to pile up. There were letters to be read and answered, bills to be reviewed and settled, messages from patients seeking consultations to be considered and dates and times set. For five minutes, he tried to keep his mind on these mundane, necessary items, then sighed, rose and called for William to have the chaise ready in fifteen minutes. There was no way he would be able to settle until at least some of the questions swirling around in his head had been answered.

Adam's plan was to arrive at The Bull Inn at Gressington as if he was returning from a lengthy journey attending to some patient close to death. He would order refreshment and spend a while talking with the landlord. Then he would make his way back to Aylsham. After a moment, he recalled he did have one or two patients not too far away from Gressington. It would never do to start a rumour that one or other of them was dying! No, on second thoughts he would use the fiction that he had been at his brother's house when he was called out in error by an over-zealous servant to visit someone in Blakeney. Since he needed to return home to deal with other medical business, it seemed best to head directly for Holt and the road to Aylsham. To stop at Trundon Hall was bound to delay him further.

It sounded weak, but it would have to suffice. At least the name of Bascom counted for a great deal in that area. With luck, the landlord would be so pleased to tell his cronies he had entertained the squire's brother that he would not look too closely at why Adam had been there.

Luckily the inn was quiet and the landlord more than willing to serve his distinguished visitor in person. Adam ordered a pint of good ale for himself and invited the landlord to join him in a drink of his own choosing. As he suspected, the man swiftly filled a tankard and drank down fully half of it at a single gulp. When Adam suggested he should fill up again at his expense, the landlord regarded him with that intense pleasure hardened drinkers have for anyone fool enough to pay for their vice. Tongues were loosened and caution thrown to the wind. Whatever information this generous visitor wanted, he should have in full.

The events of the fatal fox-hunt were still a lively topic of conversation in such a small village, so the topic arose naturally. Everyone knew Adam had been present at the inquest. What could be more natural than for him to be curious about other aspects of the affair? He had only to make a general enquiry about events at the inn that day to set the inn-keeper in full flow.

The innkeeper explained Sir Jackman himself had organised the hunt over his estate. He didn't like all and sundry wandering around close to his house, so whenever the hunt met locally, those attending would be told to assemble outside The Bull. The huntsmen and riders in their fine clothes always attracted a good number of spectators, so it was excellent for business—even though Sir Jackman was often slow to settle up for the drinks supplied to the hunt-servants and his own friends. That day, the hunt had been especially well attended. The Wennard lands included large areas of heath, full of rabbits and foxes to prey upon them. As well as Sir Jackman and his son, a good number of the neighbouring squires and most of the substantial tenant farmers had joined in. Sir Jackman's gamekeepers knew his taste for a good gallop after a fox, so they would have been out early to stop up the entrances to any earths or badger setts where the hunted animal might take refuge.

When all had assembled and drunk their stirrup cup—or two—the hunt moved off along the trackway that went more or less due south, along the western edge of the valley. The land was fairly open between there and the river, so if a fox were found, it would not easily go to ground. Unfortunately, the only scent the hounds had picked up hadn't taken them far. Either the fox managed to cross the river to break its scent trail, or the trail had been made the night before and the fox already well away. The hounds had started baying, of course, and the huntsman had blown his horn to urge them on, then their heads had come up and they pulled up in a confused mass. It was just about then that one or two of the hunt followers first noticed the absence of Sir Jackman.

"I see," Adam said. "So he had started out with all the others, I presume?"

Not at all, the innkeeper told him. Sir Jackman wasn't with the hunt from the start; he himself had known that since before they moved off.

He'd noticed Sir Jackman riding away in a great hurry a few minutes earlier. What's more, he was going in the opposite direction; north towards the roadway that led from east to west along the coast itself.

"I saw him clear as day," the innkeeper told Adam. "He set out along the track right beside the inn here—the one between us and the church. Going fast enough too, he were. Only place that track leads is to the road between Cley and Blakeney, close along the marshes by the shore."

"I wonder what he was doing?" Adam said. "You didn't get any idea, I suppose?"

The innkeeper's chest swelled visibly.

"Indeed I did, sir. Not in detail, but still plain enough. Just before the hunt moved off, the old squire as was must've seen someone in the crowd. There's allus a heap of villagers' wives, children and loungers who comes to watch the spectacle. There were a good few that day, as I said before; morn'n usual, I'd say. Now whoever old squire saw seemed to upset him mightily. He shouted several times for whoever it was to stand still and wait for him to reach them. They can't have done that, for the next time I looked, old squire were standing up in the stirrups, looking all around for 'em. Must've lost sight of whoever it was and let 'em slip away."

"Was it someone on a horse or on foot, do you think?" Adam asked.

"That I can't rightly say," the innkeeper replied. "I don't think it were anyone on a horse or in a carriage, but I can't be sure. But something must've persuaded Sir Jackman that he knew where they'd gone. He rode his horse right into the crowd, scattering people on all sides and swearing as would've made a sailor blush."

"Was it one person he was after or more?"

"I truly don't know, sir, for I never seen exactly who he was lookin' at. But, as I says, it's clear he thought they—or he—had gone off up the track towards the coast. It took him a few moments to push his horse through the mass of people. They were as keen to be out of his way as he was to get through, for that horse had a wild look in his eye. I wouldn't have put it past him to start kicking out neither. Trouble is, when people in a mass gets scared, they many times goes in the opposite direction to what would be best."

"But Sir Jackman got through?"

"Right enough. And once he was clear of the crowd, he whipped up that 'orse of his and set off at the gallop up the track like I said. Still swearing and cussing he was, fit to burst."

"Did you see him again that day?" Adam asked.

"No, I didn't, sir. Wherever he went, he didn't come back past here. More or less as soon as the hunt drew away, the brewer's dray arrived, so I was outside with them. It don't do to let 'em unload without watching 'em. Sometimes they picks up a barrel of beer somewhere else that's being returned because it's bad. Then they tries to slip it into your order and keep a good one. Good profit in selling a cask of ale to anyone willing to pay and no questions asked."

So Sir Jackman headed north towards the coast road in pursuit of some person or persons he had seen in the inn yard. Who on earth could that have been to get the man so angry? Well, if he'd reached the coast road and turned west, he would soon have been in Blakeney. If he'd come back from that direction to reach the river where his body was found, he must have passed by the inn. The innkeeper seemed sure he hadn't and he'd been outside with the draymen the whole time. But if the baronet had turned east towards Cley, he could well have come back along the eastern side of the valley, though still to the north of where the hunt was by then. Assuming he decided he'd lost whoever he was after and was in a hurry to catch up with the hunt going south, it would have been natural to follow the road to Holt, then turn down into the valley along the shortcut Adam had taken two days before. Then he would have crossed the river at precisely the place where his body was found.

That must be what had happened. Sir Jackman would almost certainly be in a great hurry. He'd lost a good deal of time on his fruitless search and the hunt was moving further away at every moment. Could he have heard the sounds of the short-lived pursuit of a fox from where he was? It was possible, if the wind had been blowing in the right direction. If he thought he'd miss his gallop and fail to arrive in time for the kill, a keen sportsman like Sir Jackman would certainly try his hardest to catch up. He might have even decided to make the shortcut still shorter by plunging more or less straight down the side of the valley. It was steep and a rider would have needed to force his way through a good deal of brambles and gorse, so that would account for the damage to the gorse and saplings.

The innkeeper could tell him no more, though he furrowed his brow a good deal and his face grew red, either from the unusual effort of thought or from the copious amounts of beer he'd drunk at Adam's expense. Still, the information provided was well worth the price of four—or was it five?—jugs of ale. It had been enough to slur the man's speech a good deal at the end anyway.

Eventually, with many empty promises to return whenever he might be passing that way, Adam took his leave and rattled away down the same side of the valley as the hunt had taken. Time to go home and try to allow it all to settle into his mind and join up with what he knew already.

Once again, Adam allowed himself to seek out his friend Lassimer to act as a sounding board. There was still enough time before dinner to allow for a short visit. To his surprise, he was shown into the parlour, where Peter soon joined him. He came accompanied by a neat young maidservant bearing the necessities for serving them coffee. She set pot and cups down carefully on the table, added a small bowl of shavings from the sugar-loaf, then turned to leave the room. Adam did not recall having seen her before, so he decided to satisfy his curiosity about her.

"You must be Jane," he said.

"No, doctor," she replied. "I'm Susan. Jane is upstairs, cleaning the master's bedroom." Then she turned once more to her master. "Will that be all, sir?"

Adam stared at her. Surely this was not the girl sent by the Overseers of the Poor? What had become of the stick-thin arms, the lank hair and the famished look? This girl was possessed of clear skin, bright eyes and the youthful plumpness that betokens a fine figure in later life.

"Thank you, Susan," Peter said. "You may go now. We need nothing more." Then he turned to Adam and began to laugh. "I see it is too long since I entertained you in my parlour, Bascom. Oh, I know you love to sit in my compounding room, but I thought you in need of refreshment. I have a strict rule that no liquids may be taken into the place where I mix my medicines, save those that belong there. One careless spill might lead to significant damage to the ingredients I store below the counters. I wished to offer you coffee, so we had to talk here."

"Susan?" Adam stuttered. "Where? How? I mean …"

"What you see, Bascom, is the result of several months of good, regular food, kindness and the resilience of youth. You will know Jane when you see her, for her hair is the colour of a fine carrot and she has more freckles than I have ever seen on a human before. But enough about my maids. Let me pour the coffee while you tell me all you have discovered in the matter of the murder since we met last."

The telling took many minutes, though Peter was a good listener and did not interrupt before the tale was complete.

"So," Peter said when Adam had finished. "We are left with the same questions as before, together with several new ones. You move sideways, not forwards. The most important question remains. Was the trap with the rope aimed at Sir Jackman? How did anyone know he would ride that way? You have progressed no further on either of those points."

"All too true," Adam said. "If the trap was meant to kill, wasn't it more likely to go wrong or fail completely? I mean, might it not merely hurt him or throw him off his horse into the water? Unless he struck the rope—for that's what I believe it was, tied between two trees—unless he struck it with considerable force, either of those outcomes would be more likely."

"I wonder why Sir Jackman didn't see the rope in time to avoid it," Peter said. "It was broad daylight. No one rides full tilt into a rope across his path unless he is going too fast to pull up. Even then, if he had crouched in the saddle, the rope must have passed over his head, surely? You said the marks suggested it was at a height of six feet above the ground or more."

"High enough that I could not see the marks clearly when I was standing by the tree. I had to get back on my horse to look at them properly. From the saddle, I would judge them to be about the height of my armpits or a little less."

"Interesting," Peter said. "From the way you've described the site, I doubt the horse would have jumped upwards in an attempt to clear the stream. Would it not rather have leapt forwards as far as it could? In such a case, its rider would surely lean forwards too, over the horse's neck. However I look at it, it makes no sense. He may have been in a hurry, but I cannot see anything to suggest Sir Jackman would try to get his horse to leap across the river. All he had to do was splash through the water and get up the opposite bank as quickly as he could. He might have urged the horse to go straight up the far bank, rather than following the zig-zag tracks made by the cattle. Nothing more."

"Once he was across the stream, he would also have been well clear of any rope, if it was tied where I imagine it was," Adam said. "Believe me; I have driven myself nearly frantic with attempts to solve the puzzle, all to no avail."

"Let's leave it for the moment, then," Peter said. "You say the innkeeper told you Sir Jackman set off northwards, in pursuit of the mystery person he had seen in the inn yard, while the hunt moved off to the south?"

"That's so. I wish I had any notion of who he saw to upset him so much. The innkeeper said he was roaring and swearing as a man possessed."

"That's simple enough. It must have been his daughter."

"His daughter?" Adam cried. "Which daughter? Did you not tell me one at least could not have been involved in what happened because she had eloped? Do you mean his other daughter?"

"Not at all," Peter said. "I mean the one who has eloped."

"But she had gone!" Adam voice was shrill. "You told me so yourself."

"It is only now you've told me of Sir Jackman's behaviour in the inn yard. Before, there was no need for me to be precise about the time or manner of her departure."

Adam's attempt to calm himself was not a great success. "Then be precise now, Lassimer, I pray you. What do you know that makes you think Sir Jackman saw his daughter that morning? Be plain, man, plain for God's sake!"

Peter's reply was a model of calmness and reason. "I was told Sir Jackman had been suspicious for some time that his daughter was defying him in the matter of meetings with Mr Lancelot Pashley. As a result, he had confined her to the house. Mr Pashley could hardly bring a carriage up to the door for them to elope in. She needed to find a way to escape far enough from the house to meet with him. Upper Cley Hall stands more or less at the eastern side of the Wennard estate and the only road is that from Cley to Holt. Of course, it passes too close to the house for her purpose, so the cunning young woman worked on her father's passion for hunting to persuade him to let her go to watch the hunt that day. She promised to travel in the little dog-cart, with father and brother riding beside her. Then, when the hunt had left, it was arranged that two of Lord George Gossett's gamekeepers would escort her back home. No chance of escape there."

"What happened instead?" Adam snapped. "Get on with it!"

"This is purely guesswork, you understand," Peter replied. "I expect she sent a message to Mr Pashley saying she would be in the inn-yard at such and such a time. He came in a carriage, stayed at the edge of the throng, waited for her to slip down from the dog-cart and ran off with her through the crowd back to his carriage. It would take but a moment for her to climb in and duck down out of sight. With luck, everyone would be so busy admiring the riders and fussing over the hounds to notice she'd gone. Once both were safely aboard, Pashley would drive off as calmly as possible."

"But her father saw them!" Adam cried. "That must be it! He saw what was going on and tried to prevent it. He must have been some way from the lovers, so thrust his horse through all the people to get to them. Pashley would have heard him shouting, realised further concealment was useless, and driven off as quickly as he could—up the track to the north and the coast road! Sir Jackman, of course, rushed off after the pair."

For a moment, Adam's face was a picture of triumph. Then his expression changed to one of disappointment.

"Why didn't he catch them? If they were in a carriage and he was on horseback, he must have overtaken them swiftly."

"That I cannot answer," Peter said. "Did your innkeeper indicate how long it might have taken Sir Jackman to get through all the people?"

"No," Adam said. "All he said was that the people in the crowd were frightened and started running about in all directions to try to get away."

"There must have been a few carriages there as well," Peter said. "Many ladies enjoy seeing the hunt set out and they would not have come on foot. I suspect it may have taken our enraged baronet longer than you think to get clear and set out on his way. As I recall, that track does not go far before it joins the coast road, nor does it run straight. There are some hedges too, are there not? It's quite likely, they would've been out of sight before he could leave the inn-yard and go after them."

"Yes! Yes!" Adam said, becoming excited again. "Once the coast road was reached, it would still be unclear whether they had turned to the left towards Blakeney or to the right towards Cley. I cannot now remember if the road is in plain view in both directions. The gorse and furze are often tall. Besides, it is a road much used. If there were many upon it that morning, even Sir Jackman in a towering rage could not have proceeded at better than a trot. Now suppose … Sir Jackman heads for Cley. He must have done so to end up where his body was found. Mr Pashley has turned towards Blakeney. Thus Sir Jackman goes some distance in the wrong direction, before realising his error. No point turning back by then; the two lovers will be far away. Instead, he decides to rejoin the hunt by heading down the road towards Holt and taking the shortcut over the river. I do believe you have solved it, Lassimer."

"I am not totally without brains, Bascom," Peter said, "even if you sometimes imply that I am."

"Never!" Adam said. "Without morals, I grant you, but I have never thought you stupid."

"And I am to be content with that?" Peter feigned irritation. "A clever rogue? A fine way to talk to your friend!"

"Hush with your nonsense! Let me think," Adam said. "You said the baronet's daughter—what's her name—has gone to Scotland?"

"Her name is Caroline. I said all assume that is where they've gone."

"Why? She is of age, I believe you said."

"No again," Peter said. "I said she is twenty or twenty-one. The difference would be crucial in this case. I do wish you would be precise, Bascom."

"You are a fine one to talk of precision! If you had been plainer about the details of this elopement from the start, you would have saved me much wasted effort."

"But why should I have thought to give you every detail?" Peter protested. "As I said a little while ago, neither of us had any reason to think the matter important."

"Well … I suppose that is true enough," Adam said. "Let's not quarrel over it. I know it now and can see its worth as part of the puzzle. With that element solved …"

"Slow down, friend," Peter said. "It makes a good story—even a convincing one—but we don't yet know it's correct. That Miss Wennard went to the inn-yard seems certain, for we know she has eloped and that was an essential part of her plan—at least if what the gossips say is true. We don't know for certain her father saw them; nor that the sight was the cause of his anger and haste. Another reason may yet emerge. Of course, once the young pair return, you may be able to ask her, but that cannot be for some days at least. Oh! She will not yet know her father is dead."

Adam was deflated.

"All you say is true, Lassimer. I am letting myself grasp at the first viable explanation, mostly for want of any others in this most tangled and murky affair."

"What will you do next?"

"I am not sure," Adam said. "I would like to know more of what happened during the hunt. How Sir Jackman's body came to be found when it was, for instance. If what the innkeeper said is true, the huntsmen, hounds and all the followers should have been several hundred yards away, milling about on the opposite side of the valley. What made anyone go down to the river and find the dead man?"

"Indeed," Peter said. "Another puzzle. Why don't you visit your patient, Mr Scudamore, again? He sounds to be a lively young fellow and must move in the right circles when he's here. Perhaps he'll know of someone who intended to follow the hunt that day. Lady Alice too must be aware of most of the people in these parts who are said to enjoy fox hunting. Between them, I don't doubt they can suggest one or more whom you could annoy with your questions."

"Pah!" Adam said. "Even when you make a sound suggestion for once, you cannot resist some ribaldry. I am the very mirror of politeness and courtesy, I would have you know."

"Is that what your young lady in London tells you?" Peter said.

Adam jumped and spluttered. "Lady? … What lady, sir?"

"I am waiting for you to tell me her name, Bascom, for I am sure enough of her existence. Your poor mother long ago gave up the task of trying to civilise you, yet the past few months have seen a marked improvement in your behaviour and your appearance. You usually affect a modest and grave demeanour, quite suitable for a physician, yet of late you show a distinct interest in the theatre and in music, both of which you lacked before. Your dress is far tidier and of better quality. It remains the dress of a doctor, while displaying something close to fashion in its details. I know you are now a wealthy man, but this overall neatness and polish indicates a feminine hand at work. It is no one here, of that I am sure, not even Miss LaSalle. These mysterious visits to London hold the answer."

"Balderdash!" Adam said. "Sheer imagination and invention! There is no mystery. I've already told you that. In London, I attend learned lectures and strive to better my mind."

"Why do I not believe you?" Peter said. "Oh, I have no doubt you do those things, but not all the time. It is what you do besides, in the evenings—and most of all at night—that intrigues me."

"By George!" Adam said. "Is that the time? I have not sufficient leisure to waste it listening to your nonsense, Lassimer. There are things I must be doing. Good day to you, my friend."

"Run away if you wish," Peter said. "I shall not give up. In time, I will have the truth out of you, even though I let it pass for today. Good day to you too, Bascom—and give my regards to your lady in London the next time you see her."

Adam had already slipped past Susan and opened the front door for himself, but as he hurried up the street towards his own door he knew his face must be burning.

It had not occurred to Adam until Peter had given the name of Miss Wennard's lover to seek out his friend Mr Jempson. Mr Jempson was a merchant and a prominent Quaker. There must have been talk about Mr Lancelot Pashley's elopement amongst the members of that sect, if he too was from a Quaker family. Many of the stricter Quakers disapproved of marriages outside the Society of Friends, as they called themselves.

Mr Jempson might not have been on Adam's mind, but the doctor was definitely on his. A young manservant from Mr Jempson came to Adam's house that same day to enquire whether the doctor might be able to spare his master some of his time. It was not urgent, he had been told to say, nor on a medical matter. Adam agreed at once to a visit and suggested the next morning. Although Mr Jempson lived barely a quarter of a mile away, on the outskirts of the little town, their paths rarely met. Much of the merchant's business was conducted in King's Lynn or Great Yarmouth. As a dealer in grain, the ports from which the bulk of the county's usually abundant harvests were shipped were of great importance to him. Indeed, to Adam's knowledge he was the part-owner of several grain ships, as well as a maltings and two substantial grain stores.

At eleven o'clock the next day, therefore, Mr Jempson came to Adam's house, exchanged warm greetings with him, and was settled in the parlour to take coffee. After the usual preliminaries, the merchant explained the main purpose of his visit was to inform Adam that his only daughter, Elisabeth, was to be married soon. He wished to extend an invitation to Adam to attend the celebrations and share in the family's pleasure. Naturally Adam accepted, since he counted both father and daughter amongst his friends. All the right things were said and Mr Jempson sat beaming with pleasure.

Within Adam himself, the news brought less welcome feelings. Elisabeth Jempson was, to his mind, the perfect material for a wife. She was beautiful, kind, gentle and yet both well-educated and fully able to hold her own in the world. Now she would be another man's wife and a veil of formality and propriety would fall between them.

Of course, he had always known he could never consider seeking Elisabeth's hand for himself, however fond his feelings towards her. Mr Jempson was a man of importance amongst the Norfolk Quakers. He would be bound to wish his only child to marry within the Society of Friends. Though Adam had great admiration for the way in which most Quakers lived, he knew he would never be able to subscribe honestly to their religious beliefs. Yet, now the inevitable had come to pass and she was promised to another, he could not help feeling sadness and regret alongside a genuine wish that Elisabeth's marriage should be happy and successful.

"What is the name of the fortunate gentleman?" he asked. "It is possible that I have heard of him or his family, if he lives in these parts."

"It is Mr Gerard Pashley," Mr Jempson replied. Adam must have jumped visibly, since Mr Jempson hesitated a moment in puzzlement. "Thou wilt certainly have heard of the family, I expect. They live not far from the village of Letheringsett, which is close by thine own family home at Trundon Hall. I believe their estate was formerly owned by a member of the Custance family, who died without issue. He directed that it should be sold, since he was a philanthropic man who wished to make a number of monetary bequests to good causes in the county. Mr Gerard Pashley's father, Horatio, is a successful tea merchant and importer. He bought the estate and now spends the greater portion of his time there."

"But indeed I have heard of the family, Mr Jempson, though I did not know they now lived in the former Custance property. Only recently too. Surely the Mr Lancelot Pashley with whom the late Sir Jackman Wennard's daughter is said to have eloped must be some relation?"

"His younger brother," Mr Jempson said. "A delightful young man. He and Mr Gerard have taken charge of the family business, so that their father may enjoy a well-deserved period of rest and retirement."

"So he is the one with whom Miss Caroline Wennard has gone to Scotland to be wed?"

"To Scotland? Why dost thou think that, doctor? They are in Norwich, to my certain knowledge, for I attended their joyful nuptials only some days past."

Adam was thoroughly confused. "You were there, Mr Jempson?" he said. "So you approve of the match."

"Most certainly, my dear doctor. Mr Lancelot Pashley will make a fine husband and he and his bride seem much devoted to one another."

"But she did not have her father's consent," Adam protested. "From what I heard, he had quite another bridegroom in mind for her."

Mr Jempson frowned.

"I welcome the death of no man, doctor, nor will I condone violence in any way. However, it is hard indeed to feel a proper degree of sadness at the killing of Sir Jackman Wennard. He was both cruel and heartless, I fear. The man whom he was trying to force—yes, force—his daughter to marry is fully sixty years of age and noted for his dissipated style of life. When she informed him of her own choice of husband, her father flew into a passion, though the Pashley family are respectable and more than wealthy enough. I suspect Mr Horatio could have bought out the baronet's estate three or four times over. When Sir Jackman heard his daughter had indicated her desire to join our Society … I can scare bring myself to tell thee of it, it is so foul. He struck her, doctor! Struck her and left her lying on the floor before him! For a man to strike another in anger is a heinous sin. To strike your own child is almost unforgivable."

"But is she of age?" Adam asked.

"Fortunately, she came of age some weeks ago. Thus her own consent to the marriage was sufficient in the eyes both of the law and of all reasonable men. She was forced to leave her home by means of a subterfuge, which is what I imagine was reported to you as an elopement. To prevent her from marrying Mr Pashley—and to punish her yet further for her brave disobedience to a tyrant's will—her father was keeping her confined within his house. Yet escape she did. The two young people came into Norwich and were married, both in the eyes of God and of the law, in the Meeting House there. All had been planned beforehand to prevent her father seeking to disrupt even that sacred ceremony."

"And she and her husband are still in Norwich?"

"So far as I know—ah, I see the purpose of thy questions now. The death of the baronet concerns thee in some way."

"I suppose men would say it concerns me, Mr Jempson," Adam said. "My brother is magistrate in those parts and was consulted by the coroner on a troubling matter. The coroner's medical examiner found signs upon the body which indicated the baronet had not died from a fall from his horse, but as a result of some deliberate act. This was bound to cause something of a sensation at the inquest, so my brother approached me in haste to ask that I might offer an independent medical opinion. My findings concurred with those of the coroner's man in every detail. Without doubt, Sir Jackman Wennard was murdered."

"Alas," Mr Jempson said. "How wicked are the ways of men, doctor. But surely thy part in the business is now over? Or has thy curiosity once more taken charge?"

Adam grinned. "I cannot deny the curiosity, Mr Jempson," he said, "but my involvement stems from another cause. My brother takes his duties as magistrate most seriously—"

"As he should," Mr Jempson said.

"Indeed. The baronet's heir, his only surviving son, now Sir Robert Wennard, is adamant in claiming his father's death was an accident. He has refused to institute any form of enquiry into the death of his father. He has also made it clear he will answer no questions about the matter. I have even heard it said he has expressly forbidden the rest of his family, and any person in his employment, to give information."

"Surely that is a most unnatural action?" Mr Jempson said. "A son to refuse to consider the evidence of two doctors, that his father's death was not accidental, but the result of violence against him?"

"So you would think," Adam said. "My brother was worried by this circumstance. Although all seem to agree that Sir Jackman was an unpleasant, even cruel man, he was still the owner of many acres of land and a person of some standing. To my brother, to walk away without seeking to establish the truth of such a dreadful crime against the King's Peace is unthinkable. He consulted the Deputy Lieutenant of the County, who agreed with him fully."

"So, doctor," Mr Jempson said, striving to keep a straight face, "since thy brother is doubtless aware that thou hast a certain level of experience and interest in solving mysteries of this type—"

"He has asked me to act in his stead. You have it, sir. It seems that all who know me conspire to take me away from my practice to delve into one mystery or another."

"On thy part, of course, there is nothing but the greatest reluctance," Mr Jempson said. "Come, my friend. Such matters as this are as meat and drink to thee! Nor could anyone find a more thorough, conscientious and thoughtful investigator in this land, I dare say. Thou needst not ask for my poor help, for I offer it to thee at once with an open hand and heart. Though I doubt I have much to offer in any practical way."

"There is one thing immediately," Adam said. "Could you send word to Mr Lancelot Pashley that I would deem it of great assistance to speak with him and his wife on this matter? I have been told they met that day where the hunt was collecting. They may have noticed something to help fill a number of gaps in my understanding of events before the death occurred. I would not intrude on the lady's grief, if it were not so important."

"I will send word this very day, doctor. I will be most surprised if they are not ready to talk to thee. I will also add my own recommendation in the matter and vouch for thy discretion. The moment I have a reply, be sure I will communicate it to thee forthwith."

A SHORTCUT TO MURDER

Five

To Norwich

ADAM'S INVESTIGATION WAS AT LONG LAST MOVING FORWARD. He had high hopes of his meeting with the former Miss Caroline Wennard. If her father had seen her at the inn with her husband-to-be, she would surely know. Seeing her in the act of eloping could explain Sir Jackman Wennard's sudden departure from the inn-yard in the opposite direction to the hunt; it might also throw light on many other matters. So far, all Adam had produced was a hundred questions, none with answers. Once again he must wait on events, though he was sure Mr Jempson would be true to his word in good Quaker fashion and arrange a meeting with the Pashleys as quickly as possible.

What he needed most were fresh insights into what he knew already, some different way to fit the information together. His present ones had failed. Maybe it would be best to turn his mind right away from the problem for a while, stand back, regain some perspective. Allow his mind to shake itself free of current preconceptions and find a better approach. He also had patients to see. It was all very well rushing off to solve the mystery his brother Giles had presented to him, but doing so would not allow him to send out suitably large bills at the end of the next quarter. He might not need the money, but it was pleasant to have it. Besides, he told himself severely, he had people depending on him to help them fight sickness. To abandon them would be a clear violation of his purpose in becoming a physician.

For the next few days, Adam devoted himself completely to his practice and his patients. Many of them suffered from chronic conditions like gout, rheumatism, cases of the pox and ailments of the stomach. Mixed in with these were the usual agues and fluxes, a bone to be set or a wound to be dressed, the routine of almost any physician. He prescribed purgatives and cordials, bled one or two—though he was coming to doubt the efficacy of that treatment—and offered others advice on their diet. Happily, the journeys demanded of him coincided with an unusual spell of warm, settled, autumn weather, so that driving along a country road became a pleasure. He loved the vast skies with their towers of white cloud so characteristic of Norfolk. It was impossible to feel gloomy, while the sun shone, huge flocks of peewits and plovers wheeled over the marshes, and the larks sang as if it were spring.

All this time, the scattered pieces of information he had about the murder of Sir Jackman Wennard slid and shifted in his mind, forming combinations, breaking apart again and reforming in fresh patterns—none of them satisfactory.

Others were active on his behalf. Charles Scudamore wrote to say that Lady Alice had sent letters to several of her late husband's acquaintances seeking any who had been part of the fox hunt on the day Sir Jackman was killed. Would they be willing to describe what they had seen? He had himself written to one or two colleagues in the legal profession who might have some insight into the affairs of the Wennard family. And though Adam had forbidden him to leave the Mossterton estate as yet, he had spent two useful hours with Lady Alice's steward probing what he knew of the attitudes of Sir Jackman's tenants towards their landlord.

According to the steward, progressive landlords, such as Sir Daniel Fouchard, understood the best way to increase revenues from their estates was to help their tenants add to their own profits. Some judicial investment of capital in land improvement, or the purchase of new farm equipment, could reap a handsome reward for both parties. The best landowners also combined holdings into larger farms, as opportunities arose, since the more substantial tenants often used their own capital to add to the landlord's spending on improvements. Finally, they were willing to give long leases to those tenants who proved the best farmers and put some of their own money into better land use. All improvements took many years to produce their full results. Short leases would deny a farmer and his family the benefit of his investment and hard work.

On all these counts, the Wennard family had proved deficient. Sir Jackman, in particular, must now derive more than two-thirds of his total income from his racehorses. He won regularly, so breeding stock from his stables commanded high prices. He had recently sold two breeding mares to the Prince of Wales, and there was always strong demand for the services of his prize stallions. Neither of his two predecessors had taken much interest in their estates. For Sir Jackman the lands were better used for hunting than for agriculture.

Even so, the late baronet, it seemed, had been as greedy for rent increases as any gentleman whose expenditures were high. The result was a tenantry who felt themselves little more than sources of cash, to be milked as much as possible, yet denied the capital they needed to bring their holdings up to a better standard.

That, however, was not the chief cause of complaint. It was common knowledge that Sir Jackman Wennard judged any pretty woman fair game for his lust, be she wife, daughter or sister of a tenant. And while some ladies might make little protest at giving him what he desired, he was not above taking others by force, if he could catch them when their menfolk were absent. There were many husbands, the steward had told

Charles, who nursed well-founded suspicions that their womenfolk had given in to the practiced words of a habitual seducer like Sir Jackman. A few had still darker thoughts, perhaps having returned home one day to find wife or daughter confused and upset, yet unwilling to explain what had happened to them. It would be understandable, Charles wrote, if one of these men had finally decided to teach the baronet a lesson. Even a trap that only threw him from his horse to suffer bruising or a broken bone or two would be better than suffering in silence. The chances of this action being brought home to an individual would not have been great.

Poor Adam! The more information he had, the more confused he felt.

Charles' final piece of information only increased the number of suspects. The young lawyer had persuaded an acquaintance, also in the legal profession, to send his clerk to look through the records of the assize courts and quarter sessions for the past two years. There, he had found four men convicted of theft against Sir Jackman Wennard, three by poaching and one servant found guilty of taking six silver spoons and a quantity of table-linen. The servant was certainly guilty and had been hanged as a result. The three poachers had also been convicted and sentenced to death. However, two were local villagers and young enough for the judges to recommend that the king should exercise mercy and commute their sentences to seven years transportation. Both had protested their innocence throughout. The third poacher, as young as the others, was a gypsy. He had been hanged, Afterwards, various members of his family had been heard to make passionate threats of revenge against Sir Jackman. It was not known if that band of gypsies was still in the area, but their hatred of the man who had brought about the death of the young man was deep. Might not a trap of the kind that killed the baronet be a likely way for gypsies to take their revenge?

By this time, Adam felt close to despair. Still he had some hopes that by focusing on a single area of suspicion at a time, he might at least serve to eliminate it and narrow the field somewhat. Whether that trap had been set by a vengeful gypsy, a disgruntled tenant, a cuckolded farmer or even a wastrel son, someone must have felt able to guess their quarry must pass that way before anyone else discovered the contrivance. Solve that conundrum and he would be well on his way to finding a sure path through his present tangle of conflicting ideas.

On the next day, Adam returned home to find a message from Mr Jempson, saying he had been called to Norwich unexpectedly and had taken the opportunity to visit the newly-weds. Mr and Mrs Lancelot Pashley would be delighted to see the doctor and tell him what little they knew about the death of the lady's father. They were, at present, available on most mornings and would wait to hear from Dr Bascom what arrangements would be most suitable for him.

Adam straightway told William to hire a carriage from The Black Boys Inn to take him into the city. He would go to Norwich the very next day, as soon as the calls he had already scheduled were complete. He could stay overnight with his mother—she had grown resigned to his sudden, unannounced visits—and send word that he wished, if possible, to see Mr and Mrs Pashley the following morning.

It was nearly two o'clock before Adam was able to set out for Norwich. That would allow him to complete his journey before nightfall, though he would probably miss dinner. Still, his mother's cook would doubtless find him something to eat. The weather was no longer quite so pleasant either. A chill wind blew in from the German Ocean and a thick covering of cloud threatened rain. He was sure those whose harvests were yet to be completed would be watching the sky with considerable anxiety.

As he expected, his mother greeted him calmly, merely remarking that it would be quite pleasant some day to have advance warning of his arrival. This was a continual theme, so Adam only grinned and said that he rarely knew himself what he might be doing more than a few days ahead. The cook made him a cold collation, which he was happy to eat alone, then he joined his mother and her companion in the drawing room to drink tea and while away the evening in conversation.

"I hear you are engaged in solving yet another of your murders," Mrs Bascom said. "It is hardly a proper activity for a gentleman; especially one who is now a wealthy man and a physician of excellent standing in local society. I declare I grow tired of my friends pressing me for news of some other terrible deed you are seeking to solve. That is, when they are not asking me when you will take a wife. There are a good many mothers in the county who have that matter on their minds, my son."

Adam swiftly sidestepped her attempt to raise what he knew must become a continual subject from now on.

"If anyone should be blamed for entangling me in yet another mystery, mother," he said, "it's my brother Giles. It's his sense of duty as a magistrate that is forcing him to undertake an investigation into Sir Jackman Wennard's death, since the man's own son will not do so. Since Giles is so busy with other matters, and knows he has little aptitude for such work, he turned to me. Would you have me refuse to help him?"

"Pah!" Adam's mother said. "If he had not involved you at once, you would have been furious. Probably sulked for weeks. Admit it, my son. You pant after mysteries of this type as a greyhound pants after hares. Is that not so, Sophia?"

Sophia LaSalle, Mrs Bascom's lady-companion, looked up from the mending she had been pretending to do and regarded Adam coldly.

"It is indeed so, Mrs Bascom," she said. "Dr Bascom has so great a love for wild-goose chases that he has dashed after his quarry without deigning to tell us what he is doing. After the assistance we were able to give him on the last occasion, I wonder he is now so disdainful of our help. I gather that coming here today is a mere convenience to him and no more."

"That is enough!" Adam's mother exclaimed, her voice sharp. "My son's affairs are his own. I do not doubt he can bring all to a successful conclusion without any assistance from you, miss."

Sophia looked so crushed by the unexpected tartness of this rebuke that Adam felt compelled to try to rescue her.

"It was not lack of willingness, Miss LaSalle, but lack of the occasion. My practice will not admit of me taking the time too often to come into the city. However, I will tell you what I know and will be most grateful for any light you can bring upon it. As you say, you have been of considerable help to me on previous occasions. Please be assured I do not seek to exclude you this time."

Before he could begin on his tale, his mother interrupted.

"Do you have any news of your future plans, Adam? I am sure you must find that modest house in Aylsham quite inadequate. Perhaps you have already given some new dwelling some thought? Your present home would not, for example, be in any way a suitable place to take a bride."

Adam groaned inwardly. Not this again! Would his mother now find some way to raise the topic of marriage every time she spoke to him? He had little doubt that she had already drawn up a list of the most eligible young ladies in the county. It was time to try to deflect her once again.

"No, mother, I have no new plans of that kind," he said, "nor do I feel in the least willing to give up my present house. It suits me very well, I find. It also has the advantage of being close to my friend Lassimer's premises. Most physicians must spend weary hours compounding their own medicines. I have the great good fortune to have a skilled apothecary to undertake such work on my behalf." He hurried on, allowing no space for his mother to speak again.

"I do have news of two weddings, however. Miss Elisabeth Jempson is to marry Mr Gerard Pashley, the elder son of a most well-respected tea merchant, Mr Horatio Pashley. The Pashley family, like the Jempsons, are Quakers, so it will, I am sure, be a most suitable match."

"Excellent!" Sophia exclaimed, then blushed furiously as both mother and son turned towards her in surprise.

After a brief pause, Adam continued.

"I have come to Norwich expressly to call on that family. Not, however, purely to add my congratulations on their son's engagement. I am to meet tomorrow with the younger brother, Mr Lancelot Pashley. It was he who eloped with Miss Caroline Wennard on the very day her father was murdered. They are now married, to the great delight of the bridegroom's relations, and are staying at their house for the time being. The reason for this visit will, however, not be apparent to you unless I explain much of what I know."

Finding herself blocked and outmanoeuvred, Mrs Bascom sighed and accepted the inevitable.

"Very well," she said. "Do not interrupt, Sophia. I know you and your constant tendency to question." Then, with this last attempt to vent her frustration on someone, she settled back in her chair and prepared to let Adam take the floor.

Adam explained the whole situation, as clearly and simply as he could. Going over things like this was always useful to him, setting events in the correct sequence and pointing out such links between them as he had discovered. It helped him clarify his thoughts. When he had finished, he waited for comments or questions. Both ladies had remained completely silent throughout his narration.

"These cousins of Lady Alice Fouchard," his mother said. "These twins. I believe you said their name is Scudamore."

"That is so," Adam replied, though what relevance such a question might have was beyond him.

"I believe that is quite an ancient lineage and a noble one. Correct?"

"Noble certainly and probably of long standing. Their father is a younger son, of course, though they tell me he is a distinguished barrister in the London courts and held in high regard by His Majesty. Somewhere in the immediate family I understand there is an earldom."

"An earldom? Really?"

By now Adam could see where this was headed. Once again he did his best to turn the conversation aside into other directions.

"The principal matter concerning me is to solve the problem of why Sir Jackman rode off in the opposite direction from the intended path of the hunt. That and what he did while he was away. He cannot, I think, have gone far. If he spotted his daughter and her lover and set out in pursuit, I cannot see how they eluded him. He was not hindered so much by spectators of the hunt that he could be far behind them. A man on a fine horse—I understand Sir Jackman kept a most expensive stable—must surely overtake a wheeled vehicle after but a modest distance."

"I can see that," Sophia said. "It is most peculiar."

"There is more," Adam said. "Even if they were still ahead of him when they reached the coastal road, he surely turned in the wrong direction to find them. He must have turned towards Cley. Nothing else could account for where his body was found and the route he had taken to try to catch up with the hunt. He came from the east, of that there can be no doubt. But what if the fugitives had taken the other direction? Sir Jackman obviously knew his daughter was of age, so he would not have assumed she was heading for Scotland, as I did at first. Yet there are many Quaker families in King's Lynn, for example, who might have been willing to give the young people refuge."

"I can think of one piece of investigation that might be of assistance," Sophia said. "It should be possible to guess at how far Sir Jackman had travelled by going over the actions of the hunt itself in detail. How far had it gone by the time the members were aware of Sir Jackman Wennard's absence? To know that will let you estimate the time Sir Jackman had been seeking his daughter, which will in turn suggest the greatest distance he could have travelled. Of course, such calculation could be an overestimate. Some might have noticed him missing, yet not considered it of any importance until his body was found."

"It is a fine idea, Miss LaSalle," Adam said, hoping to restore a little of her usual confidence and good humour. "I wonder how I might be able to collect that information?"

"Would your brother not be able to find out?"

"I doubt it," Adam replied. "Giles is no sportsman. Even if he had been told who intended to go hunting, he would not have retained the information above a few minutes. I have already asked Lady Alice Fouchard to seek out any she knows who were part of the hunting party that day. I am sure she and her late husband were welcome guests in every substantial house in the county. She has the most lively intelligence and will accomplish what I need swiftly, I'm sure. I must go to Mossterton Hall again soon and see what she had discovered."

For some inexplicable reason, this idea seemed to cast Sophia back into gloom.

"I suppose she might," she said. "There is probably no other way. Of course, I do not know the countryside, so I can be of limited use to you at present."

But Adam's mind was too far engaged in working through the implications of what they had been discussing to notice any wistfulness in Sophia's voice.

"Ah!" he said. "I can see at least one objection. I assumed the hunt intended to stay within the valley of the river. That's where the land is most even and there is least gorse and bracken to find your way through. If you wanted a fine gallop, you would seek to find a fox who might oblige you by running that way. But what if you wished to stay in Wennard lands, but were happy to go up the west side of the valley onto the flatter land above? I can't remember how far the Wennard estate stretches on that side and who owns the land beyond. It could be someone who wouldn't mind the hunt going into their fields. After Glavenbridge, all the land southwards is Bascom land, until you reach almost to Letheringsett. I cannot believe Giles would have welcomed Sir Jackman's hunt onto his fields. Of course, the baronet himself could have decided to ignore his neighbour's wishes. Yet there would be many amongst those taking part in the hunt who would not wish to antagonise Giles in such a way. I hope that tomorrow may bring me some answers."

"Interesting," Mrs Bascom said abruptly. "Yes, of definite interest, I would say."

Adam started a little, for he had virtually forgotten her presence.

"What is interesting, mother?" he asked. "You know the land around Trundon Hall well. Do you know how far the Wennard estate extends on the west, beyond the road, or whose lands it borders on there?"

"What? No, that's of no importance. Tell me. What age is Miss Ruth Scudamore? Is she fair or dark? Well-favoured or plain?"

Now it was Adam's turn to become bewildered.

"We were not talking of Miss Scudamore, mother. Haven't you been listening at all? What I want to know is—"

Mrs Bascom waved her hand with impatience. "Do pay attention, child. I asked you several important questions. Well? What are the answers?"

"I don't know, mother," Adam said. "Fair, like her brother. He told me he's twenty-three, so she'll be of the same age. To be honest, I took little enough notice of the lady, beyond thinking she was perhaps a little above the average in height, undoubtedly handsome and possessed of unusual grace when she moved."

Sophia LaSalle rose abruptly at this point. She declared she had a headache and must retire to her room at once. If it did not improve, she begged to be excused from joining them at breakfast, for she would be unable to eat anything.

After she left, Adam turned back to his mother. "I declare the inhabitants of this house are becoming most strange," he said. "You ignore all I tell you and ask questions about Miss Scudamore. Then Miss LaSalle has yet another of her unpredictable headaches and must retire to her room. Whatever is going on?"

Mrs Bascom shook her head sadly, then burst out laughing.

"Oh dear, Adam," she said. "I should have known better then to speak my thoughts aloud, or ask you to describe anyone other than one of your patients. Why you cannot see what ails Sophia amazes me. However, I should have expected no less. I am sure you will work it out in time. She is a dear soul, but not in the least suitable, of course. As for the Scudamores, why should I not take an interest in the addition of fresh people of quality to the neighbourhood, even if it is only temporary? I must ask Lady Grandison about them. I declare she reads pedigrees in the way others read the latest works of fiction—not that there is much difference in some cases. Jane Labelior might know as well. She, of course, is somewhat older, but must move in the same circles. She also spends a good deal of her time in London. Now, if we are both to be in good spirits tomorrow, it is time to retire."

She rose, then stopped in the doorway to look back at her younger son. "If you wish to be kind to Sophia, do not encourage her in false hopes, especially by allowing her to think she can play any significant part in your investigations. I am sure that would be best for both of you."

"Why ever not?" Adam asked. "She has already helped me to think of several fresh areas to investigate." Mrs Bascom only sighed and shook her head at that, then they both went upstairs to retire for the night.

Six

Escape to Happiness

THE NEXT MORNING, AS ARRANGED, ADAM WALKED DOWN THE HILL and across the river to the house where Mr and Mrs Lancelot Pashley were staying. It lay in an area off Magdalen Street much favoured by the more prosperous merchants and manufacturers of the city. The house itself proved to be of fairly recent construction, solid and four-square with five bays and three stories, the whole made of fine red brick with pale stone around door and windows. It was a house that stated, without equivocation, that the family who lived in it were people to be reckoned with.

The interior also spoke of wealth and taste, though overlaid with the simplicity Adam had seen before in the homes of Quakers. The furnishings were neat and restrained, although a cursory look proved all were of the highest quality. It was so reminiscent of Mr Jempson's home in Aylsham that Adam almost expected to be greeted by his old friend and his lovely daughter, rather than the young couple who now entered the parlour where a maidservant had taken Adam to await their coming.

Lancelot Pashley was dressed very much in the style of a Quaker, though not in any way compromising on quality and style. He was a fine, tall young man, clean-shaven and exuding energy and life. His new wife walking beside him did not resemble her father remotely. Where he had been heavily built and thick-set, she was willowy. His hair, though greying, must once have been dark. Hers was far paler, with almost a reddish tinge to it. Yet there was something about those eyes, set widely apart, and the firmness of her jaw that indicated her parentage. Despite her attractiveness and femininity, Adam guessed she would be uncompromising in her determination to live her life in her own way.

She too had adjusted to fresh surroundings. Her dress was far simpler than any she would have worn at Upper Cley Hall, a severe style in grey worsted, its plainness relieved by ruffles of creamy lace at the neck and cuffs. Though he was no judge of such things, even Adam could see this lace was of such exquisite workmanship that it probably cost more than most young women would expend on their whole ensemble.

Greetings and compliments were exchanged, coffee was provided and served, and the time finally came when Adam could ask his questions with propriety. He had expected Mrs Pashley to demand he tell her whatever he knew of her father's death. She did not. Whether because she knew enough already or through the natural pain such information might bring her, he did not know. Either way, it left Adam uncertain of how best to begin. After what felt like a pause of embarrassing length, but was probably no more than one or two seconds, he trusted to his luck and plunged ahead.

"That morning, Mrs Pashley," he began, "the day of the hunt, you travelled to where it was to meet? In company with your father and brother, I believe?"

"I did," she replied. Her voice was low and level. "It had taken a good deal of persuasion on my part to obtain my father's permission. He was determined to keep me in his sight if he could."

"When you arrived, what did you do next?"

86

"I made the excuse that the area before the inn was too crowded for me to be able to take my dog-cart there. Also, that I wanted to be able to greet a number of friends and acquaintances, all of who would be moving about and being jostled by the crowds. I therefore left the dog-cart behind the inn, in the stable yard, and had the inn's groom put my pony in the stable. Then I went around the front to the place of the meet."

"And you, Mr Pashley?" Adam asked.

"I travelled to the inn the evening before and took a room for the night. I could not risk coming into the inn yard that morning in case I was seen by Sir Jackman Wennard. I therefore stayed in the main room on the ground floor, watching as best I could to see my future wife arrive. When I did, I went to the stables and told the groom to get my horse and curricle ready at once. I told him I wished to be able to leave as soon as the crush of carriages and people about the meet would allow it. All this was as we had agreed in advance."

"What was your plan for meeting and leaving?" Adam asked.

Mrs Pashley answered first.

"I was to look out for a time when my father and brother were both distracted by speaking with others, then slip back into the inn. That I did. Indeed, I was so nervous I might have been seen that I first went to one of the front windows and spent a few moments looking out. Had anyone noticed my absence, I could return, making some excuse about wishing to escape from the crowd for a moment or two. When I was convinced all was well, I hurried through the inn to the stable yard where Mr Pashley was waiting."

"How did you get away without being seen, assuming you did?"

"We knew we must avoid as much notice as we could, doctor," Mr Pashley said. "It would be the time of greatest danger to our enterprise. To leave at once must have attracted attention, so we retreated upstairs to the room I had taken and waited until the hunt had set out and all the spectators dispersed."

"You stayed in the inn?" Idiot! Double-dyed idiot! All along he had assumed they would try to get away immediately. Mr Pashley was correct. That must have invited discovery. Why hadn't he considered Mr Pashley might simply take a room and stay out of sight?

"We believed it was the safest course," Mrs Pashley said. "We could not have left the inn in the curricle without attracting attention. We reasoned that, even if I was missed, my father and brother would assume I had slipped off to meet Mr Pashley nearby and make my escape. The dog-cart was, you recall, lodged safely at the inn. We hoped they would not think to search the inn itself—at least, not until it was too late."

"It was a weary wait," her husband continued, "for it felt as if hours had passed. All that time, we were afraid my wife's father or brother would come and discover where we were. In reality, we had to wait less than half an hour. First we heard the hunt move off, then there came a period when the sounds of other people collecting their horses and carts from the inn yard indicated they were leaving for home. Finally, all became calm."

"Even then we waited a few more minutes," Mrs Pashley added. "My father or brother might suddenly recall they had not seen me depart for home and turn back."

"When we could wait no longer," Mr Pashley said," I helped my wife into the curricle, where she concealed herself in the footwell between the seats and I covered her over with a light travelling-rug brought for that purpose. Naturally, she had no luggage. She could hardly have explained why a brief trip to see the hunt assemble would have necessitated her taking any."

"Quite," Adam said. "Nor, I imagine were you much burdened. You had stayed only one night. So which way did you go, Mr Pashley?"

"Towards Blakeney by the usual road. I had been told the hunt intended to set out southwards, so we could not risk the road to Holt. Once we reached Blakeney, we drove along the coastal road to Wells. At an isolated spot, my wife came out from under the rug and was able to sit up normally. From Wells, we journeyed first to Fakenham, then took the Norwich road from there onward."

"And no one came after you at any time?"

"No one. Why do you ask?"

"A few moments before the hunt set out from the inn," Adam said, "Sir Jackman Wennard was seen to be much agitated by something. Once he had extricated himself from the crowds, he set off northwards by the road to the right-hand side of the inn, riding at great speed. I had guessed he had caught a glimpse of you both departing and dashed off in pursuit."

"That cannot have been the case," Mr Pashley replied. "We were still inside the inn, and would be for some time."

"No," Adam said. "I see that now. I wonder what he did see to send him off like that, without a word to anyone."

"The hunt left without him?"

"Indeed it did."

"But we had heard he was … assassinated … in the course of the hunt."

"Yes and no," Adam said. "So far as I can tell, he was hurrying to catch up with the hunt when he was assaulted. What is odd is that he must have been coming from the road between Cley and Holt, not from Gressington or Blakeney. Only by assuming that, can anyone explain the spot where his body was found."

"That makes no sense," Mrs Pashley said. "I know my father was an erratic man, much given to sudden passions, but fox-hunting was his favourite recreation. He would never have left the hunt, save for some compelling reason. If he was coming in the direction you say, he must have ridden into Cley and out again. Why?"

"I have no idea," Adam said. "At least I know now it could not have been in pursuit of you. Even when you left Gressington, you went in the opposite direction to the path he must have taken. Do you have any reason to believe your plan had been betrayed or he had any inkling of it?"

"No," Mrs Pashley said. "None knew of it, save for my sister and she would never betray me. Oh, my heart aches for how she may be treated now by our brother. He would guess she knew what was afoot. I wanted her to find some reason to leave the house that day as well, but she had nowhere to go. Indeed, she argued that if we both left at the same time, a plot would be guessed at. With great bravery, she opted to stay and face our father when he returned. Neither of us could know he would not do so alive. You may think me heartless not to grieve for him, doctor, but I cannot. His behaviour had long ago turned any loving feelings I might have had towards him into a profound dislike. I can say in perfect truth that I have found more love and compassion in this house than I have known in my own home since my dear mother died, many years ago."

"Will you stay here?" Adam asked.

"For the moment," Mr Pashley replied. "I have been living here anyway. My father, Mr Horatio Pashley, has a mansion near Mousehold Heath. Since he left off day-to-day involvement in our family business, he resides there most of the time. This house is now the home of my brother, Mr Gerard Pashley and his new wife—or will be when they are wed. As soon as possible, therefore, my wife and I will rent another house for ourselves nearby."

"I believe you know my sister-to-be, doctor?" Mrs Pashley said.

"Certainly, for she and her father live close to my own home in Aylsham. I have enjoyed their acquaintance for more than a year. Your brother, Mr Pashley, could not have chosen a better person to become his wife—" A gulf loomed before his feet and Adam stumbled lamely to avoid it. "—save of course for Mrs Pashley here, and you had beaten him to that prize."

If either of the couple noticed Adam's confusion, they were too polite to say so.

Since neither could add any more to Adam's sum of knowledge about Sir Jackman's actions on that particular day, he took his leave amidst protestations of friendship and invitations to visit again whenever he might be in Norwich. Once again, his theories about the events at Gressington had been proved wrong. If Sir Jackman had left in pursuit of anyone, it was not his daughter.

By the time Adam returned to his mother's house, Mrs Bascom and Sophia had gone visiting and were not expected back before dinner. Adam felt he could not wait so long. Instead, he left a note for his mother, thanking her for her hospitality, and sent a manservant to The Maid's Head Inn to enquire of the availability of a carriage to return him to Aylsham. As luck would have it, they could supply both vehicle and driver within the hour. It would mean returning to his house without being able to warn Mrs Brigstone of his coming, but he was sure she would be able to find him something to eat. At two in the afternoon, therefore, he left Norwich and headed northwards. With dry roads and fair driving conditions, he should be home in an hour, or a little more.

All the way, Adam kept turning his mind first this way and that, trying to make a coherent pattern out of what he had been told. However hard he tried, he found himself brought back to the same conclusion— he still lacked evidence on the key points in the puzzle. What he kept getting was general information or facts without any indication of where they fitted. Had anyone who saw Sir Jackman's departure that morning noticed anything to account for it? When the hunt moved off without him, why had his son, Robert, ridden off like the rest? Did he not know his father was missing? Did he assume it would be of no use to wait for him? In a normal situation, it would be simple to ask. As it was, the young baronet's angry refusal to answer questions left him relying on information or guesses from others.

Maybe Lady Alice had found someone present at the meet and willing to talk to him. Of course, he might require discussions with several to tease out enough information to be certain of the facts. Most people were not especially observant and there had been no reason for any to consider that day important until later. Well, he would send word to Lady Alice as soon as he reached his house and ask if she would allow him another visit—preferably the next day. He could bring her and her visitors up to date on his findings and see if they had anything else of use to him.

Thinking of Lady Alice reminded him of Miss LaSalle's behaviour the day before and his mother's odd remarks about it. Miss LaSalle had not been present when he breakfasted, but she could not be unwell or she would not now be out visiting with his mother. His mother seemed to believe he should know why her lady companion was behaving in such a strange manner. How could he? He had hardly spoken to the woman and then only in his mother's presence. Why on earth could women not be straightforward, like men were? Why should they expect you to guess at their concerns and interpret their moods accurately? If a woman wanted you to understand something important, would it not be far more logical to raise the matter openly? Somehow, it always seemed that the prettier the woman, the more she demanded that the men around her should be able to read her mind.

Well, he would forget Miss LaSalle and her headaches and odd reversals of mood. He had better things to think about. For a start, he was sure his mother was plotting hard to find him a suitable wife. If he did not wish to be entangled in matrimony yet—and he did not—he must not only frustrate her plans, but cause her to leave off making more. That would not be easy. Only let him be able to bring this muddle around the death of Sir Jackman Wennard to a successful conclusion and he could find a pressing reason to go to London for a week—perhaps two or even more. He would be away from her observation—and that of her many friends—and could devote himself to the various pleasures the city could offer him. Museums, exhibitions, lectures, conversations with learned colleagues…the theatre… relaxing and most enjoyable company…"

It was on that happy note that the carriage clattered through Aylsham and reached Adam's door.

Adam arrived at Mossterton Hall promptly at noon the next day. His audience was waiting impatiently. Lady Alice, Miss Scudamore and her brother had assembled in the morning room, eager to hear whatever he would tell them of his further discoveries. They were so desirous of getting to the point that the polite niceties of greeting were omitted almost entirely.

"Well, doctor?" Miss Ruth Scudamore began. "We are agog to hear of your latest discoveries. The affair of the baronet's death has been almost the sole topic of conversation since your last visit. Now we look to you to put us out of our misery."

"You do exaggerate so, niece," Lady Alice said. "Do not believe a word of what she is telling you, doctor. We are pleased to see you, regardless of certain people's vulgar curiosity, and will not in any way badger you on that or any other subject."

"There, sister," Mr Scudamore responded. "Consider yourself suitably rebuked. Ruth has been pressing me almost every moment to recall each detail of your last visit, doctor. You might almost think—"

"Which is something you do rarely, brother," Miss Scudamore interrupted. "Our good doctor is not yet sufficiently accustomed to your manners—or lack of them—to know that you are more full of whimsies and flim-flam than a balloon is of hot air. Ignore the baby, Dr Bascom. It is only attention he seeks."

While this family banter was proceeding, Adam found himself feeling envious of the ease he could see characterised in the interactions of this household. He supposed his parents had been a little too serious for their children to relax in this way. His father had been feckless enough, in all conscience. Maybe his mother had felt she had to maintain a certain reserve and calm to counteract her husband's wilder nature.

With a slight start, he realised all faces were turned to him, expecting some response to a question he had never heard.

"I beg your pardon?" he said.

Miss Scudamore threw her hands in the air in mock despair and her brother grinned. Lady Alice regarded Adam with an odd expression he could not quite place. In another person, he might have interpreted it as a certain exasperated fondness, but that could not be so here.

"My dear doctor," she said. "I see you became so confused by the babble that passes for conversation between these two that you retreated into your own thoughts. I cannot blame you. So—the floor is yours. Please ask us any questions you wish and we will strive to assist you. If you can also bring yourself to indulge the fearful Scudamore curiosity somewhat, I, for one, will be most grateful. I do not believe I could endure many more days of being asked when you would come again and urged to press you to come sooner."

"Thank you, m'lady," Adam said. "My apologies for being so absent minded. Much has happened since my last visit and my mind is so full of questions and speculations I fear for my sanity. I do have questions to ask and counsel to seek. But I see I shall obtain a far better hearing if first I share what I have learned. It will also help you all to understand why I need to know the answers to what I will ask you.

At once Adam began to set out the situation of the baronet's death, so far as he now understood it. When he came to explain that whatever had caused Sir Jackman to leave the inn yard in such a passion, it could not have been catching sight of his daughter in the act of eloping, there were gasps of surprise. And when he set out the reasons for knowing that the baronet must have turned along the coast road towards Cley, he faced nodding heads and murmurs of agreement.

At length, his tale was finished and he awaited their responses. Lady Alice spoke first.

"Let us deal with the most pressing matters," she said. "That poor child, Charlotte Wennard, may be suffering a closer confinement than her sister did. Even if that is not the case, it is hard to believe her brother will be treating her kindly. I will invite her to visit and discover her situation for myself. If I do that, I cannot believe Sir Robert will refuse. If he does, it will prove the unsuitability of his temper towards her and we must think of other ways to get his sister out of the house and away to safety."

Adam had not thought of that, but knew he could leave such matters to Lady Alice. Though she appeared outwardly soft and gentle, he did not doubt that the blood of long generations of warlike Marcher lords ran in her veins. It would be a brave man—or an extremely foolish one—who would attempt to stand in her way.

"That is most kind, m'lady," he said. "Her sister, Caroline, is concerned for her, but has, as yet, found no means of communicating directly. She believes herself to be cut off from her family. I am glad to be able to say that she has been welcomed most warmly by her husband's kin."

"That's fine then," Mr Scudamore said with the air of a man dismissing some unimportant detail before returning to the main subject. "All the Pashley family told you, doctor, serves only to add to the mystery. If the two lovers stayed within the inn, her father could not have seen them leaving. Then, if he had noticed Caroline was missing, why should he have gone rushing off, alone, on the road heading north? He could have assembled a large number of persons to assist in his search and greatly increased the chances of finding her."

"People do not always respond in rational ways to an emergency," Miss Scudamore said, "especially those known for outbursts of bad temper. Sir Jackman's actions were probably based on no more than a guess. If he had at last noticed his daughter missing, he must surely have jumped to the conclusion that she had run away. The doctor has told us he had been keeping his daughter a virtual prisoner, and she had needed to plead for some time to be allowed to go to the meeting of the hunt. If she had slipped away, he would have known the northward road was the only path open to her. From your description of the geography of the inn and its location, to leave by any other way must have taken her through the front yard where the crowd of horsemen were assembled—including her father and brother."

"That is quite correct," Adam said. "Even so, I must wonder why Sir Jackman didn't at least alert his son. Everyone seems to agree Robert shared his views. He would have done nothing to help his sister get away."

"Speaking as a man of the law," Mr Scudamore added, "I cannot see that father or son could profit from whatever they did. If the young lady was of age, no one could stop her marrying whomsoever she wished. The worst they could do would be to cut her off without money. Given her husband-to-be and his family are rich, this would not be of much consequence. Anyway, the two of them must surely have considered the likely outcome before doing what they did. If father and brother conspired to imprison poor Caroline, her fiancé and his father could have instituted a lawsuit on her behalf and forced her father to set her at liberty."

There was a long pause while all thought deeply and seemed to arrive at no ideas worth sharing. In the end, it was Lady Alice who first spoke again.

"From all you have told us, doctor, it seems to me whoever Sir Jackman saw might well have had nothing to do with his daughter. It must rather have been someone else. Someone who was indeed leaving at the time he saw them, and by the route he took. Nothing else can explain his frantic haste to follow on his own. The difficulty is to fathom who that might be and why he wished to come up with them so much."

"I agree with you entirely, m'lady," Adam said, then stopped abruptly as his hostess was unable to suppress a giggle.

After a few moments, she managed to master herself enough to explain.

"My humblest apologies, doctor, for such unforgivable conduct. It is just that…I mean…when you address me in that way, I cannot help thinking that you sound like one of the footmen. I do wish I could find you some better mode of addressing me that would not offend against propriety."

Adam could not help grinning in return.

"Would it be of help if I spoke more deliberately and fully—more like a doctor? I could try to remember to call you 'my lady', sounding the words in full."

"I believe that would be helpful, doctor. Let us hope so, for you will have the very worst opinion if I keep laughing when you speak to me."

To Adam's immense surprise, he found himself giving a response that was almost gallant.

"Nothing you could do or say would make me have anything but the highest opinion of you," he said.

"One day," Lady Alice replied quietly, "I hope we may find still better ways to refer to one another."

At that, the Scudamore twins both appeared startled. Charles turned slowly and looked hard at Adam, before trying to smother a smile. His sister, on the other hand, looked towards her aunt in a manner that was almost hostile. Then she too returned her features to their blandest aspect.

"We still have to find an explanation for why Sir Jackman was absent long enough for the hunt to move off without him, but not so long that he would not have tried to catch them up. He had to have been close enough to be making the attempt when disaster struck," Miss Scudamore said, in her most businesslike tone. "Unless, of course, he wasn't trying to come up with the hunt, but was by the river for quite a different purpose."

Adam groaned softly.

"Each time I think I am approaching some solid facts," he said, "all I find are more questions and uncertainties. You are correct, Miss Scudamore, of course. I can only guess at how far he may have travelled while he was absent. As things stand, it appears impossible for him to have come to the spot where he met his death other than by leaving the road between Cley and Holt and taking the shortcut down the hill. All else is speculation. When I arrived, my lady…" All smiled at this. "…you assumed I must have many questions to ask. I have none save this. Have you yet found any who were part of the hunt that day? If you have, I will approach them and ask them to speak with me."

"I have found one such already," Lady Alice said. "I wrote to him myself to introduce you and explain the reason for your interest. That will ensure he'll respond favourably to you sending your card and asking for an appointment. Now, if you have indeed no further questions on the business of Sir Jackman Wennard, doctor, let us change the topic. My impetuous nephew here, Charles, is most eager to ask you when he can be released entirely from any restrictions on his actions."

Adam thanked her profusely for her help and confirmed that his patient was now restored almost to full health and could do whatever he wished. His only advice was that any activities that might demand a strain on the muscles in the chest should be avoided for a little longer.

"I suppose you are eager to return to your home in London, Mr Scudamore," he said. "I am sure you must find our country very dull by comparison."

"Not at all," Charles replied. "I find I am uncommonly attracted to this area. No, doctor, you will not be deprived of my wise counsel so soon, however hard you try. London is a devilish bad place for a young attorney to establish himself. Lawyers there are near as abundant as fleas—"

"And just as unwelcome," his sister said.

"Indeed so, sister. Both creatures are possessed of the same tendency to fasten on some poor person and suck their blood, as you have often told me. The idea of settling into a comfortable country practice, where I could avoid too much work, yet attain a modest sufficiency, attracts me greatly."

"Lazy cat!" his sister said.

"I am most uncommonly fond of the creatures, sister, as you know. I much admire their philosophy of life. They do what they wish when they wish it, eat all they can and sleep the rest of the time. Where is your kitten, aunt? I have not seen him on your lap today."

"He is near fully grown," Lady Alice replied, "so like all males who feel themselves possessed of a maturity they have yet to attain, he disports himself in hunting all day, and then demands the full attention of the ladies of the house when he deigns to return. He is also as vain as any fop, for he washes and preens himself for hours. Still, unlike that sort, his beauties are all natural to him."

"How is it, doctor, that I have the suspicion I am being rebuked?" Mr Scudamore said. "All I did was enquire after the animal. Nor should my sister be so smug in berating me. She too has fallen under the spell of these fields. You should know that she considers herself a most learned person in all aspects of the natural world. I cannot attest to the depth and genuineness of her knowledge, for I willingly accept I am as ignorant of such matters as a pig is of the movements of the stars. She does, however, keep up a voluminous correspondence with various staid and learned gentlemen of mature years—oftentimes men of the cloth with time on their hands—on such obscure topics as where swallows go in winter and why the leaves of trees turn red and orange in autumn. What is altogether remarkable is that they take her seriously."

"Which you never do, brother. I have often pointed out that, while those of superior intelligence can easily grasp the ramblings of people of the stupider kind, those possessed of a mean and scanty intellect find the thoughts of their betters incomprehensible."

Her brother ignored her.

"My sister spends long hours in the fields and woods, studying everything from insects to the meanest fungi. As you can imagine, doctor, London affords few opportunities for such an eccentric pastime. The young ladies there are more attuned to the careful observation of fashions and fabrics. They swoon at the tuneful warblings of some Italian castrato. She is entranced by the song of the thrush or the nightingale. To be amongst the gardens and trees of this estate is almost a heaven for her. She pleads with me daily to allow her to stay."

"Ignore them, doctor," Lady Alice said. "I have learned to do so, or they would drive me insane with their nonsense. The plain fact of the matter is that the attorney who has been handling the legal affairs relating to this estate is an elderly man much afflicted with a good many ailments, principally gout. His doctors have advised that he should spend a lengthy period in Bath to take the waters and restore himself. He was reluctant to leave me until I was able to convince him that my nephew, for all the levity of his manner, is fully able to undertake the necessary work. My brother has agreed his son and daughter may remain with me for as long as I wish. Ruth is indeed an accomplished naturalist and an artist of considerable talent. You must persuade her to show you some of her wonderfully detailed botanical drawings. Being here provides her with abundant fresh material. Two natural philosophers of great importance have now commissioned her to provide them with the illustrations for their next books."

"I would be greatly interested in seeing some of your work, Miss Scudamore," Adam said. "If I am not quite so ignorant of the natural world as your brother claims to be, I am always ready to learn more. I am also well aware of the importance and difficulty of accurate depictions of natural phenomena. In medicine, any publication containing fine illustrations is sought after eagerly. No mere words can convey the details of the workings of the body as an illustration can. I am sure the same is true in botany and biology."

"Take no notice of my sister's blushes and feigned modesty, doctor," Mr Scudamore said. "Your kind words will have acted upon her as the presentation of a big, meaty bone upon a starving dog. Take care that she does not capture you when you come next and subject you to hours of lectures and hundreds of paintings. It does little good to encourage anyone infected with enthusiasm, you know. You will regret it."

"Hush, nephew!" Lady Alice said. "Dr Bascom is too polite to say it, but I am sure he finds a little of your silliness is all he can take in one day. Will you stay to dinner, doctor?"

"Alas, I must with the greatest regret decline on this occasion, my lady," Adam said. "At present, my duty towards my patients is all too often fitted into brief periods between the investigations into Sir Jackman Wennard's murder."

"I understand," Lady Alice replied. "On this occasion, then, you are excused. However, the next time you visit us I shall insist. I long for at least one person at the table who can sustain a sensible conversation, instead of squabbling and teasing all the time. Goodbye, doctor. You are most welcome at any time, I assure you. I do hope your next visit will not be long delayed. I will continue to seek out any from amongst those who rode with the hunt who can supply the facts you need."

A SHORTCUT TO MURDER

Seven

The Workings of Nemesis

"THIS IS THE MOST FRUSTRATING MYSTERY I HAVE EVER DEALT WITH," Adam told Peter two days later. "Each time I begin on a promising path, it is either blocked by some new fact or runs away into a dense undergrowth of confusion and ignorance. I can no longer be sure who or what it was that sent Sir Jackman Wennard rushing away from the inn at Gressington. Something did, that is certain, but whether it was flesh, fowl or fish no one can tell me."

"Fish seems unlikely," Peter said. "The sea is at least a mile distant and the river about half the same amount."

They were sitting in Peter's parlour. When he arrived at Peter's shop, Adam ignored a warning from Peter's apprentice and went at once to the compounding room, only to back out at once, coughing and gasping. His friend's calm response to his spluttered protest was the instruction to go away and wait in the parlour until he had finished. More than fifteen minutes later, Adam's throat and eyes were still burning.

"What foul brew were you concocting in there?" he said. "It tries my friendship to discover you seeking to poison me as soon as I arrive."

"Spirits of hartshorn, my friend," Lassimer said. "A rich source of ammonia much used to counteract fainting in those of a nervous disposition—or with their corsets laced somewhat too tightly. You should try it yourself."

"I don't doubt what you were making would revive anyone who had fainted. It would wake the dead!"

"If only it could. Think what I might charge for it."

"You have the soul of a mountebank, Lassimer. Trust an apothecary to think at once of base profit."

"Just because your investigation is not proceeding well, is no reason to throw a tantrum," Peter said. "A man who barges into an apothecary's compounding room must accept the consequences. I believe my apprentice tried to warn you, yet you swept past him in that lordly manner beloved of physicians and quacks. However, let us not waste time on trivialities. We will see if the news I have will raise your spirits. I was at Saxthorpe yesterday, assisting a certain midwife there—"

"Is she a widow?" Adam asked.

"As it happens, she is, and a most comely one at that. Barely forty years of age. Youth has undoubted pleasures to offer, but a woman of experience—"

"Spare me your observations on such matters!" Adam said. "I do not doubt that she has an itch from time to time that you graciously undertake to relieve."

"Somewhat indelicately put, Bascom, but essentially correct. However, she also purchases various preparations that assist in the process of childbirth. Many of the poorer people of the area cannot afford the outrageous charges of physicians and man-midwives. To such as these, she is a godsend when the pains of labour come upon them. Indeed, it was a birth that took her to The Three Pigs Inn at Edgefield, where the publican's wife was about to produce her third child."

It had proved a brief labour and an easy birth, Peter explained. The child, a girl, was healthy and strong. All in all, a most successful delivery, which went a long way to explaining why the midwife found herself enjoying a welcome glass or two of gin with the publican afterwards—at his expense. They talked of many things and the jug of gin had become much lighter than it had been at the start, when the man began to tell her an amusing tale.

He had a cousin at Cley, he explained, who had told him a most amusing story about that old rogue Sir Jackman Wennard. He could vouch for its truth, for his cousin had seen it all with his own eyes. What's more, it had happened on the morning of the hunt, during which Sir Jackman Wennard had lost his life.

The good people of Cley, he said, had been much startled to see that same baronet come galloping into their village at about ten in the morning, riding an enormous black horse. A fine beast all agreed, but like all such high-bred animals, nervy and excitable. Once man and horse had reached a point near the windmill, Sir Jackman reined in the beast and started demanding of all nearby whether they had seen a young man and an older woman pass by, probably driving in a chaise or curricle.

"A young man and an older woman?" Adam interrupted. "Mr Lancelot Pashley is undoubtedly young, but Sir Jackman would hardly refer to his own daughter as an older woman."

"That was what he was asking. His very words, I was told," Peter said.

None in that end of the village had observed such a couple that day, but Sir Jackman was not able to go further and address his question to more, since the landlord of The Fishmonger's Arms came out to see what all the noise was about.

According to the cousin, this landlord is a man of perhaps five-and-forty with an exceedingly pretty wife some twenty years his junior. Every man in the village dreams of taking a turn with her. None try, however, since the landlord is well known to be the jealous type and more than handy with his fists. Sir Jackman, of course, had sniffed the lady out. According to the gossip, he had plied her with fine words and ample gifts until she agreed to his suggestion that he might meet her in a suitable place whenever her husband was absent on business. Naturally, the husband had found out soon enough, for there is no such thing as a secret in such a small community. Only two days earlier, the villagers had noticed the wife had a fine black eye and was being close-confined at the inn. Now, seeing right before his door the one who had defiled his marriage bed, the landlord decided it should be the adulterer's turn to suffer the consequences.

Without a word, the landlord hurried back within, while Sir Jackman, perhaps sensing danger, wheeled his horse around and began to move off the way he had come. Before he could do so, the landlord re-emerged, this time carrying the blunderbuss he used for duck shooting on the marshes in winter.

"Surely he would not have shot Sir Jackman!" Adam said.

"Oh no," Peter replied. "The cousin said the man had too much sense to put his own neck into a noose. He wished to punish, not to kill. Besides, half the village was watching by this time and however much they sided with the landlord and hated the baronet—as all did—they would never have condoned murder. No, seeing the debaucher of his wife already turned to run away, the landlord simply raised the gun into the air and let it off. It was a huge weapon, well charged-up, and made a tremendous noise which echoed back from the houses all around."

Naturally, such an explosion was enough to make the baronet's horse go into a panic. It laid its ears back flat to its head, rolled its eyes until only the whites were showing, and tore off up the road at a full gallop, totally out of control. Then, instead of turning to keep to the coastal road, it ran straight ahead, past the church and up the slope towards Kelling and Holt. All the village people were roaring with laughter. Many of them had begun shouting to increase the animal's panic. A few even seized sticks and buckets and beat them together to add to the noise. It was a tribute to Sir Jackman's horsemanship that he managed to stay on the beast's back, but even he could do nothing to slow its headlong flight.

"I wish I had been there!" Peter said. He and Adam were near crying with laughter by this time "Imagine it! Everyone laughing and shouting and yelling the horse on, while Sir Jackman clung to its back and roared curses down on the village and all within it. That's the trouble with such beasts. They're fine for racing, which is what they're bred for, and they might serve for a hunter, if you expect a good gallop. Apart from that, they're nought but a danger to themselves and all about them."

At length, when he had sated his mirth and wiped his eyes, Adam agreed that Peter's news was most welcome.

"At least we know now why Sir Jackman was on that road and had to ride down the side of the valley to get back to the hunt," he said. "I had assumed he had blundered through the gorse on his way as a form of shortcut. Now I can see that it was most likely all he could do to turn his horse in the right direction and hope to reach the river in one piece. He was riding hard because he had no other option. Even so, your news is exactly like all the rest I have discovered to date. It clears up one mystery by replacing it with two greater ones."

"How so?" Peter asked.

"First, it makes it even less likely anyone could have anticipated Sir Jackman taking the route he did—if that is possible. If you are clinging to the back of a runaway horse, you go where you must, not where you plan. Not only do we still not know why the baronet had left the hunt and ridden to Cley, we have evidence that his route back to the hunt was entirely the choice of his horse. The second extra mystery is, of course, his description of the persons he was seeking as 'a young man with an older woman'. My visit to Norwich told me his daughter could not have been his quarry, since he neither saw her leave nor knew she had in reality hidden in the inn. Now we find him in pursuit of two people who have not figured in this puzzle before—and about whom we know nothing, save that the male was young and the female older. Who could they be?"

"One of his lovers slipping away with a young buck?" Peter said. "Even the greatest lechers do not like to be reminded that their women might fancy a turn or two with someone fresher and more energetic. Sir Jackman was fifty-two or three years old at the least and had been exerting himself between the sheets—aye and almost everywhere else—for almost four decades. His experience might have been unrivalled, but his stamina would certainly be failing."

"Perhaps," Adam said. "Somehow I cannot believe it was so simple. All I have been told leads me to think Sir Jackman was solely interested in his own sexual needs. He used women and tossed them aside. Would he have worried so much if one found a young man who showed greater interest and ability in providing for her own pleasure? I doubt it. He would have been more likely to declare her a trollop and restore his wounded pride by forcing himself on some maid or pretty farm girl."

"There is that," Peter conceded. "My midwife friend said the folk who live near Upper Cley Hall hate the man for that very reason. No woman was ever safe from his attentions, unless she was old or truly ill-favoured. Nearly all claimed to know of a neighbour whose wife, daughter or maidservant had been seduced or molested. In truth, they were probably talking about their own womenfolk. Sir Jackman's death has brought nothing but joy to that locality. His son may boast of emulating him, but I gather he lacks the courage to do much more than talk about female conquests. He has tried his luck with one or two, but a well-aimed blow—or even harsh words—are usually enough to make him back away."

"I have not met the young man," Adam said, "but my brother thought him a weakling, for all his arrogance and pride. He's shut himself away in Upper Cley Hall and does nothing but repeat that his father's death was an accident. He's also near drowned in debt, so any delay in the granting of probate and him coming into his inheritance must be avoided. Not that I believe such a delay will happen."

Once again, Adam was to be proved wrong.

In keeping with the frustrating pattern that had formed about this investigation, when he returned to his home Adam was told Mr Charles Scudamore had called while he was away. Adam's servants guessed where he was, but since they had not encountered Mr Scudamore other than as a patient, they were unwilling to ask him to seek their master at the apothecary's shop. The visitor had also made light of the doctor's absence and admitted he should have sent word in advance. However, no harm was done, since he had business that must take him to Gunton Hall. He would therefore return through Aylsham on his way home to Mossterton Hall and hope to find Adam in then.

The expectation of a visit from Mr Scudamore caused Adam still more frustration, especially since his brother's groom arrived next with a message asking Adam to go to Trundon Hall to hear "some fresh items of news on the matter the squire had asked him to look into". No indication of particular urgency accompanied this message, nor did the groom have any idea of how urgent the summons might be. In the end, Adam had to weigh the balance between an obvious act of impoliteness and delaying a response to an invitation that appeared to be of no great urgency. Leaving on another errand when he knew Mr Scudamore would return could only be excused in extreme circumstances. He decided to stay and told the groom to tell his master to expect his brother in the morning.

That this was the correct choice seemed to be proved when Mr Scudamore arrived barely half an hour after. The young man was profuse in his apologies for coming to Adam's house unannounced. The news he brought was interesting, but not especially urgent. Since he was riding to Gunton anyway on a matter of boring business, he decided to call on Adam along the way. It was a mere whim, he explained, aimed at brightening his day.

All this Adam heard with a sinking heart. Talking with Peter that morning had already left him more confused than he had been before. Now he must try to listen politely to what he expected would be no more than one or two pieces of useless information.

"You know that I am presently acting for my aunt in various legal matters to do with her estate," Mr Scudamore began. "Yesterday, this required me to talk with one of her tenants who is seeking permission to vary several small aspects of his lease. I won't bore you with the details. The matter was soon concluded and he was about to leave when he mentioned that he had been part of the group of people who rode after the hounds on the day Sir Jackman Wennard was killed. Since I knew of your interest in learning more of what happened, I asked him at once how the day had gone."

Adam's disinterest evaporated a good deal. "What did he tell you?" he asked.

It seemed at first that the man had little to report of any moment, Mr Scudamore explained. The hunt moved off and the hounds quickly picked up a scent. It could not have been a fresh one though, since after 'giving tongue'—the brutes howling and barking in excitement—they ran perhaps a quarter of a mile, then lost whatever scent they were following. Up to this point, he said, no one was aware that Sir Jackman was not amongst the party. It was only when they were milling about, while the whippers-in called the pack of hounds together again, that he had heard Robert Wennard asking people if they knew where his father might be. One or two said they had noticed him pushing through the crowd outside the inn and calling out in anger. Most assumed he had seen some pickpocket at work. Crowds attracted them much as fresh dung attracted flies. It would be only natural to try to apprehend the thief. Sadly, in such a press of people it would be easy for the rascal to slip away. One person even claimed to have seen Sir Jackman ride off up the road to the north, but this was not generally believed. The baronet was known to be near obsessed with fox hunting. To imagine he would ride off in the wrong direction, just at the point the hunt was about to ride out, stretched credulity too far.

The tenant with whom Mr Scudamore had spoken, a Mr Bowright, was towards the edge of the group, so he observed all this from a little distance. All he could say was that Sir Jackman's son seemed unusually concerned to discover where his father might have gone. But since none, so far as he could tell, was able to help him, he did little more than stand in his stirrups and look around in the hope of catching sight of his parent somewhere.

"What changed him must have been the shots," Mr Scudamore said.

Adam was on him in an instant. "What shots?" he demanded. "Was it the shot from Cley?"

It was Mr Scudamore's turn to look baffled now. "From Cley? Is that not several miles distant? I mean, I am not very familiar with the geography of this area, but—"

"What shots?" Adam repeated, leaning forward. "Tell me!"

"Of course, of course. Only ... why are you staring at me like that? This is what the man said. He said that he had heard two shots, fairly close upon each other."

"Where from?" Adam snapped. "How far off?"

"He wasn't certain. Not from far off—no further than the other side of the valley. He had the impression the first was a little further off than the second, but it had been impossible to tell precisely. His own thought was that they came from the woods across the river. Others said they had come from the fields on the nearer side or from close to the river itself. One or two declared some fool of a tenant had forgotten about the hunt and decided to amuse himself by shooting at vermin like crows and magpies. That made people angry, since the sound of shooting would send any fox in the area running for cover right away."

"Two shots, you said," Adam repeated. "Close together in time, but one further away than the other. And from the area of the river and the wood beyond."

"Yes," Charles said. "That's correct. That's what Mr Bowright told me."

"So what happened then?"

"According to Bowright, Robert Wennard went tearing off at once in the direction of the shots. Not a word to anyone. Just dug his heels into his horse and rode off at a gallop. No one else was sure what to do. A few rode after him, but not with anything like the same urgency. They set their horses to a canter so they could note where he was going and be close enough to ride over if anything interesting developed. The huntsmen swore since they now had their hands full trying to keep the hounds from chasing off after Wennard's horse. All the rest stayed put, including Bowright. After all, it had nothing to do with what they had come for, which was to find a fox. When no one came back and no further shots were heard, the general belief was that whatever tenant had fired them was now receiving a blistering rebuke from Robert Wennard."

There the matter rested, Charles continued. The hunt went onward along its intended path. The hounds found a strong scent and tore off after a fox, with the riders strung out in a long line behind. They had come hoping for a good gallop and that was now what they got. They even made a kill, more or less right on the southern border of the Wennard estate. Neither Robert Wennard nor any of those who had followed after him returned, of course. It was only after the hunt had ended and many had dispersed that the news came an accident had happened. The information that the victim was Sir Jackman Wennard had not reached Mr Bowright until next day. Naturally, when he was told it was murder, he thought Sir Jackman had been shot. Not before time was his immediate thought. Not only was the man a menace, he was damn bad-tempered with it. It was a wonder some angry husband or father hadn't seen to him earlier. When the inquest showed that the baronet had died from a broken neck, he had been amazed.

"So that's it," Charles concluded. "Am I to understand from your excitement that it will be of some use in sorting out what happened?"

Adam shook his head and looked dejected. "I truly don't know," he said. "It does clear up one small part of the puzzle; how Sir Jackman's son came to be the one who found his father's body. He would have an intimate knowledge of his family estate. That must have allowed him to pinpoint the source of the shots more or less precisely and ride straight there. Whether he did so in fury at some person who might disrupt the fox hunt, or in fear for his father's safety, we cannot know unless he tells someone. At present, my brother informs me the new baronet is saying nothing to anyone. I had hoped at one time to come upon some evidence proving who might have had prior knowledge of Sir Jackman's movements. What I was told this morning has all but eliminated that hope. Your news has destroyed it completely. It was the shots that drew the son to the place, not anything else."

"Would it be presumptuous of me to ask what you learned this morning?" Charles said. "I had assumed before now that investigating a crime was little more than collecting together a group of likely suspects and questioning them closely until the guilty party confessed or gave himself away. This is truly a revelation to me. Such a puzzle! So many twists and turns! So many hopes dashed and theories destroyed! I declare it is the best mental exercise I have ever known. I will drive myself mad with it, unless you give me something to chew on as I ride onwards. Please, doctor. You would not wish to undermine the balance of my mind, would you?"

What else could Adam do but give as short a summary of his present state of knowledge as he was able? Mr Scudamore listened with rapt attention. At the end, his eyes were shining and his suppressed excitement was like an electrical charge of the kind used by showmen to flash into a great spark to dazzle their audience.

"My father should be eternally grateful to you, doctor," he declared. "I believe I mentioned he is quite an eminent barrister and prosecutor in London. He must have to grapple with this kind of thing all the time. Until now, I was certain his work consisted of nothing but dreaming up fine speeches to impress a jury, while others wrote down the plain facts of the case for him. I used to tell him that I could not understand why muddling the truth and throwing dust in the eyes of judge and jury was thought an honourable profession. No more! My respect for the old boy has increased in leaps and bounds. Just wait until I tell my sister. She will be green with jealousy that I have been here.

"I promise I will give all these matters the closest thought, doctor, and tell you anything that I may wring from them. I may appear nothing but a foolish and an idle fellow, but I have a brain—one that is trained in legal matters and accustomed to extracting whole volumes of meaning from half a dozen words within a lease or contract. That brain may be of use to you yet."

Eight

Focus and Resolve

ADAM RECEIVED BUT A COLD GREETING FROM HIS BROTHER THE NEXT MORNING. It was true that he had not hurried overmuch on his way to Trundon. The weather that year had been poor most of the time; all wind and rain and cool days with colder nights. On that day the sun shone, many of the leaves had already turned to russet and gold and it felt good to be alive and able see it all. As he drove through Letheringsett, the rich malty smell of fresh-brewed beer overlaid the more musty aromas of gentle decay that autumn produced. Even the little River Glaven, sparkling in the sunlight, sounded as if it was glad to be running through the damp meadows on its way to the sea.

When Adam arrived Giles was in the library, seated at his desk and toying with some papers. As soon as the servant had withdrawn, he jumped to his feet.

"I wonder that you did not see fit to come yesterday when I called for you, brother," he said. "When my servant brought back your message that you would not come before today, I was amazed that you should treat me so. Now I find you must have dawdled along the way, doubtless admiring the view and considering the flowers in the hedgerows. It is too much!"

"How was I to know your summons was so urgent?" Adam protested. "Your servant will bear witness that I asked him if you had said anything on that score. He assured me his only charge had been to bring me word that you wished to talk with me. Nothing more than that. I am not a mind-reader, brother, that I can sense your true wishes at a distance of more than ten miles."

Giles was deaf to such mild reasoning. Instead, he began striding towards the other end of the room, turning his back on Adam and seeming rather to address the wall before him.

"Now this," he said. "Now yet another complication. Has it anything to do with Sir Jackman Wennard's death? I don't know and I doubt you'll be able to tell me. Damn the man! Why couldn't he get himself killed in some sensible way? Fall prey to a set of highway robbers, perhaps, or even die in his bed like any honest Christian."

He turned and started back the way he had come.

"Listen to this! Another turn in this most serpentine business. A letter from Lord Weybourne, who writes for the executors of Sir Jackman's Will. He is asking for my guidance on how they should respond to a communication from a lawyer in Norwich—a lawyer acting for a lady who says she is Sir Jackman Wennard's first wife. First wife. Mark that! So far as the executors knew, Sir Jackman had but one wife, the mother of the heir and his two sisters. How could he have a first wife, I ask you?"

"Bigamy," Adam said. "It's not unknown, brother. Perhaps a woman he married long ago and left somewhere. Later, he thought she was dead—or hoped she was. The question is whether her claim is genuine."

"You think I cannot work that out for myself? All that matters to me is whether this matter of prior marriages accounts for the man's death in any way. Now you're going to tell me you don't know."

"How can I know?" Adam said. "This is the first I have heard of it."

"You would have heard of it yesterday, had you deigned to come as I asked."

Adam ignored his brother's jibe. His mind was racing furiously, trying to adjust his various theories concerning the death of Sir Jackman Wennard to accommodate Giles' revelation.

"Well, brother," Giles went on, "what else have you discovered? I beg it may be good news at last."

It took a mighty effort, but Adam swallowed his pride and indignation and explained some of his most recent discoveries. All the time he was speaking, Giles stood with his back turned and his whole body stiff with impatience and frustration. Adam had got as far as relating what he had found out concerning Sir Jackman's treatment in Cley, when Giles spun around and headed off again towards the opposite end of the room.

"Pah!" he snapped as he passed. "More trifles of little relevance! I ask you to find a murderer and you bring me a tale of an angry husband taking a pot shot at a man all knew to be a confirmed adulterer and seducer. All that shows is that Sir Jackman rode that way and departed again. Nothing about how he came to be at a precise spot where someone had set a trap for him. Nothing to say who that person might be."

Adam agreed. "Yet by ruling out alternatives—such as a pursuit of his eloping daughter—it serves to narrow the field somewhat."

Giles merely grunted. "How am I to explain the delay to his lordship? You don't think of that, do you? I assure the deputy lieutenant of the county, a peer of the realm, that my brother is by far the best person to call upon to investigate this matter. That he has done so on previous occasions and with notable success. That His Majesty even saw fit to give him a handsome reward for his services. That he would bring all to a swift and satisfactory conclusion. I gave him my word. Now weeks have passed and we are no further forward."

"This is a tangled tale indeed," Adam said. "Like a complicated knot, it needs patience to find the end that will allow all to become straight again. I cannot make events clear and simple when they are not. I am no magician. Even today you yourself have introduced another twist that must be understood and related to all else. You do not solve a mystery by attacking it with cudgel and trying to force it to give up its secrets."

Once again, Giles ignored his brother's attempt at reason. "If I take this tale to his lordship the deputy lieutenant," he said, "he will laugh in my face and tell me I should have done what he asked and applied to the Bow Street Court to send an experienced and professional investigator. Accuse me of seeking to pass off a foolish brother as someone skilled in criminal investigation. Now you bring me yet another mare's nest—"

"Sit down!" Adam could hardly believe what he had just said. "Stop pacing up and down and whining like some schoolboy who must explain to the teacher why he did not con his lesson properly. Sit down I say! Hold your tongue before I leave and abandon you to whatever fate your fantasies have woven. By God, sir, if you are not quiet at once I will not answer for my actions! You cannot make bricks without clay, nor can you discover the truth without facts enough to point the way. Sir Robert sees fit to deny us information or assistance. Is it any wonder I must rely on scraps to build up a picture of what happened? Never mind the noble lord, the deputy lieutenant. If he has a brain, he will understand and be patient as we all must. If you will not tell him as much, I swear that I will."

"You would not dare!"

"Would I not? Try me! He is a man like other men and as subject to foul moods and idle fancies as all the rest. I do not doubt that he has someone above him who also believes the way to bring matters to a successful conclusion is to hound and harry those who do the work, while preparing yourself to claim the glory of success or heap the blame for failure on someone else. I care not, even if it should be the king himself. The truth is out there and I mean to find it—and damnation to any who stand in my path!

"What we must do is press on, not give way to childish fears. This affair is more complicated than any could have imagined at the start. That is undeniable. Is that a reason to give up now? Never! It is a coward who runs away when difficulties bar his path. Listen! No, you have said more than enough. Sit down and listen!

"Stripped of all the false trails and dead-ends that always arise in such matters, we can see clearly that Sir Jackman Wennard set out that morning with no other thought in his mind than to enjoy a day's hunting. At The Bull Inn, he saw something or someone which turned all that on its head, so he left the hunt and rushed off in pursuit. He didn't find what he sought. Instead, on coming into Cley and enquiring urgently for "a young man and an older woman", he encountered an angry husband. The result was that his horse took fright and bore him off in a direction not of his choosing. When finally he gained some degree of control, he sought to rejoin the hunt. His horse, however, probably forced him to ride straight down the side of the valley, until he came to the place where the trap was set.

"It is plain he was still going at as near a full gallop as the horse could manage through the undergrowth. What does any rider do if he finds himself headed down a steep slope at high speed? He leans right back in the saddle. If he does not, the least bump or stumble by the horse will throw him off over its head. That was why a rope set at a height to catch a rider in the chest instead caught him in the throat and lodged under his chin. His sheer momentum was more than enough to jerk his head back so violently that his neck was broken on the instant. What if that trap was not meant to kill him? What if the purpose was only to tumble him from his horse? What if someone was lurking nearby, perhaps meaning to rob any who passed that way? They certainly caught one person in their trap, but could it not have been by the merest chance?"

Giles' mouth was hanging open and his eyes staring, but he made not a sound.

"No, brother. I have not been dealing in irrelevant trivialities, as you accuse me of doing. What I have done is prove that there can be several explanations for what happened that day. I had thought of the possibility of footpads a while ago, but dismissed it. I still think it unlikely. I have been told that few ever use that path through the woods save local people, and then only rarely. Your footpad plies his trade where many pass and where he may hope to come upon someone with money in his pocket, a fine ring on his finger and a watch in his waistcoat. Why waste your time on a path through the wood occasionally used by poor folk? It will not do. If I raise it, it is only to show that nothing is certain until we have amassed sufficient evidence to support it. That is what I am doing—and a slow and tedious process it is.

"If the noble lord did indeed suggest you call for someone from London to look into this matter, I can only assume he knows nothing of the temperament of the people in these parts. Would they tell such a man anything? Would they even speak to him? You know as well as I do they would mumble in broadest dialect and smile to one another when he was forced to give up. He would at last return to London, with a tale of clodhoppers and fools who neither knew nor cared what went on around them. Meanwhile, the locals would amuse their friends in the alehouse with tales of how they had "sent that Londoner who thought hisself so grand" on his way empty-handed.

"So, brother. Do you wish me to help you or not? If you do, now is not the time to soothe your own frustrations by turning on me. I have enough of my own, I assure you. Annoy me enough and I might even discover the truth on my own and keep it from you, just to pay you back for your infernal rudeness."

When Adam left Trundon Hall, his heart was still racing and his breathing uneven, for all that Giles had given him a most grovelling apology and promised to support him from now onwards, come what may. Adam had surprised even himself. To think that he had spoken to his elder brother in such a way! If their mother ever came to hear of it, she would scold him soundly. Still, there was little chance of that. He was sure his brother was far too embarrassed by his own foolishness to admit to anyone else what had passed between them. Giles was a fine man, stout-hearted enough in a fair fight on open ground. It was not his fault if fate had denied him ease in coping with such complex and ambiguous matters. There he had neither skill nor endurance. If something was not plain before him, he felt only irritation and a strong wish to leave it aside if he could.

Nonetheless, Adam now reckoned Giles' behaviour had been useful to him. In seeking to set out the facts, such as they were, in a manner plain enough for his brother to grasp, he had cleared his own mind. It had become obvious he must go once again to the spot where Sir Jackman had died and try to verify what he believed must have happened. He had not known what to look for when he went there last. True, he had seen evidence the undergrowth had been trampled, but he hadn't taken that much notice of it. Now there were also those shots to be accounted for. Was it an indignant farmer wishing to drive a trespasser off his land? Had there been someone waiting there for the hunt to come near enough for him to get a clean shot at his selected target? It would be easy enough to lay a false trail by dragging a fresh fox carcass through the fields and down to the river. All knew that the hunt would try to remain on the lands of the Wennard estate, so it was very likely they must pass along by the river at some point in the day.

Once he had inspected the site again, he would leave the how of the baronet's death aside for the moment and concentrate on the why. If he could unravel that, it might point him towards that person or persons whose actions most needed to be investigated. In the meantime, it was imperative he took the news he had at length extracted from Giles—the very news he had summoned Adam to hear—to Mossterton Hall. He needed the help of a trained legal brain.

Adam's luck held. He found all three members of the Scudamore family present, eager to hear what new items he had discovered. His long drive from Trundon Hall had served finally to calm his temper and his nerves. First, of course, there had been the niceties of polite society to consider. They sat in a delightful parlour, neatly furnished, where the afternoon sun shone through large windows to provide both warmth and good light. Lady Alice offered refreshment, each selecting what they most enjoyed. Adam was happy to accept a dish of the excellent tea Lady Alice favoured. Miss Scudamore joined in its praises. Charles Scudamore pulled a face and asked for a glass of good ale. Finally, all settled themselves and waited for Adam to begin. Only then was he able to share Giles' startling news.

As his news unfolded, the faces of his audience registered their responses clearly. Lady Alice looked saddened more than shocked. Miss Scudamore seemed excited, as if the plot of some novel had all of a sudden begun to play out in the real world. Charles grinned and clapped his hands with pleasure.

"My dear doctor," he said, "that is indeed a tale to gladden any lawyer's heart. A rival claimant to a title and a fortune! A marriage that may have been bigamous—perhaps deliberately so. A spurned wife now seeking her due. It takes little skill to prophesy years of legal claims and counter-claims, while the courts plod their elephantine steps through an undergrowth of facts and speculation and whole tribes of lawyers grow rich on the costs. Who is making the claim? What evidence can they produce in support? Oh, this is better than I could have imagined!"

"In the letter my brother showed me, Lord Weybourne merely stated he and the other executors had been approached by a lawyer acting for the supposed first wife and her son. Proofs were mentioned, but not specified. The lawyer suggested the administrative processes of applying for probate should continue, but no bequests should be made, nor ownership of the land settled, until the matter of who is indeed the rightful heir may be resolved, in the courts if necessary."

"A cautious man," Charles replied. "He is, of course, perfectly correct. The Will may still be proved, but it must be obvious to all that the final settlement of the estate cannot continue until such a claim can either be verified or dismissed. It seems Sir Robert—or maybe just Mr Wennard—will have to wait some time longer for his money. Worse! As soon as word of this gets out, no man will give him credit. Should the rival claimant prove his entitlement to title and estate, Robert Wennard will have nothing."

"He will also be proved illegitimate," Miss Scudamore added. "As will his poor sisters."

"I feel for them," Lady Alice added quietly. "This is none of their doing, even if it is true. One is now married, I know. Let us hope her husband is man enough to stand by her."

"I do not doubt that, my lady," Adam said. "When a Quaker gives his word, whether on a contract or in marriage, there can be no going back."

"Any money left to them should be safe enough," Charles said, "provided they are named in the Will. If, as I imagine, the estate is entailed to the next legitimate male heir, it must pass to that person—whoever that may be. Each heir of such a Will has only a life interest in the property. He may not sell it or dispose of all or part in any other way, though he can usually obtain a mortgage. Nor need he be named. It could be that Sir Jackman left other monies, not part of the estate proper, to his son by name. If so, those bequests would be honoured, whether he is found to be the legitimate heir or not."

"That is very much what I needed to know," Adam said. "There is no reason yet to believe the son—I mean Robert—had any prior knowledge of this claim. If it is genuine, Sir Jackman must have known it might be made some day. Had he taken any steps to guard against such a claim? Where has this first wife, and her child, been for so many years? Why has she pressed her suit now and not before?"

"I am sure you can find out," Miss Scudamore said at once. "You are so wonderfully clever."

Her brother and aunt stared at her, though neither made any comment. Adam was much too wrapped up in his own thoughts to notice.

"I asked my brother to write to Lord Weybourne saying he didn't believe it was a matter for him to become involved in as magistrate, unless there was evidence of criminal fraud. However, he was willing, in a private capacity, to provide the assistance of his brother and a lawyer known to him to interview the claimant and begin the process of testing her claim."

"Which lawyer is that?" Charles asked, clearly disappointed at his words.

"A certain Mr Charles Scudamore, I believe," Adam said. "Always assuming he is willing to accept the case."

"Oh indeed, he is, he is!"

"If Lord Weybourne accepts my brother's advice, he is to reply at once to this Norwich attorney saying his client should agree to tell her story to his emissaries and answer any questions they may put to her. Giles is sure all will be done as I suggested. None of the executors will want to be involved more than they must. Most are elderly landowners whose greatest wish is to be spared any trouble or exertion in their declining years. What must have seemed a simple task when the Will was drawn up, accompanied by suitably generous bequests for their time and trouble, now looks as if it might become more of a problem than it's worth. He thinks they'll be delighted to hand the work over to others—with a suitable payment from the estate, of course."

"Naturally. It's well known that we lawyers will send you an account for the time expended in wishing you good day."

"There's no need to be so proud of being mercenary, brother," Miss Scudamore said. "I'm sure the doctor's thoughts are far above such base motives."

"Stuff and nonsense!" her brother replied. "Physicians often extract more than blood from their patients. Is that not so, doctor?"

"Behave yourselves, both of you," Lady Alice said softly. "I am tired of your chatter. Now leave us. There are things I wish to discuss with Dr Bascom in private."

Adam could not imagine what these might be. Lady Alice appeared to be in the best of health. Besides, he was not her doctor, nor did he think it proper he should be. It would be against all propriety to be involved in intimate discussions—or, still worse, examinations—with a beautiful woman whose age was so close to his own—however pleasant a prospect it might be to place his hand... No, no! Best not indulge in any daydreams like that.

Lady Alice must have divined at least some of his thoughts in that uncanny way she had. As soon as Charles and Ruth had left them, she hastened to reassure him that it was not a medical matter on which she wished to consult him, but a family one. Her elder brother, the father of Charles and Ruth, had written to her suggesting they should soon return to London. He was certain she must have had more than enough of them by this time. Charles ought to be working to establish himself in a practice, not idling about in Norfolk. Ruth also needed to be thinking of her future. If she wished to support herself by her botanical and technical drawings, she should direct her time to seeking more commissions from the many museums and collections to be found in the capital. If she wished to marry, the years were slipping by. She would be more likely to meet a suitable man in London than in the country or a provincial city.

"What he means, as I well understand, is that he does not trust her to make a wise choice, doctor. Ruth is not without a certain statuesque attractiveness..." Coming from an undeniably beautiful but petite woman barely five years older than her niece, this was not much of a compliment. "… but her brains easily frighten most men off. She is so unused to attentions that even a small dose of gallantry could turn her head. A fortune hunter must instantly see her as easy prey."

Adam was still baffled by the notion that his advice could be of any use. True, he understood a good deal about the tribulations of establishing a professional practice. He also saw that Mr Charles Scudamore's light-hearted manner might not be what everyone thought appropriate in a lawyer, any more than it would be in a physician. However, he was surely not the correct person to be lecturing a young man of superior family background on how he should behave.

Once again, Lady Alice took him by surprise.

"Do not worry, doctor. I am not going to ask you to turn Charles into a sober-sided lawyer or give fatherly advice to Ruth on the perils of suitors. For a start, Charles would laugh in your face; and Ruth would be more likely to suppose herself helplessly in love with you than pay any attention to your words."

"In love with me?" Adam said, so startled his voice emerged in a kind of squeak.

"Why not?" Lady Alice said. "I'm sure many women must dote upon you."

"None that I know of," Adam said.

"That's why I am so sure of it." Lady Alice being enigmatic put Adam into a flutter. Then, as his mother did so often, she shook her head a little, smiled at him and continued.

"What I wish your guidance on, doctor, is simple. Do you believe there may yet be enough in this puzzle of yours to justify me in asking my brother not to press for Charles to return? In Ruth's case, it will be easy for me to point out the opportunities for her to study the natural world at first hand. I can also undertake to introduce her to suitable institutions and societies in Norwich which may be glad to exploit her talent. As for the young men, I know my brother will trust me to keep her safe. Charles is harder. You must have seen for yourself that he has a fine brain—when he can bestir himself to use it. To be blunt, I doubt he will ever make much of a success as a London lawyer. There is too much competition; too much need for exertion and a constant striving for clients. In a provincial backwater, such as a small town in Norfolk, he might well find ample work to keep him in comfort without needing to expend more effort than his nature would find acceptable. I need to know if you agree with me. If you do, I will ask you to find a way to involve him more closely in this puzzle of yours. I can give him some basic legal work on the estate, but my brother will know this cannot occupy much of his time. Your words this afternoon also gave me another idea. If I could say that he is likely to be engaged by the executors of a large estate to handle the matter of a substantial, but disputed, inheritance, his father would be appeased at once. Do you really think it will happen?"

"I do, my lady," Adam said. "My brother knows most of the executors personally. Like him, they are honest, straightforward country gentlemen, with little taste for anything complex or uncertain. He also has certain reasons to wish to please me a little."

"That sounds ominous. You are, in my direct experience, the kindest and most understanding of men, but I should not like to raise your ire, if I could avoid it. Be that as it may, I confess that my niece and nephew irritate me at times with their childish squabbles. Yet this is a very large house. It would seem desolate indeed should I be the only person here save the servants. Having them with me is the best tonic I could be given."

"Then, as a physician, I must see to it you have access to that tonic for as long as necessary, my lady. It will be no trouble to involve your nephew Charles in the matter of Sir Jackman Wennard's Will. I had hoped to be able to do so when I called here today. If it would please you, that is an even stronger reason for me to accomplish it. I have also thought for a time I might use some of your late husband's magnificent bequest to purchase properties that might yield good rents. Your nephew could act for me there as well."

"Bless you, doctor," Lady Alice said. Then she looked at him so strangely and for so long that Adam began to blush. "Alas," she said, "I must let you go now. I would invite you—nay, press you—to stay for dinner, but invitations have already been issued for our local rector and his wife and their daughters to dine with us. Charles and Ruth are dreading it! The rector is a good man, though exceedingly dull in his conversation. His wife has no thought in her head but to find husbands for the daughters. Since both are plain and lack accomplishments, it must prove a Herculean task. For their part, the daughters believe Ruth to be a fount of knowledge on the latest fashions in London. She, of course, has neither knowledge nor interest in such matters. Sadly, she has a wicked sense of humour. When two of them called with their mother one afternoon recently, she almost convinced them that 'the ton' had quite given up hats; and that the brightest of red cloth was entirely á la mode for day dresses. Had I not intervened, they would have attended morning service bare-headed and arrayed as scarlet women!"

Nine

Following Fresh Tracks

ADAM HAD FOUND IN THE PAST THAT THERE CAME A POINT IN UNRAV-
ELLING A PUZZLE where finding a way forward seems hopeless. If this was
not it, he would be most surprised. The only thing to do was to press
onwards and trust that his luck must change, despite his brother's frustration at his failure to provide a quick and simple answer to the question of
who had murdered Sir Jackman Wennard. It was not his fault the puzzle
kept growing more convoluted by the day. Sir Jackman Wennard might
have appeared on the outside to be no more than a bluff country squire
with a passion for fast horses and pretty women. Now they knew his life
held at least one secret of substantial proportions. Since he must have
wanted that secret to remain well hidden, he would hardly have made it
easy for anyone else to sniff it out. Adam could not imagine the baronet
would wish his acknowledged son and heir to know either. In many ways,
it was surprising they had advanced so far.

Adam was out early that day, riding his horse, not sitting comforta-
bly in the chaise. His plan was to arrive in Cley in time to get breakfast at
one of the inns. By doing so, he could also enquire of the landlord where

to find the home of the tenant farmer through whose holding the path down from the road to the river ran. He would need to go off the track of the shortcut and had no wish to suffer the embarrassment of explaining his actions while facing an angry farmer, probably holding a gun. The Bascom name had some power in those parts, since they bordered his family home, but it would still not do to wander over someone's farmland without their permission.

The weather was holding up at least, though there was a tartness in the air that suggested autumn rains and winter frosts could not be far away. He passed through Holt before its people were about in the streets, the scent of breakfast from the houses urging him onwards. Now he had stopped at the first inn he found on his way into Cley; a long, low building hard by the church. Its name, 'The Three Swallows', seemed entirely appropriate, for he could see a few of those birds hawking for flies over the fields about or sitting in excited rows on some of the house's eaves. Where they went in the winter, no one knew. Some believed they hibernated at the bottom of ponds; others that they hung themselves up inside trees, like bats, or flew off to some destination as yet undiscovered. Whatever the truth of the matter, it would not be many days now before they would all leave until next spring.

Fortunately, the inn could provide Adam with a fine breakfast, served by the publican's wife in person. He imagined her, on hearing the name 'Bascom' given by this unexpected guest, hastening to assume her best manners and hustling the maidservant away into some inner room. It was not every day that the brother of the squire of Trundon Hall came to her inn. She would be determined to make the most of it, so that she and her husband could boast to their regulars that they had welcomed a member of the gentry that morning.

It would doubtless also add to her sense of importance that she had at once been able to answer his question about the tenant of the land he had been passing as he came down the hill.

"That'll be Jeremiah Kingsland, sir," she said at once. "A fine farmer, they say, though he has had little enough help from his landlord in improving the fields he leases. He lives right across the way. You goes out of our door, over the road, and through the little meadow they say was once under the sea when this was a busy harbour. It's still dreadful damp in the winter rains, but more on the further edge, on towards where the village lies now. The harbour wall used to come right up to the church. Aye, this building would have stood hard alongside where fine ships were moored. But that were long ago, sir. They do say it were even afore the time of Good Queen Bess."

Adam expressed suitable interest in this sketchy history of the once flourishing haven between Cley and Blakeney, then gently asked what else she knew of Mr Kingsland.

"Indeed, sir. I be sorry for wandering in my speech, but I like to make sure our visitors knows this place was not always as small as it is today. Well … Jeremiah Kingsland. He do live in the house you'll see almost opposite the church, beyond the meadow I mentioned, the one where the land starts to rise up. No one would wish to build where the land floods, would they, sir? A man well into middle age, well set-up and prosperous enough, I dare say. No children though to take over the tenancy after him. An honest, hard-working man, who likes a drop of our good ale."

It took Adam a great deal of gentle persistence to persuade the innkeeper's wife to allow him to leave as quickly as he wished. In the end, the sight of a whole, golden guinea in her hand in payment for both breakfast and information shocked her into silence and he was able to slip out and make his way to Mr Kingsland's house. The farmer might, of course, be out in the fields somewhere. Adam could only hope that, if he was, he could be found and persuaded to return.

Mr Jeremiah Kingsland proved to be at home, having just consumed a breakfast every bit as generous as the one Adam had taken. From the look of his ruddy face and ample waistline, Adam suspected such meals formed an important part of his day. He was probably a little older than the innkeeper's wife had estimated, though hearty enough, and it was likely he tried now to confine himself to the role of overseer, while his labourers did all the hard work in the fields.

If Mr Kingsland was startled or impressed by receiving a gentleman in his home so early in the day, he did not show it. Perhaps he was not the type of person to be much swayed by a family name. Perhaps the breakfast he had just eaten was of a size to demand a great deal of his energy for its digestion. He answered Adam's questions readily enough, however, though he could not quite resist showing his anger at the previous squire.

"This is good land, sir, given some care and putting some heart into it from time to time. It only looks poor because there's so much gorse and bracken in places. As I told Sir Jackman, if you adds some good loads of marl and fold sheep on it over the winter, you quickly turns near-barren heathland into fine crops of barley. There's good profit to be had in that in London and such parts. The folk around here can't afford much better than the dust in the bottom of the sack nowadays. It's London—aye, and markets in the Low Countries and the like—what drives up the price of all grain beyond what ordinary labouring people can afford. That, and the poor harvest of recent years. But you hasn't come here to listen to me preaching to you on the cost of grain.

"That track you mentions down the hill isn't a regular road. It's more of a pathway sometimes used by local folk wanting to go down to the river. Strangers wouldn't hardly know it was there. The old squire what they say has been murdered now didn't much like people on his land—not even his tenants! Too afraid they'd steal his game. But since he used that pathway himself, he made sure it was kept open and free from those damned traps his keepers set all around to catch and maim poor folk desperate for a bit o' meat. Oh no, the gamekeepers was careful to keep the path free. It wouldn't do to shoot the squire with a swivel-gun or catch his horse's leg in a trap, would it?"

"Sir Jackman Wennard used the track himself?" Adam said. "Often?"

"Used it a good deal, especially if he was coming home late after a boozy session with his friends over Langham or Letheringsett way. Saved him from going all the way into Gressington to get on the road to Cley. Of course, he'd be in the opposite direction to the way you says he went on the day he was killed—up the hill, not down. He said it was a good deal safer at night than the road too. Robbers and footpads either didn't know it was there, or thought none but poor villagers used it. Go along the roads round here at night and you risks meeting up with smugglers and the like. They'd rob any fine gentleman what blundered into their path. That track is too narrow and steep for their wagons or packhorses, so you wouldn't find them along it."

That confirmed that Sir Jackman knew well enough where the track went to. If Adam was right, it also made it the obvious way for him to seek to turn his panicking horse to return to the hunt. He would have known where the huntsman planned to go that day. To go down the shortcut he normally used in the other direction must have seemed the quickest way to catch up.

When Adam asked about the other paths he had seen through those woods, Mr Kingsland could also supply the answer. Animal paths, he told Adam. Deer made them, but all kinds of other beasts used them afterwards: foxes, badgers, rabbits, even hares. The poachers used them too, both for concealment and because they wanted to see where the animals might be passing. Such tracks tended to wander about a bit, but they almost all went down to the river in the end. Animals needed to drink as much as people did.

That took Mr Kingsland back to the topic of Sir Jackman Wennard's gamekeepers.

"The ones he employs are not much better than ruffians," he said. "No skill in either of them, I say. Only good enough to come upon a poacher and near beat the life out of him. Still, that must be what the squire wanted. As I told you, he was frantic in his hatred of poachers. Made his keepers fill the wood with traps to catch 'em. Seems to me I'd best go with you, if you're set on blundering about in them woods and gorse patches. I knows how to spot where the keepers puts their hellish machines. I'm happy for you to go anywhere you like over my farm, sir. Still, I'd be most uneasy about a gentleman blundering through that area alone."

Adam didn't much fancy the idea either. As he thought about it, he realised that the helpful Mr Kingsland had already answered a good many of his questions. If he could set Adam straight on one or two more, there might be no need to go back to the slope at all.

"I was told," Adam began warily, "that on the day Sir Jackman was found dead, there were at least two shots heard at almost the same time as he must have been coming down the hill. Do you know who might have been shooting that day?"

"No one I can think of," Mr Kingsland replied. "It weren't me for certain. Damn silly place to go shooting anything. Damn silly time too. Trees and bushes are too dense to let you get a clean shot, save at point-blank range. We shoots the vermin from time to time, but it would be a fool who shot at anything on the day of the hunt. Squire would be bound to be there and he'd have run mad. Frightening the foxes, you see. Ruining his sport. But he weren't shot, were he? I heard someone broke his neck for him."

"No, he wasn't shot. I suppose someone might have tried though."

"Surely not. They'd be near certain to miss and then where'd they be? No chance at a clear shot and a steady aim. Besides, I heard he only went that way because he'd made a fool of hisself in the village and Dick Hanson at the Fishmonger Arm's let off his gun to frighten the horse."

Adam agreed that was the case. Anyone wanting to shoot the squire would have hidden in the woods to shoot over the clear ground beyond the river. No sense in taking a pot-shot or two at a galloping horse in thick cover. That wouldn't explain why the baronet had run into the trap in the way that he had.

"Tells you what I thinks, doctor," Mr Kingsland said. "I thinks what them folk heard was the squire's horse setting off two of them cursed swivel-guns. If his horse strayed off the track and down one of them animal paths, he'd very likely set off some trap or other. Wood's full o' them."

"The horse wasn't hurt," Adam objected. "At least, not so far as I know."

"Them guns is designed to hit a man creeping through the wood, not a galloping horse. Ten to one they'd miss, I reckons. Can't be sure, of course. I'm no gamekeeper. But that's how it seems to me."

Adam cursed himself for not thinking of that before. But then, he was neither a landowner nor a poacher and his father had been too soft-hearted to use such implements on his own land. It was so simple! Think what it would have done to the horse, already panicked by what had happened in Cley. Not only would swivel-guns firing explain the shots, it must also have been what caused Sir Jackman Wennard's horse to take him into the rope at such speed. Even if the rider had seen the trap, he wouldn't have been able to avoid it in time.

Mr Kingsland proved such a fine source of information Adam decided there was no need to go again to the place where Sir Jackman Wennard had met his fate. What happened was as clear in his mind as if he had been there. The great horse charging down the hillside while Sir Jackman fought to gain control, leaving the proper track, plunging onwards headlong into tangled gorse and bracken. Then the tripping of the two swivel-guns, whose reports so close to its hindquarters must have further terrified the horse, Sir Jackman lying back in the saddle to try to curb the horse's speed and keep his place on its back. Finally horse and rider rushing out of dense undergrowth to where the rope caught under the man's chin and snapped his neck in an instant, so he tumbled out of the saddle and the horse was set free to rush on over the river and out into the fields beyond. The only question which remained now was whether that rope had been put there to catch Sir Jackman or for some other reason, as yet unknown.

Not a bad outcome for an early morning ride, especially if you added the fine breakfast at the inn. Time now to head for home again.

Adam was tempted to forego another call on his brother, especially after the tense exchange of the last visit. If he pressed on into Holt, he might be at his own house again within an hour or so. Still, it would not do. If Giles heard his brother had been at Cley—which he must, gossip of any kind being traded eagerly in remote villages such as that—to avoid the usual courtesy call would hurt his feelings and suggest Adam had yet to forgive him for his previous outburst. So Adam turned his horse and took the by-road over the river to Gressington, then on through Glavenbridge and thus to Trundon Hall again.

He found Giles once more in his library, seated at his desk, a tumbled mass of papers and letters before him. This time, however, the source of Giles' agitation had nothing to do with his brother. A new gang of highwaymen had chosen the area between Letheringsett, Blakeney and Salthouse for their operations. Over the past few nights, they had robbed travellers of anything of value they might be carrying. The day before, growing yet bolder, they stopped a local farmer and his wife coming home from market in broad daylight and stole the cash the farmer had been paid for the sale of six fine pigs. Everyone from the deputy lieutenant to the local clergy were demanding Giles find the gang at once and send them for trial.

"There are three of them," Giles told his brother. "All wear masks and are well armed. Their leader sports a fine hat with a cockade and a bright blue coat with scarlet buttons. No one has been hurt so far, but it's probably only a matter of time before robbery turns into assault and murder."

"Is it the smugglers, do you think?" Adam said.

"No, I don't think so. They'll make more by sticking to their usual trade. There's been quite an upsurge in smuggling along this part of the coast. The Revenue's Riding Officers are hard pressed and there's talk of calling on the Yeomanry or dragoons to assist them. Of course, I'm in the middle. The Revenue keep demanding I help them more, though how I don't know. To be honest, I wish the deputy lieutenant would summon help from the military. That would take me out of it altogether."

"So, regular robbers or footpads possibly. Has there been any other crime in this area recently?"

"Someone raided the home of the Creston family at Glavenbridge when the family were away and the house left empty. A neighbour says he saw three men riding off from there late in the evening, going in the direction of Gressington. When the Crestons returned home, they found the house broken into and all the silver missing, along with Mrs Creston's jewellery and two fine duelling pistols in a case. Some people are crediting the highwaymen with that crime too. Is that correct? The neighbour may have seen three men, or he may have imagined it, being certain any crime must be carried out by these highway robbers. Even criminals have their specialisations. Burglars rarely turn to robbery on the road. Why should a successful band of highwaymen decide to rob a house? I tell you, brother, I am being driven made with claims, counter-claims and demands for instant action. If I had known a magistrate's life would include so much criticism and thankless work, I would never have accepted the position when it was offered."

"People are frightened," Adam said, "and frightened people always want someone else to take away their fears. I wonder where these highwaymen have come from of a sudden? Why are they operating around here? It cannot be all that profitable. Why aren't they looking to the busier roads nearer to the towns? Country roads at night are like to be empty, while a good many merchants and farmers can be found on the main routes at almost any time of day—gentry too."

"Please tell them so then," Giles replied. "Maybe they will heed your advice and move off to rob folk around Cromer or Holt, or even Aylsham. Anywhere out of the area for which I am responsible. I'm sorry, brother. I will have to leave you to your own devices regarding that other matter, at least for the present. You can understand I have to concentrate on smoking out these thieves."

That suited Adam very well, though he was careful not to say so. He spoke a few more sympathetic words, promised nothing and headed back home as soon as he could do so with politeness. Highwaymen were not his problem, thank God. Yet he still wondered exactly what the three of them were doing, plying their trade amongst poor folk and empty roads.

There was still no word from the lawyer representing the rival claimant to the Wennard estate, so Adam could not go further on that score either for the present. Nor was there a letter or message from Lady Alice to tell him he might call on someone who was part of the hunting party on that fateful day. He knew he should be grateful and turn his attention back to where it belonged—his practice—but he knew he couldn't. His curiosity had been brought up to fever pitch. It could not be quieted. His restlessness only forced him to rehearse his existing knowledge again and again in the hope some new meaning could be wrung from it. After barely half an hour therefore, he decided to go and see Peter to bring him up to date.

Peter was grateful for Adam's call, since he too had exhausted his mind by endless repetition of the inadequate information he had already. Now he listened carefully to the new information. There was no doubt what most intrigued him—the rival claimant to the Wennard estate. The news of this development had not yet reached folk in Aylsham, though it must do so soon.

"What a surprise it will be!" Peter said. "There's been no material like it for gossip in many a year, I'm sure. Everyone will be talking of it. Don't worry, Bascom! I'll be certain to listen out for whatever may be useful. Highwaymen too! Let's hope they stick to back roads north of Holt and avoid the main roads. Pickings will be easy, I fancy, but rather thin. My guess, like yours, is that they'll soon tire of robbing farmers and farm servants. If they want to be able to prey on the gentry or professional men like yourself, they should turn instead to the coaches that run regularly between Holt and Norwich and Cromer and Norwich. Both pass through Aylsham. Both are much used. There's also the mail coach which runs along the turnpike road. Even a few of the gentry use that to get to London in a hurry."

"Won't they be well guarded?" Adam said. "When last I used the mail coach, the guard had gun, powder and shot enough to slaughter half the county."

"Even the best-armed guard can be made of no effect by surprise, Bascom. The passengers won't help, though they'll be eager to suggest whatever they lost was worth twice what they actually paid for it. Most people find their bravery dissipates instantly when they're looking at the barrel of a loaded gun. Mine would, I assure you."

"Mine too," Adam agreed. "Never mind. These robberies are not what I have been asked to deal with. Do you have any news you think might be useful to me?"

"It's not much, but you're welcome to it. Word has spread that Sir Robert Wennard is close to bankruptcy. Indeed, I have heard talk of several shopkeepers and traders refusing to sell provisions, even coal, to Upper Cley Hall, except for ready money. You'd think the executors of the Wennard estates would make sure the heir had ample money for daily necessities. Either that isn't the case, or such money as they do allow him is being used in other ways."

"The latter, I would think," Adam said. "My brother told me young Robert likes to spend most of his time gambling and drinking. It's a sickness with people like that. Whatever money they can get goes to support their habit. They always believe the next hand of cards or wager on a race will be the one that will restore their fortunes. It never is."

"The man is also being uncooperative in allowing the taking of the inventory needed for probate purposes to be completed," Peter said. "I heard he's been raising objections to what he calls the valuers "prying into the family's personal effects and valuables". He's also dismissed two maids and a footman for theft, though all three deny having touched anything at all."

"I imagine the theft was his," Adam said, "and he's trying to shift the blame elsewhere. Been selling the family silver, probably, or his mother's jewellery—if there's any left after all this time. She died when he was still quite a small boy, I think. Somehow I can't imagine Sir Jackman keeping his wife's valuables for reasons of sentiment, can you? Still, you never can tell." A thought came to him. "Ah! There's an opportunity perhaps. Can you find who the dismissed servants were and where they are now? They won't have any love for their former master, so might be willing to tell anything they know. If he's dismissed them already, he can't bring any more pressure to bear to keep their mouths shut. I doubt he could produce actual evidence to support his charges—especially if whatever he alleges they stole has been lost at the gaming tables. This could be the chink in Sir Robert's armour. Through it we can spy out something of what may have been happening in the house, before and after Sir Jackman's death. It's worth a try."

A SHORTCUT TO MURDER

Ten

Making Plans

ADAM HAD REACHED THAT IMPOSSIBLE STAGE IN INVESTIGATING ANY PUZZLE when he found himself regretting every moment spent away from it. Nevertheless, he must try to recall he had a medical practice that he owed some of his attention. Thanks to other sources of income, he'd reduced the need to rely solely on his patients in matters of finance, but he was still a doctor and intended to act like one. Visits must still be arranged and consultations undertaken, however often his mind wandered off towards reviewing evidence and the formulating of yet more hypotheses.

The periods riding, or more often driving his chaise, between his home and his patients' houses gave him some of the best opportunities for thought, even if it wasn't always productive. Like most people, his moods rose and fell in response to the state of the weather or the roads. If the sun shone, his mood became optimistic. When it rained, as it had done all that day, he fell into gloom, conscious of the mistakes he had made and how tangled the mass of conflicting evidence had become. Then he would return home moody and disheartened.

It was in just such a state of gloom that Adam arrived back in Aylsham, water dripping from his heavy coat, his face stinging from the wind and his hands chilled, despite the gloves he wore. Darkness was closing in earlier and earlier as the year spun into late autumn and he was already treating patients for the agues, rheumatic symptoms and bronchial ailments that would plague them all winter. He had prescribed bed rest, purgatives, opiates and cupping of the chest wall all day long. Yet what lowered his spirits the most was the recognition he could do so little to help these people in their pain and discomfort. He knew some of them, at least, would not see another spring.

In this glum mood he surrendered his chaise and horse to his groom, William.

"Message for you in the 'ouse, master," William said. "I met up with the Norwich carter this morning and 'e gave it to me to bring back. I left in on the desk in your library."

It was a letter from the lawyer handling the claim of the lady who said she was the first Mrs Wennard. He had written to say that Mrs Sarah Wennard—so she must not have remarried or reverted to her maiden name—would be willing to receive Dr Bascom in the lawyer's office in Norwich to answer all his questions. She would make herself available at any time between the hours of eleven o'clock and two o'clock on any of the next four days. After that, she was planning to return home to await the outcome of her legal action.

Adam knew much would hinge on this single conversation. If he mishandled it, or left important matters out, he might not get a second chance. He was determined to shut himself away in his library for the whole of the next day to plan what he would ask of the lady.

So rigid was his adherence to this decision next morning, that he refused even to leave off his task and emerge for meals. Mrs Bridgestone had to send Hannah in with food and drink enough to sustain him.

"He didn't even speak," the maid said when she returned to the kitchen after delivering her master's breakfast. "Just glanced up at me and flapped his hands, like you might to shoo the chickens away. I think all this runnin' about and mullin' over terrible murders has quite overset 'is mind. It ain't natural to lock yourself away like that. Anyway, I left the tray on a side table, so 'e can 'ave it if 'e wants."

All that day, the servants crept about as quietly as they could and stayed well away from the library. Darkness came, and still Adam stayed in the room. A dim light under the door showed he must have lit a candle, but there was no sound of activity. By the time the servants went to their beds, their master was still there.

What was Adam doing all that time? Going over and over what he knew, or thought he knew, seeking for any indication of a pattern that could explain all the elements of the puzzle. Who had Sir Jackman been seeking when he left the inn-yard in such a passion? How could a killer know his victim would not follow the hunt that day? How could he have known as well the track his victim would then take to return and catch up with the others? If Sir Jackman hadn't been riding full tilt, the rope would only have knocked him off his horse. How could the murderer have brought this about—if he had? Had robbery been the motive? Was the killer hiding nearby, ready to pounce on the fallen man and take what he could? If so, why kill him?

So far, there was little trace of answers to any of these questions. The son, Robert, was deep in debt and kept very dubious company, yet his father was wealthy and debt free so far as anyone knew. He mingled with the local nobility and gentry, attended assemblies and balls and doubtless enjoyed a good deal of hospitality. He was a successful horse breeder, who had sold horses to royal patrons. Yes, Sir Jackman was a confirmed lecher, but if all the upper class men who were known adulterers and woman-isers were murdered, the country houses and merchants' homes of the entire county must be wholly depopulated.

No one in the house save him knew what time Adam finally went to bed, yet in the morning he rose and ordered his breakfast as usual. He looked pale, his eyes were rimmed in red, but he showed no other ill effects of the day before. After drinking two cups of coffee, he announced he was going to see Mr Lassimer, but would not be absent long. His breakfast must be ready for him to take as soon as he returned. William must have the chaise standing outside for him by eleven o'clock. He would drive himself. And with that, he swept out of the house.

Peter was startled by such an early visit, but assumed there must be a good reason for it. Naturally, he invited Adam to join him in taking something to eat or drinking a little coffee, but these small acts of politeness were ignored. It was obvious his friend's mind was elsewhere.

What Adam wanted to ask was whether Peter knew the carter who travelled regularly between Holt, Aylsham and Norwich. When Peter said that he did, Adam gave his orders, for there was no other way of describing what he asked. Peter must ask the carter if he had carried any packages or boxes recently from Upper Cley Hall into Norwich. If he had, Peter must ask him where he delivered them in the city. The information was vital, so Peter must seek out the man as soon as possible. On second thoughts, he must also ask the carter who travelled to King's Lynn the same questions. Norwich was most likely, but it would not do to overlook other possibilities. Their responses should be conveyed at once to Adam's home and a suitable message left if he should be out. Then Adam left as abruptly as he came, all without further explanation.

Back home, Adam ate his breakfast in silence, then returned to his study. There he busied himself writing several letters. Finally, he called William and gave further orders. William must take Adam's old horse, Betty, and take the local letters to the people whose names were written on each without delay. All were most urgent. The other letter was for his mother in Norwich. William should pay a groom or other servant from

The Black Boys Inn to deliver that one, again in haste. Never mind what it cost. Adam himself was leaving at once for Mossterton Hall.

As the day progressed, Adam was to find it full of surprises. He had ridden to Mossterton mostly to bring Charles Scudamore up to date and ask the young lawyer to accompany him to Norwich. It would be helpful to have a legal person on his side in case Mrs Wennard's lawyer wanted to involve himself in their discussions. He also wanted to warn everyone at the hall about the highwaymen now operating in the locality.

At first all progressed much as he expected. Lady Alice, Mr Scudamore and his sister listened attentively to what he had to say, interrupting only to seek clarification or more details. He also reminded them he still needed confirmation of exactly what had happened during the hunt itself. So far, he had received evidence only from a single person, who might have forgotten something vital or never seen it at all. That was not safe, and he was certain others must be willing to answer his questions. In such a complex and tangled series of events, missing even a single critical piece of information could leave them blind. He'd hoped he would have been able to obtain details from many more people by this time.

Charles either failed to understand who these remarks were aimed at or thought it was best to keep quiet. He was far too eager to hear how he could take part with Adam in interviewing Mrs Wennard to worry about anything else. Adam, recognising this, decided to move on. Lady Alice had other ideas. She was much too sharp to have missed Adam's implied criticism of her nephew. It was time to set that young man straight.

Before Adam could say more, she asked Charles bluntly what new information he had to report to the doctor. Of course, it turned out to be nothing. How could there be anything, Charles protested? He had hardly left the house since the doctor's last visit. This was the response her ladyship expected and her temper boiled over. For several minutes, she raged at her nephew, berating him for his laziness, his willingness to be content with superficial actions and his general lack of attention. When would he grow up? When would he realise he needed to stop playing the dilettante and apply himself? If he thought he could drift through life as he was doing now, he would very soon find he was wrong. She wasn't going to stand for it and she knew his father wouldn't either. One word from her and Charles would find himself with his allowance cut in half and his father demanding he account for every minute of his day. Then she returned to the death of Sir Jackman Wennard. How many tenants did he have, she asked Charles? Ten? Fifteen? Most would have been at the hunt. So how many had Charles spoken to? One. Had he spoken to her steward again? No. Had he asked her if there were any other neighbours she might be able to arrange for him to visit? No again. He was a disgrace to her and to their family!

Adam sat in some embarrassment, wincing at Charles' weak attempts to excuse himself. He should have seen Lady Alice was in no mood to be forgiving. He would have done better to admit his fault at once and resign himself to the additional rebukes which must surely follow. As it was, his aunt found his feeble answers unsatisfactory and his attitude deplorable. Petite as she was, she now proved to be a colossus in terms of authority. There were to be strict conditions set on her nephew for the future. He must stop lazing around and undertake with the utmost diligence all tasks the doctor might set him. If he did not, she would pack him off to London in disgrace by the next coach. Then she would write to her brother laying out his son's failings in full.

It was at this point Charles' sister Ruth made the grave error of sniggering. The silence which followed this sad display of levity was deafening. Lady Alice turned her head with a kind of grim determination and regarded the poor girl much as Bloody Queen Mary must have looked at the protestant heretics she was about to condemn to be burned alive. It was to be Ruth's turn to face the wrath of her ladyship.

Where had Ruth been to make preliminary sketches or seek out fresh specimens to draw? How often had she been to Norwich to consult books in the fine libraries there? Why had Lady Alice not seen her with pens, paints and papers for many days? Where were the books she was studying, the letters from learned correspondents? How many visits had she made to the private collectors and men of substance Lady Alice had approached on her behalf? She was as bad as her brother; feckless, idle and feather-brained. It was not to be born!

"Stop making sheep's eyes at poor Dr Bascom too, miss," Lady Alice said. "It's high time you stopped behaving like some French coquette and attended to some serious work. No man of any worth, especially not one like the doctor, is going to be impressed by a silly girl flutter-ing her eyelashes and handing out extravagant compliments. You're not beautiful enough and have far too few accomplishments to be of any use in the marriage market as things stand. I'm warning you. If you do not reform—and quickly—you too will be on your way back to London at an hour's notice."

Adam was stupefied. He had always thought of Lady Alice as the most gentle, kind and forbearing of people, a woman moulded entirely in the loveliest, softest and most feminine of styles. Now she had giv-en him a glimpse of the hard steel which lay within. He did not know whether to be terrified or enchanted.

"Very well," this wholly unexpected tigress said. "Ruth! You and I will go about our business while these two men make the necessary arrangements to go to Norwich and pursue their investigations. Come now, I have not sent you from my house yet. Tears are inappropriate and completely wasted on me. Charles, you cannot hide in that chair, how-ever hard you try. Good day to you, doctor. I trust your investigations will prosper and you will be able to report better progress next time you call." With those final words, she rose, beckoned Ruth to follow her and left the room.

Adam wondered when it might be safe to breathe again. Charles stayed slumped in his chair like a man facing the threat of instant decapitation should he raise his head any further.

"By God, doctor," he said at length, his voice shaking. "I have never seen her ladyship behave like that before—and I hope never to see it again. That I swear! It would need a far braver and stronger man than I am to provoke such a spitfire and survive! Who would dare to argue with her in such a mood? Not I, for sure. I have long known my aunt could be fierce over matters of importance to her. What she just revealed goes far beyond fierce! I haven't been so frightened in my whole life!"

"It amazed me too," Adam said.

"You weren't on the receiving end! My father once warned me that if his littlest sister set her heart on something, she would have it, though Hell itself stood in her way. Now I see what he meant."

"Maybe we should do what she asks of us," Adam said. "Quickly too."

Charles was still shaking his head in disbelief. "She grew up amongst a mass of much older brothers, all towering over her. Most girls, my father said, would have resorted to playing on being one of the weaker sex to get their way. Alice never did. She joined in all the boys' games, handing out blow for blow, though she was half the size of any of them. They all learned to fear her anger and never dared to treat her as weak or timid. He claimed they loved her all the better for it."

"I can see that. But now, Mr Scudamore—"

"Just Scudamore, please. After seeing me laid low like that, giving never a squeak of protest, I cannot claim the respect of a 'Mister'. Indeed, I feel I should be grovelling at your feet, not just my aunt's."

The sight of Charles' contrition, theatrical as ever, quite restored Adam's good humour.

"Very well, Scudamore," he said. "Let us turn to practicalities and prepare for tomorrow's meeting."

"Indeed, Bascom. We shall do that and do it thoroughly. I mean henceforward to display such zeal that Lady Alice will not treat me thus ever again. My sister Ruth will also be regretting she has spent even half an hour away from her drawing and her studies. If either of us were to be sent home in disgrace for upsetting my father's favourite sister, I assure you it would go extremely hard with us there too. My God, life would be unbearable! To practicalities, as you said. What do you hope to discover from Sir Jackman's supposed first wife? What is my part to be in whatever takes place?"

"To put it most plainly," Adam said, "I want you to protect me from her legal adviser. Norwich lawyers are proverbial for their cantankerousness and eagerness to start litigation on the slightest pretext. I hope this man may leave us to speak with his client alone—or at least sit in silence while we do, but I fear that may be unlikely. If he sees I also have a legal mind on my side, it may lessen his willingness to try to browbeat me."

"I doubt that," Charles said. "It may even provoke him into showing off his talent to protect his client's interest by advancing his own. We shall see. I can but promise to do my best."

"No man can do more," Adam replied. "I am certain you will do very well. I still hope it will not come to that. Nothing the lady tells us can have any bearing on the strength of her legal claim on behalf of her son. That I will neither dispute nor endorse. I am only interested in the death of the man she says was her husband."

"We should make that clear at the outset," Charles said. "It may go a long way to drawing the teeth of even the most litigious legal dog."

"Very well, we will do that. What I do want is to ask the lady to tell me all she will about the circumstances of her marriage to Sir Jackman and what she has been doing since then. Where has she been? How has she lived? Why has she appeared only now? If I am right, everything that happened on the day of Sir Jackman's death started from the point when this lady discovered he had married again after leaving her. The roots of this puzzle undoubtedly extend far back into the past, but whatever set all in motion must be recent.

"I have also written to my brother. I want him to enquire urgently, probably through the mayors of the main towns in the county, for any trace of Sir Robert selling or trying to sell valuable items from Upper Cley Hall. It matters not whether it is before or after his father's death. I told him he should ask them to focus on jewellery, clocks, watches and fine sporting guns."

"Ah," Charles said, "you think he has been funding his gambling habit by taking valuable items unnoticed from his father's house and selling them."

Adam made no reply to this, for none was needed.

"Lastly," he went on, "but by no means least, I hope to learn everything I can of where this Mrs Sarah Wennard has been, and what she has done since coming into Norfolk. As I said, the baronet's murder must have been provoked by something recent, not events long past. I do not think she or her son was involved in that crime in any way. I hope not. However, it is possible that her presence or actions became the stimulus for the killer to put his own plans in motion. Logically, Sir Jackman could have been killed at any time. Why now? Why at the point when his son's inheritance is about to be called into question?"

"I know you said you do not suspect the lady, or her son, but Sir Jackman Wennard's death certainly makes Mrs Wennard's legal case a good deal less easy to challenge," Charles said. "I would not set her involvement aside so easily. Had he lived, Sir Jackman would without doubt have denied contracting a legal marriage with her—and perhaps been able to do so successfully. It would depend on the nature and extent of the proofs she can set before any court. Whichever way that went, he would certainly dispute her son's parentage. I do not doubt that his lawyers would represent this lady as little short of a harlot and her son the bastard child of any one of multiple men. How could she then be so sure Sir Jackman fathered her boy? She would deny wantonness or adultery, of course, but would be unlikely to be able to offer more than that. It is easier to prove what you have done than what you say you have not. Much would depend on whether the men of the jury believed her. Though she may claim she had not yielded her virtue to any man before Sir Jackman married her, that's easily challenged as no more than a lie to save face. With Sir Jackman unable to give evidence of his own involvement with her—always supposing he admitted to any at all—his son here will have a far harder task before him."

"I suppose you are correct about the lady's possible involvement in the death," Adam said. "The trouble is I cannot imagine how she would have been able to bring it about without substantial local knowledge and assistance. She has never been here before, so far as I know. How would she know of the shortcut, or when Sir Jackman planned to go fox-hunting over his own lands? Your other point seems to me more weighty. Since his father's death, Sir Robert must have been quieting the complaints of his creditors by reminding them he would soon have access to his father's accumulated wealth. That prospect has now retreated far into the future. It may, in fact, never become a reality. How will they react?"

"Badly, I should imagine. Yet would even one of them have stooped to the murder of the man's father, just to accelerate his inheritance, and thus his ability to pay them off?"

"Remember it would also provide the opportunity to fleece him even more in the future, should he retain his gambling habit."

"I suppose that makes it more understandable. Not much though."

The details of the visit were agreed quickly. Adam would send a message as soon as he could, indicating the date chosen and making an appointment for noon on that day. In the meantime, Charles would visit all the tenant farmers he could on the Fouchard estates to seek confirmation of events during the hunt. Then, on the appointed day, Adam was to rise early and ride to Mossterton Hall, where Charles would be waiting with one of her ladyship's carriages. Adam could stable his horse and he and Charles would travel to Norwich together.

"That will allow me to tell you whatever I have learned," Charles said, "and you to instruct me further on my part in the meeting."

Once they arrived in the city, the coachman would be told to take them to The Angel Inn in the market place, where the servants would wait until it was time to return to Mossterton Hall. Adam and Charles would purchase a late breakfast and walk the short distance to the lawyer's house in London Street, where the meeting was to take place.

"I do not think it will take more than two hours," Adam said. "So there will still be daylight enough for me to ride home again that afternoon."

Charles would not hear of it. He was certain Lady Alice would wish to hear how things had progressed the minute they got back. What he meant, of course, was that he was eager to impress upon her how diligent he had been in supporting the doctor in their joint endeavour. Adam must stay to dinner—a dinner delayed, if need be—and sleep that night at Mossterton Hall. He could ride home the next morning after breakfast.

In the end, Adam gave way and agreed to this plan. To be away from his own table and bed one more night made little enough difference when he had already spent probably one quarter of his time absent on one errand or another—and few of them associated with his medical practice.

When the day came, everything proceeded exactly as the two had decided. The weather proved dry, which was a bonus, though grey clouds covered the sky and the wind was a bitter easterly. The summer had mostly been poor. Autumn now looked set to be just a interlude before winter made an early appearance, then stayed for a considerable time. Already many of the trees had lost all their leaves and the bracken lay brown and dead along the sides of the road. The first frosts could not be far off.

Lady Alice provided them with a comfortable carriage, well protected against this early morning blast of frigid air, with a coachman and postilion to take it in charge. As a result, they covered the twelve or so miles into the city at good speed and in fair comfort. Along the way, Charles eagerly explained his actions of the day before. He had visited no fewer than six tenants and found four who had been at the hunt. Taken together, their testimonies confirmed in every detail what Adam had been told before. The only question that remained was why Robert Wennard had ridden off so quickly and so directly towards the point where his father was found. He could have been able to fix upon it from the sound of the shots, of course. Yet all the rest said they had been so surprised by the noise of the first shot that none of them paid much attention to where it had come from. When a second followed so soon, they could gauge the broad direction from where they were, but it would have taken a third or a fourth to be certain. Those, of course, never came. Yet Robert had turned at once in the direction of the ford and the wood. Two of them even thought he had set his horse at a gallop in that direction before the second shot had happened. Charles had puzzled over this, but could find no satisfactory explanation. Adam seemed entirely at ease with it.

"You have done exceedingly well," he said, "and I will tell your aunt as much when I see her. I expected something like that, but it is gratifying to have it confirmed. Still, it leaves many parts of this puzzle as uncertain as before. So, let's turn to what lies before us instead. Much hangs upon how freely Mrs Wennard is willing to speak, and how clear her recollection is of the precise chronology of events since she came into Norfolk. I am almost there, but my theories could still be overset if things happened in a different order or at a slower pace."

He would not be drawn further, much to Charles' frustration, so both turned to their other fear for the day ahead.

"Your part, Scudamore," Adam said, "will be to deal with any objections this attorney may raise to his client telling us all she knows. I may also need you to keep him silent, if he turns out to be the kind who wishes to impress the client by interrupting to ask for clarification or object to some minor uncertainty in a question. To be plain, I would be happiest if he took himself elsewhere and left us to speak with Mrs Wennard alone. I doubt that will happen, but I suppose there is just a chance he may be lazy enough to do it."

"If he is, her chances of proving her case must fall somewhat," Charles said. "Juries in such cases of disputed inheritance are easily distracted by a defence lawyer introducing fine-sounding quibbles or demanding proof of some minor matter. If her lawyer does not have every fact at his fingertips, he must stumble and appear uncertain of his own case. That could be fatal."

"Well, that is for her to worry about," Adam replied. "Aside from helping me persuade this lawyer to keep his nose from places where it's unwanted, your most important job must be to listen and consider what she tells us. You have a legal training which must help you sift out the truth from a mass of excuses or deliberate falsehoods. Fortunately for me, the lies my patients tell me—and they are many—are usually disproved by their physical symptoms. Almost none have sufficient knowledge of their own bodies to concoct a convincing tale, whether it be to hide something they fear may be the true cause of their pain, or invent yet another ailment to keep their relatives or servants dancing attendance upon them."

"You flatter me," Charles said.

"I think not. You may play the part of a careless young fool who puts off the day of serious employment for as long as he may. I am not taken in any more than Lady Alice has been. As soon as you apply yourself, your brain is keen and your attention to detail remarkable. I must know, above all else, whether the supposed Mrs Wennard is telling the truth. If she has concocted a clever story to obtain wealth and advancement, whether for herself or her son, whatever she says will be worthless to me in understanding Sir Jackman's murder. That is my main concern. The fate of the Wennard estate is irrelevant."

"To the murder too?" Charles was startled.

"Completely," Adam replied and would not be drawn further on his reasons for certainty on this point.

In the event, neither of them need have worried about what lay ahead. Mrs Wennard's attorney listened carefully to Adam's explanation of his need to question his client in person and the reasons the two had agreed in advance to account for Charles' presence. He noted Adam's assurances that he took no side in the question of Mrs Wennard's claim against the Wennard estate. Then, having thought for a moment, he professed himself satisfied. He would stay, he said, purely to see the visitors stuck to what they had promised. Otherwise he would play no part in the meeting.

Mrs Wennard herself turned out to be eager to tell her story and entirely open to questions. Perhaps because her very openness suggested a degree of honesty, Adam felt able to relax and allow her to relate events in her own way. It was a wise decision. Once she had begun, she clarified all he had come to ask of her, then added a good deal more. If she maintained the same demeanour before judge and jury, he reflected, Sir Robert would be hard put to make even the smallest dent in her case. How his creditors would react should he lose his title and his wealth, they would have to wait and see.

This is how Adam and Charles recalled what she said.

A SHORTCUT TO MURDER

Eleven

Mrs Wennard's Evidence

I WAS BORN IN CHESTER, THE ELDEST DAUGHTER OF MR GEORGE MUS-
KETT, corn chandler and agricultural merchant; not a rich man, but of
comfortable means and sound prospects. That was how it seemed, at any
rate. Fate determined otherwise. It subjected our family to several hard
blows before too many more years had passed. First, my mother died
when I was but eight and my father took a second wife. She proved more
of a burden than a help, for she was a poor housekeeper and careless in
her expenditure, nor did she care much for the three of us children who
survived from his first marriage.

Times grew hard, then harder. A succession of poor harvests caused
a general depression in the agriculture of the area. My father did his best,
but his customers were suffering themselves and had little enough to
spend on anything save necessities. My stepmother grew ever more frac-
tious at the economies she had to make, berating her husband for being a
poor businessman and dragging her down in the world. I believe he was
at his wits' end when he made the momentous decision to move us all to
Dublin, in Ireland.

159

My stepmother had been born in that city and never ceased telling all and sundry what a wonderful place it was. How the town boasted the best of society. How fine its buildings were and how fashionable its shops and merchandise. In the end, she convinced him that all would be well again in our lives, if he would only move there. We could not, of course, afford the kind of fashionable house she desired, but my father's business and properties in England sold for a good price, despite the short-term depression in his markets. People could see war would soon come, for few had forgiven our old enemies in France for their support of the American colonists in their rebellion against the king. Nothing would suit the French better than to see Canada join the Americans in independence, thus depriving us of the profitable trade with them across the Atlantic. If war broke out, imports of wheat from the New World would fall and the price of corn at home would rise.

At first, it seemed she might have been correct in urging the move. My father managed to attract business from the gentry who lived within The Pale. The common people in Ireland had long been hostile to their landlords, being nearly all Catholics and labouring under what they saw as the oppression of their English masters. As a result, those of the better sort of Anglo-Irish, those who adhered to the Established Church, had taken up residence in an English enclave, which men called The Pale, referring to the protective fence and ditch which had once surrounded the whole area. Dublin lies within it, or course, but it extends along the coast north and south for many miles. These gentry owned extensive lands throughout the whole of Ireland, but few ever ventured beyond The Pale itself. They left the management of those other estates to stewards, being content to draw the rents and leave the difficulties and dangers of a surly population to others.

Gradually, our prosperity revived and my stepmother was able to move a little in society. She had produced no children from this marriage, but that was of little concern to her. Indeed, it set her free to indulge herself as much as my father would allow. He, of course, attended mostly to the well-being and education of his two sons. As the only daughter, I was left a great deal to my own devices by both of them.

As I said, the native Irish are a great source of trouble, being always urged on by the priests and their local leaders to dream of independence from England. Many at the time believed the French must welcome an Irish rebellion and support it with troops and money. To counter such a threat, the British maintained a substantial military force garrisoned around Dublin and in the north of the island, where the majority are Protestants of Scottish descent. The officers of these regiments are a mainstay of Dublin society, their scarlet uniforms much in evidence at assemblies and balls and adding colour to the boxes at the theatre.

That was how I came to meet Mr Jackman Wennard. He had no title then. As the younger son of a younger son of a well born English family, he had to find his own way in the world and had no prospect of inheriting an estate. His father had bought him a Captain's commission in a second or third-rate regiment. Commissions in the cavalry, or in the most fashionable regiments of foot, were beyond their means, though Mr Wennard, like his father, was even then passionate about horses and horsemanship.

I will spare you the details, for I am sure you can guess what happened. I was seventeen and Jackman Wennard four years my senior. He was also a tall and handsome man and his uniform flattered him. For myself, I can say without false modesty that I was as lovely a girl as any whom I knew. Hard work and want had not removed the bloom from my skin or lessened the elegance and fullness of my figure. I fell in love with him and thought he loved me in the same way, for I was an innocent amongst those possessed of worldly cunning. Later I was to learn just what drove his eagerness to make my acquaintance and flatter me with fine words.

My stepmother was as besotted with Jackman as I was. Indeed, I have little doubt that she would have succumbed to his advances without a moment's hesitation, had he made any. However, she had neither beauty enough—nor wealth enough—to tempt him. The attentions of older women were easily available to handsome young officers, I believe, and he had probably already taken suitable advantage of women far more handsome than her. What he wanted was youth and innocence.

I think the fact that I resisted him shocked him at first. Then it served to increase his ardour. Men often are most drawn to what is hardest to attain. Others had tried my virtue and resolve and been sent away empty-handed. He was determined to be able to boast success where they had failed. If marriage was the only key that would unlock my chastity, so be it. Only it must be secret. Officers of his rank were forbidden to marry, he told me, lest concern for wives left behind should cool their ardour in following wherever their generals demanded. He would very soon be able to purchase a higher-ranked commission, which would free him to declare our marriage openly.

I believed his lies, fool that I was.

We were married, legally, but without fuss. To smooth the way, I told my father my mother approved and assured her that I had the consent of my father. In the end, he gave that consent in reality, for he was also tempted by the prospect of his daughter marrying into an aristocratic family. Never mind that it was but a cadet branch without lands or prospects. The night of our wedding, Jackman took what he wanted—not gently either. In the days and weeks that followed, he took it again, many times, until he grew tired of me. After four months, I suspected I was bearing his child, but told no one. I was still naïve enough to believe he should be the first to know—and that he would receive the news with joy.

I waited until I was sure, then gave him my news. He said little, yet his eyes told me he found my new state entirely unwelcome. Scarcely two weeks later, he informed me that he had purchased a commission in a cavalry regiment, currently stationed near Liverpool, but shortly to depart for service overseas. He would be gone for a little while, but would soon write and tell me where I might join him. That was the last time I saw him until I came into Norfolk.

For perhaps a year after that, I received occasional letters from my husband and small sums of money. Then both ceased. My son had been born, but I had no means to support him. Nor did I know where I might apply for my husband to be found and called upon to meet his responsibilities. My stepmother claimed she had always known Mr Jackman Wennard was a rake and a scoundrel and would have opposed my marriage, had she not been persuaded by her husband's approval of it. In return, my father expressed his amazement. Had she not been entirely in favour? Had I not assured him of her strong wish to see the marriage go ahead, he would have withheld his consent.

Thus my deceit was discovered and the affection of both my parents withdrawn. In my stepmother's case, that counted for little. I had always loved my father deeply, however, and his sudden coldness hurt me to the core of my soul. Worse, he declared he was unwilling to support another man's child. I must fend for myself.

Perhaps it was only his own hurt and disappointment that caused him to speak so cruelly at the start. When I made it clear I could do nothing save turn to the Overseers of the Poor for help, he relented. No child of his, he declared, should ever enter the workhouse, no matter how foolishly and wickedly she had behaved.

After that, he found me a home with an elderly great-aunt who was in need of someone to assist her through her declining years. There I must go. In return for attending on her and nursing her through her many illnesses, she would grant bed and board for myself and my son.

I went, having no other choice.

Miss Payne-Powell, for that was her name, lived in a neat house on the edge of a small village in the English Lake District. That sounds well enough, but when I arrived I thought it must be the most desolate place on this earth. I had been used first to the thriving town of Chester, then to the fine city of Dublin. Now I was to live in a place more than a dozen miles from the nearest town—if that little place even deserved the name. Still, having no better place to live, I determined to make the best of it for the few years left to Miss Payne-Powell. Then I would truly have to fend for myself in the world.

It will probably come as no great shock to a doctor like yourself that Miss Payne-Powell's illnesses were mostly imaginary. Being elderly and alone, she welcomed any diversion and was willing to pay for it, if there was no other way. The local doctor no doubt understood very well her true condition. However, she paid his bills promptly and rarely made more than a token complaint at their size and frequency. Being, in reality, healthy and strong for her age, she placed many demands on his patience and time, but precious few on his medical expertise.

Of course, she kept me hard at work too ministering to her every whim. She way buying my attendance, in her view, and would extract full value for her money. She was never unkind, only demanding. She treated me as if I were little but a superior kind of servant. What kept me there—apart from the fact I had nowhere else to go—was that she doted on my son.

Miss Payne-Powell was an ardent member of a small congregation of independent dissidents of the Unitarian persuasion. I had never encountered them before, but, being expected to attend her whenever she went to their meetings, I soon learned a great deal about their doctrines. One of these was a strong belief that each should find his or her own way to God, relying not on doctrines or priests, but their own ability to follow the paths of reason. Like the Quakers, these Unitarians valued learning and knowledge highly. So did Miss Payne-Powell. She may have grudged me a few shillings for my own use, but she determined my son should have as good an education as she could afford. I did nothing to discourage her from this. No mother would seek to prevent her son obtaining the best possible start in life.

To Miss Payne-Powell's delight, my son and I found a welcome amongst these unorthodox Christians and strove to repay their kindness whenever we could. Our protectress sent my son first to the school in the local town, then, when his abilities outgrew that, to a better school in Whitehaven. He was a fine scholar and Miss Payne-Powell's love for him grew in step with his attainments and learning.

When he reached seventeen, she arranged he should attend The Manchester Academy to complete a higher education than any school could provide. The universities were barred to such as him, of course, as to all dissenters. To counter this, thedissidents established their own places of higher education, the Unitarians taking the lead and supplying many of the most renowned teachers and lecturers. Some who attended saw themselves destined for future ministry in the church. A few, I believe, even took Anglican orders. Yet all were free to choose their own paths in life, be they sacred or secular. Because of this, the academies offered instruction beyond the narrow confines of studying the Greek and Latin Classics so typical of Oxford or Cambridge.

While he was studying in Manchester, my son discovered a passionate interest in Natural Philosophy and a natural aptitude for mathematics and the principles of engineering. He did well and was able, on leaving the Academy, to obtain employment under the wing of a leading engineer, one of the builders of the new canals. That is why I am here alone. My son is now twenty-eight years old and well advanced in his profession. He is also held in high regard by his employer and could not be released to accompany me. I will do nothing to stand in his way.

Miss Payne-Powell and I returned to our quiet ways until, once again, fate took a hand and pointed me into an unexpected path. Some eight months ago, Miss Payne-Powell fell ill. As I told you, illness came naturally to her, so none of us felt perturbed. She said she felt worse. Even then neither I nor her doctor felt alarm. However, this illness proved to be real. Before we could register that a crisis threatened, she died.

Long though I had chafed and fretted under Miss Payne-Powell's demands, I felt lost without her. Where was I to go? How would I live? It would not be fair to expect my son to keep me. He had his own life to lead. Nor could I turn to my father, for he had died several years before. Of my stepmother, I knew little and cared less. The little congregation of the Unitarian church rallied around and we buried the old lady with dignity and honour. She had been an active supporter of their ministry and they would miss her sorely.

When her Will was read, there were surprises enough. She had not been as wealthy as we all thought. Either that or a life of generosity to those she deemed worthy had almost exhausted her funds. Half her remaining investments she bequeathed to the chapel, save for a hundred pounds left to me. Her house and its contents she left to my son, stating that he should sell it as soon as he could and use the money to advance his career. She also left him the other half of her investments.

My son, of course, declared that he would do nothing to sell the house so long as I should have need of it. I loved him for that, but also determined that I would not prevent a sale for longer than I must. It will not be worth a great deal, but he is at that stage of his career when any money is welcome.

So I stayed where I was, alone now, and might have been there still had I not continued to take delivery of the Carlisle newspaper as Miss Payne-Powell had done. It was almost her sole indulgence. She read it every week from the front to the back, often regaling me with stories and items she had found there. Now, with abundant time on my hands, I started to do the same. That was how I happened upon a report of the purchase of two fine racehorses by The Prince of Wales from a noted Norfolk horse-breeder and landowner—one Sir Jackman Wennard, baronet.

I was shaken. Could that be my husband? The name was unusual enough. Few, if any, men would share it with him. But my Jackman had been plain mister, with no expectation of such advancement. I told my son, of course, but he showed little interest. He said he was not even sure he would be allowed to become a baronet, given that he was a dissenter. Besides, he could make his own way in the world and wanted nothing from the father who had abandoned both of us before his child had even been born.

At first, I professed to agree with him. Then, in the silence of the house I now shared only with a single servant, I began to turn matters over in my mind. Was this the Jackman Wennard I had married twenty-eight years before in Dublin? If it was, surely it was right, even now, that he should acknowledge his son? If he was wealthy, why should he not pay to make up for all the years when he had contributed nothing to wife or son? I had to know the answers.

First I consulted the minister at our church. He advised me to let matters rest. Why return to times that had been so hurtful? God would surely bring justice upon my husband in good time; there was no need for me to intervene. Then, when he saw I could not be dissuaded, he agreed to help me trace whether or not the man I had read of was indeed my husband. If he proved to be another Jackman Wennard, my mind would be at rest and I could forget the whole matter.

It took the two of us several months, but slowly the truth was put together. My husband had indeed joined a regiment posted abroad, but he had not gone with them. At almost the same time, three of his relatives had died in quick succession, leaving his father heir-presumptive to the baronetcy. It was a considerable surprise, I imagine, but he and his father were more than ready to take whatever chances might be on offer. I can imagine them, staying as close to the baronet of the time as they could and striving to display a proper family affection, all the while watching like hungry eagles eying a sickly deer. The fourth baronet, my husband's great-uncle, was busily engaged on drinking himself to death. He did not take long about it.

Jackman's father was now the fifth baronet and his only son's future was assured. To seal his coming eminence, that son now married one of the daughters of the Earl of Hunstanton. She bore him three children.

When I heard of this, I near fainted away. Not only had my husband left me once he had taken the maidenhead he so prized, he had placed so little value on our marriage that he ignored it entirely within barely a year to marry another woman of better birth and fortune! That was why he had been so insistent on secrecy. He meant, even as we exchanged vows before the altar, to pretend it had never happened as soon as someone better came along. I had despised him before. Now I hated him.

Had he honoured being married to me, I might in time have taken the advice of the minister and let the matter lie. But if this Sir Jackman Wennard was indeed the man I had married, he was a bigamist as well as everything else. What of his second wife? Had he not insulted her as much as he had me? She had doubtless married him in good faith, while he knew their marriage was a sham. She had born him three children to my one, but mine had the prior claim. He must be exposed for what he was, even though it meant admitting myself to have been a love-sick fool taken in by a common seducer. Then I found the poor woman had died in childbed some nineteen years ago. She had not deserved to have her life ruined, but now she could no longer be hurt by the truth coming out. My mind was made up.

Once again my son and the minister tried to dissuade me. The minister pointed out the bigamous marriage had already been brought to an end and the man had not sought to marry a third time. My son repeated his complete disinterest in any baronetcy. Probably, he said, from what little he knew of his father, all any heir of his would inherit would be debts.

I would not be turned from my purpose. I meant to know if this sixth baronet was indeed my first husband. If he was, I should decide later what action to take. At the very least, I thought I would force him to make proper provision for me. Whether I was willing to tell all openly and make his other children illegitimate in the eyes of the law and the world, I did not know. The most I would promise the minister and my son was that I would find out all I could of his family once I arrived in Norfolk, and I would find some means to see this Sir Jackman Wennard clearly before taking any action. I never doubted I would know him again, for all the years that had passed, if he was the one I had married.

I came south and found where the man I sought was living. By means of careful enquiries, I also found he intended to marry his elder daughter, a girl of barely twenty-one, to a man forty years her senior—and that this was to be done to persuade her future husband to part with a racehorse the baronet coveted. That sounded like my husband. I also learned his son, Robert, was a wastrel and a reckless gambler. Once again the old saying 'like father, like son' was proving true. Finally I learned this Sir Jackman loved to hunt foxes and had arranged a hunt over his own land in a few days.

This would be my chance to set eyes on him. I hired a chaise to take me to The Bull Inn at the village called Gressington. That was where the hunt was to meet the next morning. After I arrived, I approached the landlord to take a room for that night. He shook his head and told me his was but a small inn and all the rooms were already taken. I suppose I became distraught, for he took pity on me and said he knew of a single lady with a cottage not far from his inn who would give me a bed. I could take my meals at the inn, though I could not sleep there. I could not thank him enough.

I had given my name as Mrs Muskett. Should this man I had come to see prove not to be my husband, I had no wish to excite speculation by using his name openly. As Mrs Muskett I ate dinner at the inn. As Mrs Muskett I agreed with a Miss Kemp to hire a room in her cottage for a single night.

I was therefore already at the inn finishing my breakfast when the hunt began to assemble. I stayed inside at first. I wanted to be able to choose the time and place to set eyes on the man who had so wronged me many years before. What I had totally failed to understand was how many people would attend the meet. As well as those on horseback who would follow huntsmen and hounds, a mass of local people came to view the spectacle. It made it easy to hide myself, but near impossible to see anyone, even those on horseback. You can see I am not a tall woman.

In the end, I found a small pony harnessed to a dog-cart left in the care of a groom near the side of the inn yard. I climbed into it to get a better view and looked over the mass of people straight into the eyes of a man on a great, black horse. I had no more doubts. That was my husband. I would have known him anywhere.

What I had not realised at first was that he must also have recognised me. I thought myself too changed to appear anything like the girl he had deceived. That was why, though I tried not to reveal myself too openly, I had not thought it unwise to stand up in the dog-cart for a better view. He stared, then frowned and stared again. By this time, my only thought was to get away. Without a moment's hesitation, I sat down on the driver's bench, slapped the reins and urged the pony into a trot. The young groom leaped in beside me,—trying to stop me stealing the dog-cart, I expect—but I took no notice, for I did not mean to take it far. I could not outpace a man on such a great horse as my husband had, but I could at least get round to the yard behind the inn. From there I could slip through the garden and make my way back to the cottage where I had spent the night. I heard Jackman's roar and the great oaths he let fly as he sought to get his horse though the packed mass of people in the yard. If his face had not already convinced me, his voice would have done. Then I was away, jumping down from the dog-cart in the rear yard and fleeing through the gardens as fast as I could. What my husband did, I do not know, though I heard a great noise of hooves outside as I shut the door of the cottage. For a few moments, I feared he must have seen where I went, but the noise died away and I breathed again.

There is little more to tell. As soon as all had dispersed from the road and grass in front of the inn and I felt it was safe, I paid Miss Kemp what we had agreed and walked back to the inn. There I paid the landlord to drive me into Holt. From there, he assured me, I could take a coach later in the day into Norwich. As soon as I returned to this city, I sought out an attorney to represent me. The rest you know. I have not the funds to stay here indefinitely, so I shall soon return to what is now my son's house to await the outcome of my claim. I did not know of Jackman's death until I was told of it by the landlord of the inn where I am now staying. I had given him my true name and he was intrigued to see the same one in the newspaper he kept for the use of his guests. He asked me if I thought I was any blood relation of the dead man. I could tell him quite truthfully that I was sure I was not. After that, he lost interest in me.

I will not be such a hypocrite as to say my husband's death has caused me sorrow. I long ago passed the point of feeling anything for the man. I do not glory in it either. I wish no man harm, not even the one who ruined my life. Of the son—the one who expected to succeed him—I know nothing save his name. Believe me; I thought hard on my way back into Norwich that day whether I was truly prepared to make three young people illegitimate. I do regret how it will make his daughters feel; though if it stops that old man from taking one of them as his wife, I will have done her a great service. The other, I believe, is but nineteen. Both of them will, I hope, be able to forgive me in time. The son, Robert I think his name is, I care nothing for. He is unworthy of any distinction, as I have heard, and would spend all his father's money within a few years. If that money passes now to my own son, I trust him to know how best to use it. Some he may keep to assure his future. Some he may use to assure mine. But if he wishes to use all of it for charitable and philanthropic purposes, I shall not seek by so much as a look to dissuade him. Still, that is to jump too far ahead. My claim has yet to go before a court.

What proofs do I have to support it? I have brought a signed and witnessed affidavit from the minister now in charge of the church where we were married. In it he attests to the presence in the church records of a legal marriage between Sarah Muskett, spinster, and Jackman Wennard, bachelor, on the date I had given him. I also have a letter from the lady who attended me as bridesmaid and a note from the one surviving formal witness. Both will state on oath that they were present and saw the marriage take place. My father is dead, as I told you, but the willingness of the vicar of the time—a most upright and well-respected man—to conduct the marriage should be proof enough he had given his consent. Jackman was twenty-two, so did not need any consent from his father to contract a legal marriage. Whether all that will be enough for a court to decide in my favour, I do not know, but I have no more.

There, I have told you what I know. As I said, my husband's death brings me no pain, but if he was indeed murdered, whatever the reason might be, I believe I must help to bring the murderer to justice. 'Thou shalt do no murder' the commandment says. If a man has ignored this and wilfully killed another, he cannot blame his subsequent punishment on any but himself.

If it is possible, I will keep my son free of the prosecution of this claim. As I told you, he has declared he neither covets the title nor whatever wealth and possessions his father has left. I admire his principles, but question his wisdom. Someone must inherit those lands and serve to manage them—aye, and all those whose livelihoods depend on lands, house and even the racehorses. Why not my son? It may not be the path he has chosen for himself, but none of us can forecast when fate may choose to ignore our wishes. Each must do his or her best in the station to which the Lord has called them.

See, again I run ahead of myself. Let us leave matters there, for I'm sure you have no interest in what may happen if my claim is upheld. Your interest, you have told me, is only in helping your brother to bring a killer to justice. Am I sad that Jackman is dead? No, I feel nothing on that score. Do I applaud the one who killed him? Assuredly I do not, though it may be he deserves our compassion more than his victim did. To be driven to commit murder suggests desperation. Only madmen kill for the pleasure of it.

So, Dr Bascom, Mr Scudamore, if you have both heard enough I will take my leave. Thank you for allowing me to tell my story and for listening to me so diligently. If you need to speak with me again, my lawyer here knows where I may be found. Good day to you, sirs, and a safe journey back to your homes.

A SHORTCUT TO MURDER

Twelve

Kidnapped

ADAM AND CHARLES PASSED THE FIRST PART OF THE JOURNEY BACK FROM NORWICH TO MOSSTERTON HALL in silence, each too busy with his own thoughts for conversation. Charles was puzzling over the things Mrs Wennard had told them, since to him all were new and unforeseen. Adam had anticipated a good deal of it, in outline if not in detail. What occupied his mind was fitting what she had told them into the pattern he'd been constructing from all he now knew. He was almost there, yet the central question still seemed as inexplicable as ever. How had anyone been able to anticipate Sir Jackman Wennard's exact movements on the day of his death? Not just foretell what he would do, but accurately enough to set a trap for him at an exact place and time. Could it still turn out to be no more than a bizarre accident? No, that could not be so. What had been done at the edge of that wood had been directed only at Sir Jackman Wennard, of that he was sure.

They were almost halfway along their road before either man spoke, then Adam asked a question.

"What's your impression, Scudamore? Do you think Mrs Wennard was telling us the truth?"

"I do, Bascom," Charles said after a lengthy pause. "Oh, I don't doubt one or two details had been polished to create a better tale, a few gaps filled in with a little imagination. All witnesses do that. The past events happened twenty and more years ago. No one's memory can remain sharp over such a time span. When she spoke of recent happenings, nothing she said struck me as unlikely or even especially dramatic. People who make up stories try to produce a better tale than that."

"I agree. It seemed too banal to be invention."

"I tell you this, my friend. I'm very glad I won't be the one to find myself before judge and jury, charged with undermining her evidence or claiming she concocted it for some dubious purpose. I've considered her testimony as if I were a lawyer briefed to defend my client against what she claims. In that endeavour, I confess, I would expect to be defeated. She'll be the kind of witness the other side always fears most—straightforward, calm and precise. It's the devil's own job to cast doubt on that sort of testimony. No obvious signs of lying, as we both agree, and no stumbling or confusion to be exploited. No, I'm certain any jury would think as I think myself. She's telling the truth. There's an end of it."

"Very well," Adam said. "We both believe what she has told us is true. I cannot find any reason to cast doubt on her words either."

"Why would you wish to doubt her? Surely you should be happy to have some near to proven facts at your disposal?"

"The most common reason a physician makes a bad mistake in diagnosis is simple. We've all done it, especially when we're young and freshly qualified. We examine the patient and begin to form a diagnosis. Before we speak, fearing to appear foolish, we seek confirmation of what we have in mind. Put plainly, we look for things to support what we already believe to be correct."

Adam leaned forward and turned his head to look directly into Charles' eyes.

"When you get older and wiser, you do exactly the opposite. The more certain you feel of your diagnosis, the more carefully you try by every means at your disposal to prove yourself wrong. It's too easy to overlook a crucial point that doesn't accord with what you believe to be right or dismiss it as of little importance—even call it random and unimportant. Then your patient dies and you discover you could have done something useful, if only you'd paid attention to the neglected indications that you were on the wrong track. It is the same with an investigation like this. A great deal of what Mrs Wennard told us fits very neatly into the hypothesis I've formed. That is why I've been trying as hard as I can to find ways to disbelieve it. An amateur in natural philosophy or medicine seeks to prove his theory correct. A professional knows that what matters most is trying to prove he's got it all wrong. Only a theory which stands up to the most cynical critic has a chance of proving true."

"You're right, of course," Charles replied. "I hadn't thought of that. Maybe we lawyers have an easier time of it. There's always a lawyer for the other side making every effort to disprove whatever you claim, so we have no need to do it for ourselves. There are also some damn sharp judges out there whose greatest pleasure lies in making the lawyers on both sides look foolish."

Once again, they lapsed into silence. Much later, Charles asked, "Do you think you know who was responsible for killing Sir Jackman Wennard?"

"I do," Adam replied. "Sadly, I cannot prove it as yet."

Then he would say no more.

When they reached Mossterton Hall, Lady Alice and Ruth were waiting for them in the parlour.

"Before you refresh yourself from your journey, doctor," Lady Alice said, "I have an urgent message for you. Your brother's servant went to your house this afternoon. Finding you absent, he used his brain and sought you out here. I persuaded him to give me the message and assured him I would pass it on the moment you arrived. Your brother wishes to tell you Sir Robert Wennard has been kidnapped. A ransom note has been sent to Lord Weybourne, who is, I believe, the principal executor of the father's Will. In it, the kidnappers demand a great deal of money to secure Sir Robert's release. If it is not paid, they say they will kill him. Since I know for a fact Lord Weybourne could not decide on his own whether to eat rolls for breakfast or plain bread, he sent at once to your brother to ask what to do. Your brother has, I believe, told him to do nothing until you have been consulted. He therefore asks that you go to Trundon Hall to discuss the matter as soon as you can."

Adam looked stunned. "So soon," he muttered. "So soon. I had expected ... but not this ... not so quickly ..."

With a great effort, he pulled himself together and declared he must leave again at once.

Lady Alice was adamant. "That you will most certainly not do, doctor," she said. "It is already late and will soon be dark. You are not familiar with the road between here and Letheringsett. It passes across a large area of barren heathland, which is a favourite spot for footpads and highwaymen to lurk. You yourself warned us that a gang of such men have been operating in this area. Nothing will be lost by taking dinner with us, as you planned, and setting out on your journey in the daylight tomorrow. No, please do not argue. I insist upon it and I will not be contradicted in my own house."

That fresh glimpse of steel was enough to stop Adam in his tracks.

"Very well, my lady," he said. "I will do as you say. I admit to being tired out by today's activities. Now this news has thrown my mind into a ferment. I therefore beg of you all, do not question me about it. If you wish to be of help, let's ignore the whole topic and have as relaxed an evening as may be possible. I need to clear my head. I won't do that by plunging at once into explanations and still more theorising. I will merely tell you this. I had expected something important to occur as a direct result of Mrs Wennard making her claim of a prior marriage to Sir Jackman Wennard. That event has now happened, but far more quickly that I imagined and in more dramatic fashion. There has been no time to make our preparations, as I hoped there would be. Oh—one thing more, my lady. You said that you would invite Sir Robert's sister here and encourage her to stay for a few days. Will you please write that invitation this very evening and give it to me? I will bear it with me to Trundon Hall in the morning and see it is delivered with all speed."

"I will do it at once," Lady Alice said. "Now, Charles, Ruth. You've heard what Dr Bascom has asked of us. Be sure you do as he says, or you will answer to me. Charles, go to the stables and tell the grooms to have the doctor's horse ready, saddled and waiting outside the front door for him by dawn. Ruth, instruct the cook to have coffee—you do prefer coffee in the morning, doctor?—coffee and two fresh rolls set on a tray in the morning room for the doctor to be able to eat something before he leaves. We will say our goodbyes this evening before we retire. That way none of us will delay Dr Bascom in the morning. Now, a room has been made ready for you, doctor, and one of the maids will bring you hot water to wash away the dust from the road. Dinner will be in an hour."

With her ladyship in such a mood, no one hesitated to do what she wished. The three of them dined together, talking resolutely of anything else but the thing uppermost in all their minds. Then they took tea and played a few games of whist, before retiring early. As agreed, they said their goodbyes before going to their respective rooms. Charles grasped

Adam's hand and declared he would go with him, should he wish it, an offer that Adam declined with as much grace as he could. Ruth shook his hand demurely and wished him God's speed. Then, perhaps by prior arrangement, they both left.

Lady Alice took Adam's hand in her own small one, looked up at him with the huge, soft eyes that drew him so much and enjoined him earnestly to take care of himself.

"I have every faith in you, doctor," she said. "You know that. There can be no doubt that you will solve this mystery and see the killer brought to justice. All I ask is that you take good care of yourself along the way and return to us, unharmed and in good spirits, as soon as you may. All the resources that I have are at your disposal at any time. Now, go well and my … my blessing go with you."

As she turned away and hurried from the room, Adam, as stunned by her words as he had been by the news of Sir Robert Wennard's being taken for ransom, could do no more that stare after her.

Thanks to Lady Alice's instructions to her household, Adam was at Trundon Hall just before eight o'clock next morning. He found his brother waiting for him in the small parlour, pacing up and down and muttering under his breath.

"Thank goodness you're here!" Giles said. "I declare Lord Weybourne is close to driving me mad. He sent me two more messages yesterday evening, almost imploring me to tell him what to do. It's really too much for the old chap. First he's told someone is out to prove Sir Robert shouldn't be 'sir' anything and isn't the legitimate son of Sir Jackman Wennard. Then he's told the fellow has been kidnapped and he must pay a thousand guineas to get him back alive. The first of his letters was full of indignation at the idea of making any payment for what he referred to as 'a bastard son'. The second wailed on about the importance of saving an innocent man's life. What on earth am I to say to him? What do I tell him he must do? He seems to think me the fount of all wisdom in the matter."

"Nothing," Adam said. "Nothing at all at present. Write at once and tell him he must not meet the demands of the kidnappers, whatever threats are made. Instead he must prevaricate as much as he can, but without actually refusing payment. That is vital."

"Prevarication comes very easily to him." Giles said. "That is, so long as I can get him to keep his nerve. The first thing he will ask is whether what I suggest will endanger Sir Robert's life."

"Tell him Sir Robert is in no danger whatsoever, despite what the kidnappers threaten. I am totally certain of that. All the danger lies to others. The worst danger of all is that lives will be put at risk and still the killer will escape. If we do not take this chance to seize him and bring him to justice, I am afraid we will never have another."

"How should Lord Weybourne put off a firm reply on the demand that has been made—a thousand guineas or Sir Robert dies?"

"Suggest he asks for proof that Robert has been kidnapped. Then proof that he is still alive. Have him question the amount demanded. Let him say it will take him some time to raise the money. All of those things, but not all at once. Each time he gets an answer, he must raise another objection. We need time! The killer has caught us unprepared. I should have realised he might become desperate and rush into action as soon as he heard about Mrs Wennard's claims."

"You knew this would happen?" Giles said. "You knew?"

"Not knew ... and not this precise response. I suspected a crisis. My mistake was not to speak of my thoughts in case I was wrong. Now we have to catch up. Look, Giles, don't try to make me explain now. There's action to be taken if we are to prevent further bloodshed and trap the killer."

Giles was always at his best in a crisis. Ask him to ponder things and weigh up alternatives and he would become irritable and unhappy. Give him firm instructions, however difficult, and he was in his element. Now he proved the truth of that again.

"Tell me exactly what you want of me," he demanded.

"First," Adam said, "we have people to protect from harm. This killer is out of control and likely to lash out at anyone whom he thinks might be a threat to him. I want you to go right away to Upper Cley Hall and ask to see Miss Charlotte Wennard, Robert's younger sister. Give her this note from Lady Alice Fouchard. It is an urgent invitation for Miss Wennard to go to stay at Mossterton Hall. There she will be safe. Tell her to take nothing but the most essential items. Lady Alice will provide the rest. Then you must escort her to Mossterton Hall yourself. Go armed, brother! Take the greatest care along the way—and hurry. We must get her away before the killer can strike again."

"What will you do?" Giles asked. "I have more than one brace of pistols if you need them."

"I will come to that in a moment. Before you leave, send your most trusted man to ride to Mossterton Hall at full speed. Make sure he is armed too. Once there, he is to ask for Mr Charles Scudamore, who is staying with Lady Alice, and give him this message from me. Mr Scudamore must take Lady Alice's fastest horse and a brace of good pistols and ride like the wind for Norwich. There he must go to the lawyer's office where we were yesterday and find out where Mrs Wennard is staying. It is at an inn somewhere in the city. Tell him to find her, wherever she is, and escort her out of the city and back on her way to her home in the North Country with all possible speed. I'm not sure where she can get a suitable coach, but she'll know. He must impress upon her that her life is in danger every moment she stays in Norwich. She must leave at once and tell no one where she is headed. Will you do that?"

"At once!" Giles said. "I'll get another pair of pistols and leave these here, on this table. Take them when you're ready. I need to understand just one thing. Is there any danger to Amelia and our children if they remain here? Your mother and Miss LaSalle are here as well."

"None at all, I assure you," Adam said. "The danger lies with those who are involved directly in the question of the Wennard inheritance. Miss Wennard is in danger because she alone can give us certain vital information we need. This damnable murderer has stolen a march on us, brother. Now let us prove that we too can move quickly—more quickly that he will expect. Once you have delivered Miss Wennard safely, come back here and write to Lord Weybourne immediately, sending your message by a trusted servant. Either that or go to him yourself. When our treasures are safe, and I have spoken with Miss Wennard, we will be in position to set up our trap. Until then, delay is our worst enemy."

Giles merely nodded, then rushed from the room, calling loudly for his servants to make ready his fastest horse. Adam paused and considered his next moves. It was imperative he push the killer into a panic, so that he would act without thought. It would be exceedingly dangerous, but he could see no other way of bringing him out into the open. What he was doing now was trying to protect those most at risk. For the rest, he had no means of knowing exactly how the killer would respond to the pressure he planned to bring upon him. However much he hated the idea, he could imagine no response that would not hazard innocent lives. Even to do nothing and yield to the kidnappers' demands would bring severe risks.

At that moment, Giles' wife Amelia, Mrs Bascom and Miss Lasalle rushed into the room together.

"What is going on?" Amelia demanded. "My house is in an uproar. People are running about, fetching and carrying things. I can hear the grooms crashing about in the stable yard and horses making a dreadful noise. My husband rushed into my room, wearing his outdoor coat and clutching a brace of pistols, kissed me and said he would be back in an hour or so. I am quite bewildered!"

"I just saw a fellow dash past my window towards the stables," Adam's mother said. "He was also dressed for travel and I could see a pistol tucked into his belt. Now you're standing here with still more pistols on the table beside you. Have the French invaded? You must tell us what is going on."

"Do not delay me, I pray of you both," Adam said. "I too must leave at once. No, you are safe from the French. Indeed, you are quite safe so long as you stay here. This is all to do with the matter of the death of Sir Jackman Wennard, the kidnapping of his son and the taking of his killer. Giles should indeed be back within an hour or so and will, I expect, come to no harm. The pistols are merely a precaution, given the troubles with highwaymen of late. Now, sister. I need to know whether you have a trusted servant who would be willing to make all haste to Cley to find out whether anyone has disappeared unexpectedly—anyone other than Sir Robert Wennard, I mean. It will not be someone from amongst the better class of people, I think. Maybe an artisan, or even two. Perhaps a servant or a person connected with Upper Cley Hall in some way. I cannot be more precise. I simply suspect that one or two people, likely ones connected with Sir Jackman Wennard in the past, will have left the village within the last day or so and told no one where they were going. Let your servant find out their names, if possible, and what work they did. They must make haste, yet not cause too much alarm when they get there. I am going to speak with the parish constables in Holt and Cromer, if I can. Then I will go to my home, at least for tonight. Let any news be sent to me there. Tomorrow I expect to visit Mossterton Hall, but will return to Aylsham afterwards."

Amelia looked at him, then nodded her assent. She asked no questions and Adam knew he could trust her to do all that he asked. Before she left the room, she stepped forward and kissed him on the cheek.

"Be safe, brother," she said. "God go with you."

Adam's mother also kissed him. "We trust you, Adam," she said. "You have never let us down yet. I too will pray for your safe return." Then she allowed one flash of her natural spirit to show. "Once all this haste is over, I will demand a full explanation. I allow no one, not even my sons, to turn my life upside down and leave me in suspense for longer than is essential. Remember that."

Adam had entirely forgotten about Miss LaSalle. Only when he turned to leave did he notice her again, her face twisted by fear and entirely drained of colour. In his surprise, he hesitated for a moment. As he did, she sprang forward and clutched him in a fierce embrace. He could feel her heart thumping and her whole body trembling as she pulled him against her and pressed her face into his chest.

"Sophia, you forget yourself," he heard his mother say quietly. "Worse, you are delaying my son. Let him go. Now!"

The young woman leapt back as if Adam were red hot and rushed from the room in tears. All Adam could do was stand still in amazement. He had no idea what had just happened.

"Don't worry about Sophia," his mother said. "I will deal with her. Now, off you go. We have kept you back long enough."

Adam's horse was ready in the stable yard. When he arrived, he had told the grooms to give her water and a little food, but not to take off her saddle or bridle. Now he put Giles' pistols into his saddle bags, heaved himself up into the saddle yet again and set off for Holt at a brisk trot. If he could, he would hire a chaise in Holt to take him to Cromer and leave the horse, Fancy, to await his return. He had some distance to go, all of it at the best speed he could make. Fancy was not used to long journeys or going at a trot or a canter all the way. If he didn't allow her time to rest, she would most likely become exhausted somewhere along the road.

He decided to take the back road into Holt, since that would avoid him having to make his horse carry him up the steep hill out of the

Glaven valley and into the town. He just hoped that he could find the constable quickly. It would be another eight miles to get to Cromer afterwards, then eight miles back to get his own horse again. His backside was going to be extremely sore by the end of the day.

He found the constable easily enough and gave him his message, extracting a solemn promise from the man that he would be sure to do exactly as he had been instructed. Then he headed for The Feathers Hotel, from where he hoped he could hire a chaise for the next stage of his journeying.

As he clattered into the inn yard, whom should he meet but his old friend, Captain Mimms. The retired sea captain had a house in Holt, so it was hardly a surprise to find him there. Even so, Adam felt some irritation at seeing him. Capt Mimms was an inveterate gossip and talker. Though Adam could afford no delay, he would not wish to hurt his friend's feelings in any way either.

"Doctor!" Capt Mimms called out. "You seem to be in a deuced hurry. Someone dying?"

"Not so far as I know," Adam replied. "I am trying to hire a carriage to take me to Cromer. I have already come far this morning and my horse is tired. Look, I mean no disrespect, but my errand will brook no delay. Lives may be at risk."

"Lives at risk? Say no more, doctor. My chaise is here, for I was about to set out for Norwich when you came hurtling into the yard. Norwich can wait! I'll move over, you jump in, and we can be on our way at once. Then along the way you can tell me how I can be of assistance to you. I assume all this has to do with that fellow from Cley who was killed the other week. Heard you were on the trail again. Right! Up you jump. This is a sturdy vehicle, doctor, and my horse is fresh. Drive on as fast as you want and don't worry about anything else."

Within moments, Adam had handed his horse over to an inn groom, given instructions for her to be fed and rested, and they were out of the yard, across the Market Place and heading down White Lion Street towards the Cromer Road. Along the way, Adam brought his old friend up to date as best he could.

"Bad business!" Capt Mimms said when he had finished. "Still, I agree you're tackling it the right way. Smoke the fellow out into the open. It's the only thing to do. Remember several times when I had to take the same kind of risk with my ship. Let me think while you're talking to the constable. I know the chap there. He's a stout-hearted man, but not quite as bright as you might wish. If you'll take my advice, don't waste time trying to help him grasp the reasons for what you want. Just tell him, as clearly as you can what he must do. If you want, tell him I'm outside and he'll need to explain to me if he fails. That should stir him into action. He served under me once, so he knows I mean what I say. Maybe on the way back I'll be able to see how I can help."

Capt Mimms knew where the constable lived, which saved Adam a good deal of time trying to find his way around the narrow, winding streets of the little fishing town. They stopped the chaise outside the constable's door and Adam banged hard upon it. When the constable came in answer to this summons, the first thing he saw, over Adam's shoulder, was Captain Mimms in the chaise.

"Rawlings!" the old man roared in the kind of voice that would cut through a howling gale. "Doctor has instructions for you. Listen hard and do as he says. No arguing, man. That's an order!"

The constable snapped to attention, turned to Adam and said, "Orders, sir?" as if he was back on the deck of a warship heading into battle. Adam snapped out his instructions, the constable replied with a firm, "aye, aye, sir", turned on his heel and set off towards the centre of the town without a backward glance.

"That's the way to get things done, doctor," Capt Mimms said. "Don't give them any option save to obey you on the instant. Now, back into the chaise and we'll be on our way again."

For the next mile or so, the captain sat in total silence, his brow wrinkled and his eyes seemingly seeing nothing. Then he sat up and got back to business.

"Now, doctor," he said. "Here's what I think I can do. You want to get everyone who travels along these roads, especially the coachmen, to be on the alert for this gang of highwaymen. Until now, they've confined themselves to a narrow area around Cley and Blakeney and taken no risks. All they've done is catch a few lone travellers or a single carriage, waved their guns and taken whatever they could. Small pickings, mostly. Now you think something has changed and their leader will be in great need of as much money as he can get. Gold and silver for preference. Also jewels, watches, rings and anything else of high value that can be carried easily. These men are dangerous, but not yet hardened criminals. They're likely to be nervous, which may make them even more tricky to handle."

"That's right, captain," Adam said. "They know their only chance now lies in getting as much money as they can and then going far, far away. To get the funds they need quickly they must rob the stagecoaches or the mail coaches. They have no experience of how to bring such robberies off successfully. I think they're desperate enough to try, but I cannot be sure. What I am sure of is that if they happen upon some wealthy travellers, they'll go for them instead. They're almost certainly terrified, and frightened men are the most dangerous of all. To make matters worse, what I'm trying to do is increase their fear that time is running out. I told the constables to warn the coach drivers to go well armed and be alert at all times. I also told them to spread the word that these robberies have reached the ears of the government. As a result, several companies of the dragoons and yeomanry are being moved into the area. Once they get here, they'll patrol the roads by day and night. They'll also be joined by a number of additional riding officers from the Revenue, in case the robbers prove to be connected with the smugglers in these parts. None of it's true, but the highwaymen aren't to know that and nor are the people who, I believe, are even now closing in on the highwaymen's leader. He owes them a great deal of money, which he has no means of paying, save by robbery."

"I understand, doctor." Capt Mimms said. "You want to make him rush into action before these imaginary troops can get here. That way, he'll likely make a bad mistake—bite off more than he can chew—and then you'll have him. Those creditors you mentioned will never see a brass farthing, believe me. What I don't understand is how these robbers have anything to do with the death of that Wennard fellow."

"They killed him," Adam said. "It was a robbery gone very wrong."

"But, as I heard, he was killed in broad daylight in the course of a fox hunt," the captain protested. "What kind of highwaymen go out robbing people while they're hunting? Lots of other folk about. Hounds. You'd never get away with it."

"It's a complicated tale," Adam said. "I don't really have the leisure to go into it now. You said you also could help me? What will you do?"

"Same as you told those constables. Get the word out. Only my words won't go to coachmen and the like. I'll take a large bet that these highwaymen plan to escape overseas, if they can get the money to do so. Most ships hereabouts sail up and down the coast between Leith or Newcastle and London. They're not the ones that matter. The only ships of use to those robbers are the ones that sail to the Low Countries or to Scandinavia and the Baltic. France is more or less closed to trade now. My sons and I know just about every ship's captain between King's Lynn and Great Yarmouth. I'll make sure they're all on the lookout for anyone offering a large amount of ready cash to be taken on the next voyage. If that happens, they'll grab them and hand them over to the authorities."

"What about the smugglers?" Adam asked. "They'd just take the money, wouldn't they?"

"Aye, then like as not kill the men and drop their bodies in the ocean. They don't want to make the authorities start sniffing around on the hunt for people who are nothing to do with them. All it will need is to add a little extra to your tale of the dragoons and the Revenue men. Let the smugglers believe the best way to free the coast from nosey parkers out to shut down their trade, is to make sure these amateur robbers are taken as quickly as possible. Once they're on their way to the hangman, the fuss will die down and the troops and all the rest go somewhere else. If your robbers are fool enough to try to buy a passage with one of the smuggling gangs, you'll soon find them on the beach, waiting for you. If they're lucky, they'll be tied up neatly. If they aren't, they'll have had their throats cut as a reward for causing so much trouble."

Thirteen

Unravelling the Knots

WHILE ADAM RODE HIS HORSE TOWARDS MOSSTERTON HALL THE NEXT
MORNING, he reflected on the strange twists and turns his life had taken
in the past year. It felt as if he had no control of the direction he would
follow, nor even the ways in which he would spend his time. He made
decisions only to see them overturned within hours or days and fresh
ones take their place. Barely a year ago he had been no more than a young
physician hoping to be able to earn a modest living in a country town.
Now he was a man of some wealth, if not yet of property—one who must
strive to find any time in his life for the practice of medicine amongst the
torrent of other demands and expectations.

Take this journey. His first visit to Mossterton Hall had been made
with no greater aim than to help a patient and maybe make a good impression on the family of gentry who lived there. That had turned into
further visits composed of both joy and bitter sorrow. The excitement
and pleasure at finding a fine man willing to give him the advice and
comfort his own father had never been able to provide. The wretched-
ness and regret that it must soon be taken from him by the older man's

191

looming death, which he could do nothing to prevent. After Sir Daniel Fouchard died, his trips to Mossterton Hall had become few and far between for a time. Lady Alice, Sir Daniel's young second wife, had been weighed down by grief. Adam, feeling almost as bereft, felt he could offer her no comfort and feared her pain would but increase his.

Now, once again, the journey to Mossterton Hall had become almost a daily event. The pain was still there in the background, but there was something else—something of importance, something vital to his future. Adam would neither name it nor allow himself to explore it too far. It was too new, too fragile. If he should bring it into the open and accept it as part of who he now was, it might evaporate and leave a yet greater loss behind.

Good Lord! He was a grown man of twenty-six, a trained physician, a professional man of substance, not some youth consumed by a poetic frenzy. Wasn't it time to pull himself together and concentrate on concluding the task Giles had imposed upon him? Then he could get back to his proper activities and concerns. Shouldn't he also be considering what his mother might be planning for him—or rather whom she had set her eyes on to make into his wife? He didn't even think he wanted one—not at present certainly. Marriage brought responsibilities, children, other people to be considered and provided for. It could wait. Even so ... no, he would not let his thoughts stray there ... not yet ... not yet ...

If Sir Jackman Wennard had not looked upon the young Sarah Muskett and been consumed with desire, he wouldn't have been tempted into marrying her in secret, solely as a means to bring her to bed. If he had been an honest man, he wouldn't have abandoned her when he grew tired of what she had to offer; nor would he have refused to accept the child she would bear him. Worst of all, when fortune came his way, he put away all he had done before as of no account and contracted another, more advantageous marriage. It was that great sin, that act of callousness and selfish greed, hidden for more than twenty-five years, that had burst into the open, fouled his memory and besmirched the lives of his children. Even in his youth Sir Jackman used and discarded women on all sides. What had been so special about Miss Muskett? Was it the fact that she had refused him—been proof against his urging, while letting him see how much she wanted to give in? Adam was ready to accept that he knew very little about the odd ways of women. He had desired several, of course, but kept himself in check ... well, in most cases ... until now anyway. Had Sir Jackman any better knowledge of the fair sex? Did he know anything more profound about women than how to force himself on those too poor and weak to resist him, or seduce others too foolish, fond or lusty themselves to be able to say no?

More useless musings. This investigation will drive you mad, Adam, if you allow it, he told himself. You know why Sir Jackman met his end and you are almost certain about how it was done. You even know the name of at least one of the people responsible for bringing it about. It is proof you lack. You cannot ask Giles to instigate legal proceedings against anyone yet. Not until you can offer him more than deductions and guesswork.

That is why you're back on this road again. Not seeking information, but the means of substantiating what you know already. Whether Miss Charlotte can provide anything of that, you don't know. You can only ask your questions and hope.

The previous evening, at his home in Aylsham, Adam had received word from his brother Giles that Miss Charlotte Wennard had been delivered safely to Mossterton Hall as he had asked. Giles had found her well, but totally bewildered by events. The fact that she might be proved to be the offspring of a bigamous marriage did not, it appeared, so much upset her as cause her great anger. It was what Sir Jackman had done to her mother that appalled her, not any threat of illegitimacy hanging over herself. As for the kidnapping of her brother, she had neither knowledge nor much concern. Her father treated both his daughters with contempt, and his son repeated the same behaviour. In the eyes of both, women were either a means of momentary pleasure or useful inducements to be offered to men they wished to win over. Her father married for money and status, then treated his wife as a convenient outlet for passing moments of lust and a source of legitimate heirs. She had proved willing to suffer the one and produce the other. When he had the heir he craved and his desire faded, he had no further use for her. By the time she died, he had ceased visiting her bedroom in favour of seducing her acquaintances and pestering her maid, who was too pretty for her own good.

All this Miss Charlotte Wennard had poured out to Giles as her maidservant collected together the few necessities she required and they awaited the carriage to take her to Mossterton Hall. The next morning, when Adam arrived she was calmer, but no less resolute in proclaiming no sense of regret or sorrow for what had befallen her father and a complete indifference to her brother's fate.

"I am happy to see you, Dr Bascom," she said after Lady Alice had introduced them. "I understand it is you I must thank for having your brother whisk me away from my home in such a romantic manner. I must also declare my gratitude for suggesting to Lady Alice that she take me in. This is a lovely house and far grander than ours. I have no doubt I shall find it much more than a simple refuge. Sadly, I do not think I can tell you much. I will not pretend the death of my father caused me any deep pain; he was too cold a parent for that. Still, a father is a father and I do not believe anyone could avoid feeling some sadness in the same circumstances. As for my brother, I care not a jot whether he lives or dies."

The two of them were seated in Lady Alice's small parlour, the light streaming in through the windows to reveal the fine grain of the walnut furniture and the deep scarlet of the damask on the walls. After seeing them seated and provided with coffee, Lady Alice withdrew to leave them to their conversation. She was wearing the purple of half-mourning that day, not the black that had begun to look almost part of her. Adam thought the rich colour became her very well. Very well indeed. Miss Charlotte was wearing black, of course, but probably more in deference to social expectations than by personal choice. It did not suit her at all, but brought out a certain sallowness in her complexion.

"Before we begin on your questions, doctor, may I ask one of you?" the young lady continued. "Do you believe my wretched brother really has been kidnapped?"

Taken a little by surprise, Adam decided to sidestep that question.

"I do not know where your brother is," he said, "or his current circumstances. All I am sure of is that he is in no great danger, despite the threats made in the letter to Lord Weybourne."

"Your reasons?" Miss Charlotte demanded. So, there were at least two traits she had inherited from her father. Giles had said Sir Jackman was noted for his curt speech and imperious manner.

"If he has been kidnapped, madam, he is too valuable a commodity to subject to ill-treatment—at least at this stage. If the whole affair is a sham ... well, you can draw your own conclusions."

"Sound," she said. It was like a governess speaking to a prize pupil. "Very well. Ask your questions, doctor, and I will do my best to answer them."

"What I most need to understand," Adam said, "are the precise events of the day before your father met his end. What was he doing? Where did he go? What did he say of his intentions?"

Miss Wennard was clearly taken aback.

"The day before his death? Not what he did before he left the house to join the hunt? You are sure about that?"

"Very sure. I need to understand all he did on the previous day— and maybe even one or two days prior to that."

"Let me think," Miss Wennard replied. "You have surprised me greatly, sir. I prepared myself for this meeting by running over all that happened on the day of my father's death, so that I might miss nothing out. Now you ask of the day—or days—before. Let me collect my thoughts a moment."

Adam waited. He could hear the distant sound of sheep in the parkland by the house and the ticking of the fine carriage clock on the shelf above the hearth. Miss Wennard stared at the wall, then down at the silver coffeepot on the table.

"You have spoken with my sister, I believe?" she said at last. "Good. That will save me much tedious explanation. I knew what she planned, of course. We have always been close. That was my father's final piece of cruelty as it turned out; trying to marry her off to an old goat even older than himself. Have you met her new husband? Of course you have. I thought him a fine fellow, for all his strange, Quaker ways."

Adam began to worry that Miss Charlotte would wander so far from the point it would take him a good deal of effort to bring her back. He need not have done so.

"Very well," she said. "The day before my father's death. As I recall, he spent much of the morning, as was his habit, either out riding in his estate or fussing over his horses. Had he been even half as fond of his children as he was of those silly beasts, we would have been pampered beyond measure. Horses were, I am sure, his only genuine passion in life, not money and definitely not women, for all the number he bedded then cast aside. He was a fine rider and had a true talent for the breeding and training of racing horses and hunters. I believe he also made a good deal of money from them, though that was never the primary factor for him. He simply loved everything to do with horses. For myself, I think them stupid and far too highly strung. I can ride indifferent well, of course. My father saw to that for both his daughters. Yet I am never happy on the back of a horse. It is too uncomfortable and too far above the ground. I much prefer a chaise or a carriage for transport."

Inwardly, Adam ground his teeth. Could she never keep to the point for more than a moment or two?

"So … your father spent the morning with his horses," he ventured. "What then?"

"He set off for Field Dalling. He had arranged to visit one of his cronies—a friend from the world of horse racing, Mr Thomas Croome."

"A social visit?"

"Only in part. Mr Croome had recently purchased one—no, two—part-trained racehorses from my father and the time had fallen due to make the necessary payment. My father expected to receive his money that day."

"Do you know how it would have been paid? A banker's draft? A letter of credit? Banknotes or coin even?"

"Not really. It mattered little to me. Wait … I can say my father was not greatly fond of bankers. He put little faith in anyone, save himself. I recall him droning on one day about certain country bankers. He said they accepted your money, then either squandered it or gambled it away on foolish loans. In the end, their banks collapsed and you were left with nothing. Instead he had a special strongroom constructed near the servants' hall. It's a strange place. Thick walls of brick, of course. Even the ceiling is vaulted in brick to protect from fire. Iron bars on the windows and a great iron door, almost too heavy to move, secured with several locks. He kept all the estate deeds and documents there, present and past. He also had a strongbox set there, made of iron. As I recall it is hexagonal in shape and painted black, with two locks in the lid. What he kept in there, I don't know. I never saw it open."

Giles could ask the executors, Adam thought. They must be able to open all parts of the house to make their inventory. Unless someone within—someone who had tried to delay that inventory as long as possible— had beaten them to it.

"Where did your father keep the keys?" he asked.

"I have no idea. He was, you must understand, naturally suspicious. He told no one more than he had too. Wait! Do you think that was what my brother has been doing since my father's death? Searching for his keys? He has been turning the whole house upside down looking for something, certainly."

"Very likely," Adam said. It was time to get back to the main point. "Do you know whether this Mr Croome had actually given your father the money he owed him?"

"Oh yes," Miss Charlotte said. "That I can confirm."

"Your father brought it back with him on that day?"

"No. I believe he intended to return in the afternoon, before it became dark, but he did not come home until early the next morning. When he did, he caused an uproar in the house by rushing around, demanding breakfast, fuming at his manservant for not having his hunting clothes ready. He worked himself into an even greater rage than usual. Is it not odd that my last memories of my father alive show him red-faced with anger?"

Adam's face must have shown something of the surprise this last piece of information had caused him. Why had he not considered such a possibility before? Like everyone else, he had so focused on the day of the murder that he'd made a good many assumptions about what had preceded it. What a fool. What a blind fool.

"You look quite startled, doctor," Miss Charlotte said. "Have I shocked you? Should I feign a sadness I do not feel?"

"No, no," Adam said, "it is not that at all. Please believe that I would always have you be honest about yourself. No, it is something else; something I had not even considered until now."

"I cannot imagine what that may be," she said. "My father did not come home until the next morning for a simple reason. He and Mr Croome fell to drinking to seal their bargain. One glass led to another, until the bottle was empty. Then, of course, another bottle had to be called for, and so on. My father became so drunk it would have been impossible for him to get on his horse, let alone ride several miles home along uncertain roads. It must also have become dark by that time. Even in his befuddled state, my father would never have taken the risk of riding home in the dark bearing such a large amount of money with him. His rage next day could well have been as much to do with an aching head and sickly stomach as anything else."

"Do you know the route your father would have taken home from Mr Croome's house?"

"Well ..." She thought for a moment. "If he had taken his usual path, he would have come through the village of Letheringsett a little way, then turned onto the road towards Blakeney—the one that runs almost past your brother's house. Then he would most probably have used the shortcut through our estate, especially if he was in a hurry. That would have brought him out onto the road less than three or four hundred yards from Upper Cley Hall. As you know, our house stands some little way from the village. If he did not cut across the fields in that way, he would be forced to go to Gressington to find a bridge over the river, adding more than a mile to his journey. However, I believe he did take the longer route that morning. Yes, that's correct. He said he wished to make certain all the preparations were in hand at the Bull Inn. It brought him back even later, but I know he came that way for I heard him growl at his manservant that at least the innkeeper of The Bull knew how to be ready in good time."

They missed him because he didn't come home when he was expected, nor by the usual route. That trap wasn't set for anyone riding down the rough path towards the river. It was intended for a large man on a tall horse who would be riding up it. A man coming the other way."

"And he definitely had the money from Mr Croome with him?"

"As I told you, I know because he passed me with a leather bag in his hand. I asked him where he was going and he said he had something Mr Croome had given him to see put safe into his strongbox."

Later that day, Adam at length found he had time to visit his old friend, Peter Lassimer. He'd been kept so busy riding to and fro between Trundon Hall, Mossterton Hall and Norwich that he'd scarcely spent more than a few hours in his own home for several days. By now Peter would be impatient for fresh news and dismayed he had been so neglected. It was high time he told Peter nearly all he knew. Not quite all, for the last part was still no more than conjecture in his mind. The last thing Adam needed was one of Peter's instant answers composed of hearsay, guesswork and inexperience. Such responses were rarely correct and served only to make things more obscure.

They sat in Peter's compounding room once again and Adam told his tale while Peter rolled wax into pills and counted them out into small boxes.

"You seem to be very excited about Miss Wennard's tale of when and how her father came home," the apothecary said. "Is it relevant?"

"Don't you see?" Adam said. "It explains everything about the actual murder."

"No," Peter said. "I do not see. Explain it to me."

"It seemed quite impossible to explain how a trap set up in such an unlikely place could have any chance of success. How could the murderer know Sir Jackman Wennard would ride along that shortcut on that particular morning? Why would he believe he would fail to see the rope stretched across his path? He would be riding in full daylight, right on the edge of the wood. All must be in plain view. Yet everything I have learned points to the same conclusion. Sir Jackman only rode down the hill towards the river as a result of a series of chance happenings. Seeing his first wife—or someone he thought looked like her—at the meet of the hunt. Hurrying after the woman he'd seen and going further than necessary in a vain attempt to catch her up. Imagining it was his son who was with her in the dog-cart at the inn. That was why he asked everyone if they had seen an older woman and a young man. He forgot how old his son must be by now.

"Then he encountered the angry husband in Cley—a husband with quick access to a blunderbuss. Through the husband's spur of the moment reaction, Sir Jackman's highly-strung horse tore off in a panic and took the wrong road, the one towards Holt, not the one back to Gressington. Finally, he tried to rejoin the hunt by plunging down that hill, well off the pathway, thus setting off the two swivel-guns which threw the horse into a further frenzy. All chance!"

"So what is the truth? I tell you, Bascom, I cannot see it."

"The trap should have been sprung the day before—the day Sir Jackman went to collect his money from Mr Croome. It was not set to kill him. It was set to knock him off his horse so that he could be robbed."

"His son? No common footpad could have known he would go that way carrying so much money."

"Of course! Robert knew all about the visit to Mr Croome and what his father would be bringing back with him. He must also have known Sir Jackman nearly always took the shortcut over the river and up the hill through the woods. His father had refused him the money to pay his debts and he was becoming desperate. His plan was to stage a robbery to get the funds he needed so badly."

"Surely his father would recognise him?"

"He would not do it himself, would he? No, he paid someone else to carry out the deed. More than one person, I guess. They were to pose as common footpads, so they would bear the blame if things went wrong. I imagine Robert Wennard found a way to convince them they would never be discovered. He would find some way of throwing any pursuit off the scent. Perhaps he also said they could take all else of value his father had about him, so long as they brought him the leather bag his father was carrying. After the event, people would believe felons had set out to rob a rich gentlemen of a few pounds and come upon what they must have seen as unbelievable riches."

"Very well," Peter said, "I am with you so far. But wouldn't Sir Jackman still have seen the trap set for him? You told me his daughter said he would never have ridden back in the dark."

"It would not have been dark—at least, not fully so. Let's assume Robert guessed his father and Mr Croome would share a few drinks before he set out. They were old acquaintances, if not close friends. Sir Jackman must have reached Mr Croome's house at Field Dalling sometime between noon and one o'clock. Mr Croome probably dines at four. His guest takes his leave at, say, half past three. He has around three quarters of an hour's ride ahead of him. He doesn't dawdle, but he's in no particular hurry. Dusk falls by four and it is quite dark within an hour at most. It was also a day of heavy cloud and drizzle, which would make it still gloomier. By the time Sir Jackman would have turned off over the fields, the dusk would be well advanced."

"I still don't see …"

"You haven't visited the spot. I have. Assuming you are coming from the Letheringsett road, as Sir Jackman would have been, you would have crossed an open area of field, then come down to the ford over the river. On the other side, the land rises fairly steeply and is thickly wooded. You would have come from light into darkness—and you would be facing uphill."

"Why should that matter?"

"Think! You're probably urging your horse forward after slowing to cross the water. Even so, you'd be unlikely to be going any faster than a brisk walk. Even if you were looking out for anything in your path, which is most unlikely, you would either be concentrating on finding the right path or at least looking up into the trees. Eyes take a few moments to adjust. Coming from the light, your vision in the dark would still be poor."

"So you would ride right into the rope?"

"That was the plan. Going at a walk and sitting fairly upright—it was a tall horse remember—the rope was set to catch Sir Jackman full in the chest. That, and his surprise, would be more than enough to knock him backwards and make him fall to the ground. Then the 'robbers' would be upon him in a moment. Probably two or three of them, as I said. One or two to hold him down—or give him a crack on the head—one to catch the horse and rifle through the saddlebags."

"But Sir Jackman Wennard never turned up."

"Precisely! Rather, he fell into the trap next morning when, for some reason I do not know yet, it had not been cleared away. Only this time he was coming down the hill at a gallop, desperately trying to get his horse under control and unable to stop however much he wanted to. I doubt he would have seen the rope in time, even in full daylight. Instead, he hit it at high speed, not with his chest but full in the throat. It snapped his neck like a twig."

"So the death was an accident?"

"Exactly as Robert Wennard claimed from the first. He was speaking the truth. The problem was he could not explain why he was so sure without disclosing his earlier plan to rob his father. The death itself was indeed accidental—that strutting young braggart is no killer—but it would never have happened had he not had the path rigged with a trap. I'm no lawyer to know how the judge at the assizes would view the result.

Murder, or assault and manslaughter? Either way, young Robert would face public disgrace, followed by transportation or the hangman's rope."

"So he kept quiet."

"Of course. At first, he must have thought his troubles were nearly over. Even if the executors delayed his inheritance a little, while some small investigation took place to try to find his father's murderer, it was still assured. No one would find the men he paid to set the trap. He could either buy them off or frighten them into silence. For himself, he was sitting on his horse, in full view of dozens of people, several hundred yards away. His creditors might fuss and fume at more delay, but they would believe payment was certain."

"Until the first Mrs Wennard made her claim."

"Exactly. That was the catalyst for all that has happened since. Suddenly, the newly-minted Sir Robert faced losing everything—title, estate and money. The moment such news reached his creditors, they would be on him again. His renewed desperation must be terrible. He thought it was all over, then it comes back worse than ever."

"So what is he doing now?"

"Trying in every way he can to get a large sum of money into his hands. I am sure he knew, like his sister, that his father had placed the payment from Mr Croome into that strongbox at Upper Cley Hall. Unfortunately, he didn't know where his father kept the key. Sir Jackman Wennard was suspicious of everyone, so he made sure the key was hidden somewhere extremely secure. That was why his son has tried to prevent the executors from making their inventory and why he has been turning the house upside down."

"He's been looking for the key."

"Yes. All that money under his nose and still out of reach. I imagine he knows his father must either have left a duplicate key with his executors, or a sealed note telling them where the key can be found. That precaution would be necessary for his Will to be proved in the event of his death. Of course, if the executors get to the money it's as good as lost to Robert. They would add it into the estate, to be handed over to the rightful heir only when that could be determined. When that will be, who can tell?"

"So this business of the kidnapping is another ruse to obtain money?"

"Yes, I am almost sure it must be. That's why I have asked Giles to impress upon the executors that no ransom must be paid. I suppose there is just a faint chance Robert has been taken by his accomplices in the killing of his father. I don't think so, but I've tried to deal with that by suggesting they delay rather than refuse outright to pay."

"And now? It seems to me you fear more must happen."

"I do," Adam said, "but all we can do is wait."

Both men fell silent, their minds full of possible outcomes. At length Adam smiled and turned to a final part of the puzzle.

"You know, Lassimer. Miss Charlotte's testimony also cleared up one other strange matter."

"What was that?"

"Why Robert Wennard rode so quickly and surely to where his father lay. He heard the commotion in the wood and the firing of the guns, so he jumped at once to the conclusion it must be his father coming down the shortcut. By some means I do not yet understand, he also knew the rope was still in place."

"So he rushed to take it down before it could be noticed?"

"No, not that. There would not be time. As soon as he rode off, others would follow. As for the rope, I imagine he would have stuck to his earlier tale of footpads. In the end it was not necessary. The violence of the collision broke the rope. The two ends, hanging down against the trees, would hardly be noticeable, especially when everyone's attention was on the dead man lying on the ground. That rope was removed later, either by Robert or someone he sent there to do it. By the time the coroner and his medical examiner came on the scene, it must definitely have been gone. All they found were marks where something had been tied around the trees and cut away later."

"Sir Robert knew his father would be killed by coming that way?"

"Not knew. Not until he found him. At first he would only have feared he'd been injured—maybe quite badly. Then, once he could see the man was dead, he had to fix in everyone's mind that whatever had befallen him was an accident—and get them away from the spot before anyone began to look around too carefully. If you recall, those present said he went on and on about his father's death being a terrible accident. He also demanded his father's body be moved at once, saying to leave it where it had fallen was too disrespectful. As a result, the whole party set off alongside the river, bearing the body on its way to Upper Cley Hall. By the time the coroner had arrived, that was where it was, safely in a bedroom."

"Mr Robert Wennard, as I suppose we must call him again, may be an arrogant braggart and a spendthrift," Peter said, "but he has an uncommonly quick mind in a crisis."

"That's what's worrying me," Adam replied.

Fourteen

Daughters and Sons

ADAM DID NOT HAVE TO WAIT LONG FOR MORE NEWS. Just as he had finished breakfast the next morning, a servant arrived from Mossterton Hall
with a message for him from Charles Scudamore. He reported that he
had seen Mrs Wennard safely on her way via the coach to London. Her
son had written her a letter which reached her just before he had arrived.
The son had been asked to go to London for several months to supervise
work on various repairs and improvements being made at the docks. He
wished his mother to go there as well, for he thought it would do her no
good to be alone and isolated in the house in the north. This suited her
very well, so there had been no problem in persuading her to leave right
away—especially after Charles had offered to explain all to her Norwich
attorney and make sure he knew how he might contact her. If any person
wishing her harm tried to seek her out now, he would most likely look
for her travelling northwards, not towards London. Charles had told the
attorney to keep her present whereabouts a close secret.

Adam could now relax a little, knowing that the others under threat
if the ransom demand for Mr Robert Wennard failed were protected.

Mrs Pashley was safe in her husband's home in Norwich, Miss Charlotte Wennard under the watchful eyes of Lady Alice at Mossterton Hall and Mrs Wennard on her way in the opposite direction to the one expected.

Such respite as that news brought him did not last. A groom came from Trundon Hall in great haste, asking the doctor to return there as soon as he could. The squire wanted him to know that Sir Jackman Wennard's son had been found early that morning, injured but alive. There had also been an attempt to rob the mail coach from Cromer to Norwich the previous evening, apparently by the same gang of highwaymen who had carried out the earlier robberies in the area. The groom was sent back to reassure his master the doctor was on his way and William summoned to make the chaise ready and act as driver.

By the time Adam reached Trundon Hall, his brother Giles was once again pacing up and down the library in a fine state of excitement.

"It was that young fool Robert Wennard all the time!" he called out while Adam was still barely stepping through the door to join him.

"What was?" Adam said.

"The leader of the highwaymen. The one who wore the blue coat with red buttons. He was wearing it when his servants found him near dawn this morning."

"I do wish you wouldn't get so excited," Adam said. "Take a deep breath and tell me what has happened. Do it clearly and in the proper order."

"You knew!" His brother cried. "I swear you've known for ages. Just wanted to be able to show off when it happened and act in that superior way you have!"

"Knew what, brother?" Adam replied. "And I have never pretended to be superior."

"You do, all the time. Think I'm just about good enough to be a clodhopping squire."

"This is getting us nowhere," Adam said, controlling his anger with some difficulty. "Tell me what you know and be done with it."

"Near dawn this morning, someone hammered on the main door of Upper Cley Hall," Giles said. It was obvious he too was trying to stop himself saying things he would regret. "When a servant went to see what all the noise was about, he found Robert Wennard lying bleeding on the ground in front of the door, no one else in sight. The servants took their master in, put him in his bed and sent at once for the local medical man—that's the surgeon you met at the inquest on Sir Jackman Wennard. When they came to remove their master's blood-soaked clothes, they found him wearing a blue coat with red buttons. None of them had ever seen such a coat before. They're quite positive about that. The surgeon came, attended to Wennard's wound, which was serious, and came here at once. As you know, he used to be a ship's surgeon in the Royal Navy and is well acquainted with gunshot wounds. He's certain Robert Wennard was shot at close range."

"Will his wound prove mortal?' Adam asked.

"The surgeon thinks not, though it must be a while before anyone can be certain. The man has lost a good deal of blood. He may take a putrid fever, either as a result of the wound or from lying on the wet ground outside the door of the hall."

"Has the man himself said anything to explain what happened?"

"Not one word." Giles was eager to press his earlier point. "You did know, didn't you brother? You told me to expect something to happen and you knew what it was. Why didn't you share your knowledge with me?"

"Because I had none," Adam said. "None whatsoever, despite your suspicions. It's true I thought Robert Wennard must be behind the gang of highwaymen, but there was no reason to assume he would lead it himself—he could easily have persuaded another to do that. Yes, I suspected he must try to bring off a robbery that would let him obtain a good amount of money at one time. What it would be, and where, once again I had no notion. All I knew was he must be near frantic with the need to obtain cash enough to be able to flee the country, as much to escape some very angry and vicious creditors as to avoid justice. By removing both his sisters and Mrs Wennard as targets for more kidnapping—real this time—the only option I left him was another attack somewhere along our roads. My idea was to force him into rash action which might result in his capture, as it has."

"You certainly managed it well," Giles said. "Forgive my suspicions, brother. I am overwrought."

Adam merely nodded and smiled. "What more has been told you?" he asked.

"The local constable in Cromer warned the coachmen to be on the alert for highwaymen and go well armed. That was you too, I believe. They took him at his word. The moment the three robbers appeared, the guard let fly with a great blunderbuss, the highwaymen's leader was wounded and his companions took fright. One managed to support him just enough to stay on his horse and they rode away as fast as they could manage."

"The others won't get far," Adam said, "especially since they delayed enough to take Mr Robert Wennard back to Upper Cley Hall first. I suppose that showed some humanity. They might easily have left him by the roadside and looked only to their own safety."

Giles ignored this remark. For him, felony and humanity could not possibly be found in the same person at the same time.

"We even know who they are," he said. "The masks they were wearing came off in the struggle to hold Wennard on his horse. A Mr Parker from Salthouse, a keen huntsman who often went out with Sir Jackman Wennard, was riding in the mailcoach. He says he recognised them as two of the gamekeepers from the Wennard Estate."

"I asked Captain Mimms a few days ago to put out the word among the ship's captains all along this coast to watch out for men willing to pay a great deal to be taken out of the country at once," Adam said. "That route too will be blocked. I suggest you send word to as many of the constables between here and Norwich as you can. Tell them to be on watch for these men. Aye, and in the direction of King's Lynn too, if that is possible."

"If they're on foot or horseback," Giles replied, "their obvious course would be towards Norwich, then to London. It's easiest to disappear in a big city."

Adam agreed. Giles sent all the grooms and servants he could spare to carry the word to the neighbouring parishes. They, in turn, would pass it on further. With the hue and cry raised after them and their identity known, the two men's chances of escape were now slim.

Once again, there was nothing to do but wait. Mrs Bascom and Sophia were still at Trundon Hall and were said to be eager for news, so Adam occupied an hour or so in explaining to them much the same things he had told Peter Lassimer a day earlier. He had decided to show no sign of recalling Miss LaSalle's behaviour when they met last, as much from embarrassment as politeness. Now, when the young woman followed his mother into the room, it was clear she had reached the same decision. She greeted the doctor politely, but carefully kept from meeting his eyes and even sat herself somewhat behind Mrs Bascom. During all the time Adam was reciting what he knew and what he was doing as a result, she spoke not a single word. It was his mother who asked the questions and exclaimed at the wickedness of Sir Jackman Wennard's profligate son. Giles added one or two remarks from time to time, but he too appeared abashed by his unwarranted suspicion of his brother's behaviour and stayed quiet when he could. All in all, a most uncomfortable meeting Adam hoped might not be prolonged.

Indeed, by the time he had finished Adam felt more tired than he had in a very long time. His mother, alert to his well-being, noticed this fatigue at once and told Giles in no uncertain terms that his brother should be given a room where he could rest for a time.

Much to Adam's surprise, once he was alone he must straightway have fallen asleep for it was nearly four in the afternoon when he awoke, too late to think of returning to Aylsham that day. Adam therefore washed his face—some light-footed servant had managed to leave a jug of warm water in the room without waking him—and made what toilet he could. It would soon be time for dinner.

Giles intercepted him on his way towards the dining room.

"Those two rascals are taken, brother," he said. "They got no further than Holt. There they tried to hire a chaise from The King's Head, asking to go to Norwich. They said they were in a hurry to get there before dark and offered a guinea in gold in payment. That made the landlord suspicious, given their dusty and ragged appearance. He also noticed one had a large stain on his sleeve that looked like blood. The Holt constable had been around earlier with my message, so the landlord said he had no chaise or any other vehicle available. As soon as the men left to try elsewhere, he sent his boy to call the constable. The men went next to The Feathers, where they were also refused, then to The White Lion. By that time, the constable and his helpers were waiting for them and they were taken without resistance."

"Where are they now?" Adam asked.

"In the lock-up in Holt. They aren't proper criminals, brother, just greedy fools led astray by their master. The prospect of facing a judge, then the hangman, terrifies them. They couldn't wait to offer to turn King's evidence against their master to save their own necks. I'm having them kept in Holt overnight, then brought before me for questioning first thing tomorrow. You're very welcome to be present, if you wish."

The men who stood before Giles and Adam Bascom the next morning certainly didn't look the part of ruthless highwaymen. The older of the two could best have been taken for a petty tradesman or a shopkeeper. His clothes, though crumpled and stained by several nights of living rough, must once have been better than those worn by the normal run of labourers. Aside from that, he was well into middle age and running to a plumpness about his stomach that bore witness to many pints of beer consumed along with good, regular meals. The younger man assumed the unconcerned look of one who would have loved to shout defiance at these men of authority, yet knew he had neither the strength nor the intelligence to do so and escape still worse punishment.

Giles and Adam were careful to choose a place to conduct this impromptu court which might intimidate the prisoners and bring home to them the seriousness of their position. They therefore had a heavy table placed at the opposite end of the entrance hall of Giles' mansion from the stairway, with two chairs set behind it for themselves and another for Giles' clerk. He would record the proceedings.

Adam glanced around. The fine plaster walls and enormous mirrors of the Great Hall at Trundon, rising more than twenty-five feet above his head to a ceiling rich with plaster decoration, ought to be more than enough to represent the majesty of the law—and the wretched state of insignificance of ordinary folk who dared defy it. The Wennard house at Upper Cley Hall, he knew, was old-fashioned and unassuming in comparison. None of its owners over the past century and more had cared much for domestic grandeur or changing fashions. The land was what mattered to them, whether they hunted over it or sought to turn it into profit.

Adam's grandfather, in contrast, had dreamed impossible dreams of becoming the first Lord Bascom. So he set about proving his new status by transforming Trundon Hall into a home fit for an earl at the least. Much of the never abundant Bascom wealth had been spent on lavish building and decoration at Trundon in the latest classical style. Sadly for its owner, his home might have looked fit for a peer of the realm, but he never attained any such honour and threw away much of his wealth on the process.

The men they were to question were now brought to stand before them. For long moments, Giles Bascom left them standing in silence while he appeared to consult a sheaf of papers set on the table for this express purpose. Then he spoke first to the Parish Constable of Holt who, with two burly assistants, had brought the prisoners from their most uncomfortable overnight lodgings in his lock-up.

"What are the names of these men, Constable?" he began. "Are they mere vagabonds or men of honest employment until now?"

"Elias Thaxter and his son Jonas, sir" the constable said. "Both employed as gamekeepers on the estate of that Sir Jackman Wennard as was killed hereabouts not long ago."

"Have they been lawbreakers before this, do you know?"

"Aye, sir. Many times to my certain knowledge and I daresay if you asked the constable at Cley he could mention more. Petty thieving mostly. That and fighting and drinking overmuch. I had cause to lay hands on them a good few times on market days in Holt."

"I am amazed Sir Jackman Wennard would be willing to employ such men," Giles said.

"That Sir Jackman was always most protective of his game, sir. Hated poachers, he did. He wanted gamekeepers who would do as he wanted without concern for what the law said. That's why he hired ones more skilled at fighting and setting traps and the like than caring for pheasants or partridge."

"It seems so," Giles added. "Now. You two men. I have a copy here of the Bible. My clerk will bring it to each of you in turn and you will repeat after him the oath that you will tell the truth, the whole truth and nothing but the truth in this court. When you have done that, we will begin."

The clerk, an elderly man who was otherwise a schoolmaster in the nearby village of Glavenbridge, administered the oath in the form prescribed.

"Very well," Giles Bascom said. "You are now under oath, which means you face a heavy punishment if you do not speak the truth. Elias Thaxter. You are charged with robbery on the King's Highway. How do you plead to the charge?"

"Guilty, your worship," the older Thaxter said.

"Jonas Thaxter," Giles Bascom continued. "How do you plead?"

"Guilty, I suppose," the youth muttered, rebellion in every syllable. "My son and I wants to turns King's evidence, your worship. 'Twas that one who's now our master, Sir Robert Wennard as now is, what led us astray into doin' what we did. He said as how his father allus kept 'im mighty short o' money, even though 'e was fair rollin' in it 'imself. Then, when 'e was dead an' gone, them miserable ol' fools o' executors of 'is Will was doin' the same. It was now 'is money and 'e should rightly 'ave it."

"I advise you to speak with greater respect of your betters, man. It will do you no good before my court or any other to talk in that way."

Jonas Thaxter, the son, could no longer contain himself. "What betters? That Robert Wennard is the thief, not us. What we did, we did at 'is bidding. Aye, and 'e would have seen us in the workhouse or starvin' if we'd 'ave refused. The likes of 'im—and 'is father—ain't no better an' anyone else! As Tom Paine says, all men 'as natural rights, only them as 'as the wealth an' power denies 'em to all the rest. When we gets a revolution—"

"Silence!" Giles thundered. "If you speak again before I tell you, I will have you given a good whipping for contempt of this court. I've heard of men like you—stupid, ignorant labouring folk led astray by the ravings of that traitor and firebrand Paine. Most of them end their days on the gallows, which is exactly what they deserve. Speak when you're spoken to and not before. Yes, and take care to quote no sedition either, or you'll soon be dangling at the end of a rope, King's evidence or no."

"Please forgive my son, your worship," Elias Thaxter said. "He be hot-headed like all of 'is age. Hold your mouth, Jonas, you young fool! You'll get us both 'anged if you goes on like that!"

"We will start again," Giles said. "Elias Thaxter. What have you to say for yourself before I commit you to the next assize for highway robbery?"

"We acted under orders," Thaxter said. "Our master, who was the ringleader, forced us to take part in the robberies. That's why we wants to turn King's evidence against him."

"We will set that aside for the moment. The only matter this court must decide is whether you should be committed for trial at the assize. If you are sent there, it will be up to the lawyer acting for the Crown and the judge to decide whether or not to accept your offer. I will send them an account of what you have said today, so I advise you to answer my questions fully and truthfully if you want them to see your evidence against others as worth the cost of saving your wretched necks."

"I'll speak for my son, if it please your worship," Elias Thaxter added now. "He's not all that clever, if you see my point. Not too strong in 'is head and more apt to using 'is fists than 'is brains. Very likely he'll give you the wrong impression." The vicious look he turned on his son at this point was eloquent of delayed retribution.

"Very well," Giles said. "The gentleman on my right is Dr Adam Bascom, my brother. You may have heard of him. I have asked him to be present to hear what you say, but you will address your words to me as magistrate. Elias Thaxter, you have pleaded guilty to this charge. However, before I come to a decision on the cases of you and your son, I have

216

several questions. Tell the court how you came to turn highway robber and what other crimes you committed beyond attempting to rob the coach travelling between Cromer and Norwich."

Elias Thaxter's testimony was confused and rambling, though the main points were clear enough. As the constable had indicated, neither man knew much more about the business of keeping and breeding game than any simple countryman might have done. They had been employed as bruisers to frighten off poachers and enforce Sir Jackman Wennard's iron policy of ensuring no one, however poor or desperate, should take a single rabbit that rightfully belonged to him as owner of the estate. They only turned to robbery after Sir Jackman's death, as they told the story. That was when his son, now their master, had approached them with an offer. Since he had need of ready money, and the executors were most unreasonably making him wait for what was his, he had a plan. They would dress up as highwaymen and steal small sums from people using the roads in the area. There would be little or no danger involved and they should not need to use violence. The mere threat of a pistol pointed at their victims should be enough. Sir Robert would choose whom to attack, since he knew many of their likely victims and could select the ones he thought might have most worth stealing and be least likely to put up a struggle. To do this, he would put on a disguise and act as their leader. They too would be cloaked and masked, so no one would recognise them, and the robberies would all take place near dusk or in dark lanes or woods. Whatever they got from each robbery was to be shared out. Half for him, as leader, and the rest for them.

The first two robberies had been easy, but the takings poor. They robbed a few local tradesmen and one or two clergymen. Sir Robert had called these thefts simple practice, a chance to get used to their roles and gain confidence for better things. When he heard that word had spread about that a ruthless gang of highwaymen were working in the area it seemed to amuse him. He said no one liked to be taken for a fool or a coward, so their victims would be bound to exaggerate their fierceness and the threats they made. They could use that to their advantage to make future robberies even easier. He also began to wear the blue coat with red buttons, so he could be identified as the supposed leader of this ruthless gang. This trick had worked too. Most of their victims were so terrified from the start they handed over all their valuables without being asked. In time, they and their master raised their sights to richer prey, robbing successful farmers and traders on their way home from market, their pockets and saddle bags filled with the day's takings.

Suddenly, the man claimed, all had changed. What had been almost fun turned deadly serious. Sir Robert told them the takings from these local robberies were too small to be worth the risks involved. He had no wish to continue until they were caught, for he said he'd heard militia and dragoons were to be brought in to patrol the roads and seize the robbers. No sense in ending on the gallows for a few pounds. They must do two things. First, they would shift the area in which they sought their prey. If the forces of the law were seeking them around the valley of the Glaven, they must go further afield. It would mean leaving their homes for a few days, but it would make them safer. The other part of his plan was to obtain a great deal of money through carrying out one final robbery. For this, they must arm themselves heavily and be prepared to fire their guns if necessary. As Elias Thaxter told it, he wished to draw back, but Sir Robert would have none of it, saying he would pretend he himself had been threatened but had seized one of the highwaymen. Then he would personally hand Elias over to the magistrate. There was to be no hanging back. One last successful robbery and they could disband for ever. He would go abroad for a while. They could go wherever they wished.

That was how they came to attack the mail coach. Unfortunately, the guard was on the alert and fired at them before they had had the time to do more than draw their own weapons from under their cloaks. Sir Robert was badly wounded. They managed to get him away, but he could not ride any great distance in the state he was in. Indeed, he could barely ride at all. In the end, they slung him over his horse's saddle and headed back towards Cley. There they left him on the doorstep of his own house, banging hard on the door to attract attention before slipping away. At least his servants would be able to call for a doctor.

They weren't sure what was best for them to do next. They could have gone home and brazened it out, but the events of the night had unnerved them. It seemed better to get some distance away and wait for the fuss to die down. Neither, it appeared, had any concern for Mrs Thaxter and her other children, who would be left without any means of support. Indeed, it was clear Elias rather relished the notion of starting afresh, probably with a new woman to replace the wife he tired of long ago.

Giles was about to sum up and make a formal committal to the next assize, when Adam passed him a note. He read it, read it again, looked surprised then nodded assent.

"I have another matter to raise," he said. "Once again, I warn you to hold nothing back, if you wish your plea of King's evidence to be accepted."

A SHORTCUT TO MURDER

Fifteen

King's Evidence

"TELL THE COURT THE DETAILS OF THE PART YOU PLAYED IN THE DEATH of the late Sir Jackman Wennard. Remember you are under oath and have sworn to tell the truth—all the truth. The penalties for perjury—concealing evidence or lying to this court—are extremely severe. You would do well to think carefully before you try to come up with a pack of lies."

Giles Bascom's words produced looks of terror from both men.

"That weren't nothing to do with us!" young Jonas Thaxter cried out. "You can't make out it were, either. We knows nothing about it. 'Tis allus the same. Rich men wants to make the poor folk pay for what they done themselves. Like Tom Paine says—"

"Shut up, you young fool!" his father cried out, backing up his command with a stinging open-handed blow across his son's face. "You'll send us both to the gallows with your cursed Tom Paine. They knows, I tell you. Stands to reason, or they wouldn't raise the matter. Now hold your tongue before I gives you another clout as will hold it for you for good."

He turned back to the table where Giles and Adam sat, then fell on his knees.

"I begs you to overlook what my son said, your worships. I told you he be weak in 'is 'ead. Bad company 'as filled it with nonsense about rights and revolutions and the Lord knows what else. Only he's too feeble in 'is wits to see these men be making a fool of 'im."

"Oy!" his son cried. "Who you be saying is feeble in 'is wits? I knows a good deal more o' the rights and wrongs o' the world than you does, old man!"

His father sprang to his feet at that and punched his son so hard the lad staggered backwards, coughing and spitting bits of tooth from his mouth. The son fought back and the constables finally had to separate them. They did not do it gently either. By the time order had been restored, both men were breathing heavily. The young man's face was badly swollen and his father's left eye was shut. They looked a sorry pair.

"One more interruption from you," Giles said to Jonas Thaxter, "and I'll have the constables remove you from this room. I'll also inform the judge at the assize that you are totally infected with these wild and seditious views; any testimony you may give against Sir Robert Wennard must therefore be worthless and prompted only by malice. Then you will surely hang."

He paused to see what the young man might say, but the lad had the sense to keep his mouth firmly shut. Either that or he feared his father would kill him if he said one more word.

"Very well. Elias Thaxter. Once again I ask you. What part did you and your son here play in bringing about the death of the late Sir Jackman Wennard?"

"We was told to knock the old squire off 'is 'orse, then set upon him and rob him. Sir Robert what be squire now, it was he who come up with the scheme. Said he knew his father would be riding 'ome across the fields and over the river carrying a good amount of cash in a leather bag, or something of such. We was to put on masks he gave us to disguise who we was, steal the bag and take it to Sir Robert without opening it.

Anything else we took from the old squire was ours to keep as payment for what we done. We hadn't taken up with highway robbery then, your worship. So far as we was told, this was to be a single piece of work. I wasn't keen on it, to tell you the truth, but then Mr Robert, as he was then, said he'd give us each five golden guineas in advance to seal the deal between us. That's much more than I earns in a month o' damned 'ard work. We didn't have any love for the old squire neither. 'Ard as nails, he were. Allus complainin' at us and threatening to see us thrown out of our cottage and put in the workhouse if we let so much as a single rabbit or pheasant be taken by a poacher. 'E would have done it too."

"So you agreed," Giles said.

"Aye, sir. We agreed. We wasn't to 'urt the man, you understands. Not hurt him bad. We just had to stop 'im passing and get him on the ground so we could take what he had. My job was to give him a small crack on the head with my cudgel to keep 'im quiet like, then go through his pockets. Jonas 'ere would catch the 'orse and take a look in the saddlebags."

"How were you to get him from his horse?" Giles asked.

"With a rope across his path. Mr Robert said it wouldn't be seen in the dusk—at least, not until it were too late. His father wouldn't be coming in any great hurry, he said, but he was sure he'd 'ave taken a good drop o' liquor before setting out. He wouldn't be expecting trouble either, not on his own land."

"He was sure his father would ride that way?"

"Aye, sir. Seems the old squire always used that path when he was coming from Letheringsett or places over that side of his estate. Saved 'im a good mile or more going into Gressington and riding over the bridge back towards Cley. As I'm sure you knows, the Glaven ain't much more than a good stream along there. Over the years, all the cattle comin' down to drink has broken down the banks and made a kind o' shallows between two or three deeper pools. Good sea-trout there ... as I 'eard tell," he added quickly.

Giles ignored this tacit admission of the man's own poaching. "So," he said, "you were to catch Sir Jackman unawares by the river."

"Just t'other side," Elias Thaxter continued. "The path starts to go up the hill, you sees, and there's a good number o' trees and bushes. Mr Robert says to string the rope tight between two sturdy tree trunks, 'bout six or seven foot above the ground. Then it would catch his father full in the chest and throw him off his great horse, back over its arse. Once he was on the ground, we knew what to do."

"Did Robert Wennard lie in wait with you?"

"Not 'im! He's too fine a gentleman to wait about in the cold and damp with the likes of us. No, he said he had to stay at the hall, so as to make sure no one knew 'e was involved in any way. Once we had the bag he wanted, we was to take it to him at first light. 'Twas the fox hunt the next day, he said, so he was bound to be up and doing early. Then we could take ourselves off and lie low. So long as we kept mum about our part, he would see as no one knew what we 'ad done."

"So what went wrong?"

"The old squire never came, that's what went wrong. We hid ourselves close by the path an' waited an' waited, long after it got dark. Just in case he was delayed like. But he never come along. It were a powerful cold night too, like to freeze a man's balls off ... beggin' your pardon, your worships. We knew it would be cold, but we hadn't expected to be there that long. At least we'd used some of the money Mr Robert gave us to take along a good jug o' gin each. That kept us warm enough for a while, then we both falls asleep. You see, your honour, it were so dull, squatting there. We didn't even see as much as a rabbit or a hare as we could 'ave ... I means, we didn't even see any animals come along. The old owls were making a fair noise, but there's no use in them."

"When did you wake?" Giles asked.

"Not till well after dawn, we reckoned. It were full daylight. We both had thick 'eads from the gin and I was fair stiff from lying on the cold ground at my age. We talked about what to do and decided in the end we should go over to the hall and tell Mr Robert what had happened—which was nothing at all."

There they found everyone up and getting ready for the hunt when they arrived. Robert Wennard was already outside in the yard looking over his horse. That made it easier to speak to him. Nobody would remark on two of the gamekeepers coming up to him. They'd assume they were telling him where they'd seen a fox, or something like that. It was while they were making their way over to where he was that they heard his father clattering into the yard and calling out for his grooms to take his horse and bring him his hunter instead. He was in a foul mood, shouting and swearing and demanding something to eat and drink be brought out to him right away. It was clear he had as bad a hangover as they did, which probably explained why he hadn't come home the evening before as had been expected. Some servant brought him a slab of bread and butter and a piece of cheese. Another scuttled over with a tankard of ale or cider, they couldn't tell which. Sir Jackman Wennard sat down on a bench by one of the stables and ate and drank in silence. Since it would be clear enough to Sir Jackman's son by this stage what must have happened, they both thought they could leave things at that. They went home and looked for some breakfast for themselves.

"Were you supposed to remove the rope before you left the river bank?" Giles asked. "If you left it in place, surely someone else might be caught in your trap and hurt?"

No, the older man said, that wouldn't happen. Nobody else used the path save a few locals and they wouldn't be foolish enough to go along it on the day of a hunt. If the old squire had seen them, there would have been hell to pay. They had indeed forgotten the rope and only went back for it later that morning. When they got there it was broken anyway. At the time, they had no idea how that had happened. They just used their knives to cut the two ends away from round the tree trunks. They only realised much later that Sir Jackman Wennard must have ridden into it somehow during the hunt and broken his neck falling off his horse.

"Sir Robert Wennard, as he now was, told us that hisself, your worship," Elias Thaxter said. "He said as how we had brought about his father's death and would swing for it, if we was ever found out. I don't mind telling you that fair froze my blood, sir. We didn't ever mean to hurt the man more'n what was necessary. Not kill him. Never that!"

Jonas Thaxter suddenly found his voice. "That was 'ow the new squire first forced us to do what 'e said and 'elp him with those robberies," he said. "Told us he'd say he'd seen us creepin' about in the place where 'is father was killed. Claim we had a grudge against the man and 'ad sworn to kill 'im. It'd be 'is word against ours, and 'e was now a baronet, or some such thing, and a man o' property. Who did we think a judge would believe? A rich man like 'im or two snivellin' wretches such as us. Those was his true words, sir. Called us snivellin' wretches in that high-and-mighty voice o' his."

"'Sright!" his father added. "That was exactly what he said. What else could poor men like us do, your worship? We had to obey him, whether we wanted to or not. That's why we wants to turn King's evidence ...." The older man was determined the magistrate shouldn't forget that part. "... Sir Robert, as he now is, would cheerfully 'ave sent us to the gallows to save his own neck. It's only fair we should do the same in return."

There was little more to be got from them after this. The father confirmed he'd set up swivel-guns in the wood by the path, along with two man-traps. Neither of those traps had been sprung, but both guns must have fired at some time. He hadn't thought that especially important. Sometimes animals like badgers or even rabbits blundered into the trip-wires and set off the guns. Since the guns were set at a height to catch a man in the thighs or thereabouts, it was rare to find an animal had been hit. The pellets would fly over their heads.

For the rest, they had indeed feared their trap might have played some part in the baronet's death, but they didn't know for sure. Didn't want to know either. If it had, it was an accident. He should never have been riding that way, nor going quickly enough for the fall to break his neck. In their muddled but convenient way of thinking, he had caused his own death, and they had nothing to do with it.

Giles now ended the proceedings and stated formally that both men should be remanded in custody until the next convenient assizes or quarter sessions. There they would be tried for highway robbery and, he thought, for manslaughter as well. It would be up to others to decide whether to allow them to escape punishment by turning King's evidence against their master.

The clerk was still writing out the men's testimony when Giles and Adam left the room. Once that was done, the accused would make their marks and it would stand as evidence against them. Giles would add his own signature to the necessary documents and his role as magistrate would be completed. In the meantime, the two brothers could return to the library to refresh themselves and discuss the morning's events.

"Was that what you thought had happened?" Giles asked.

"In almost every particular," Adam replied. "Well, you have your evidence. What happens now to Robert Wennard? Will he hang?"

"The highway robberies alone will be enough to send him to the gallows," Giles said. "As regards his father's death, he planned the robbery which caused it. He may not have intended to kill Sir Jackman, but it was his actions which brought it about. I'm no lawyer, brother, but I would have thought that might bring a charge of attempted murder against him. What the penalty would be, I have no idea. Still, that's of no consequence. Whether he hangs for one crime or two, he'll still be dead."

"I suppose if any man deserves that fate, he does," Adam replied.

Giles began to pace slowly up and down again.

"How long have you known all this?" he asked. "You might have told me, instead of letting me worry myself sick trying to think of ways to seize the highway robbers and find Sir Jackman Wennard's murderer." His face was growing red, his voice betraying renewed agitation and anger.

Adam made his way to stand by his brother's side. He did not look into his brother's face, but stared instead at their reflection in the long mirror to the left of the hearth. After a pause that seemed long, but could only have been a second or so, he spoke, keeping his voice low and even.

"Please do not travel down that road again, Giles," he said. "You asked me to investigate Sir Jackman Wennard's death and that is where I began. The rest came upon me without warning, as it did upon you. At the start, I knew nothing. Then, slowly, small facts started to emerge and I tried to fit them together into a pattern that would make sense. I thought many things, brother, but still knew—truly knew—no more than I had at the outset. That is the way of things. If I do not share every thought in my head with you—or with anyone else—the reason is simple. Like all men, I do not relish showing myself to be a fool."

"But—"

"No 'buts'! Once a puzzle is solved, there is no mystery about it. All seems plain and obvious. Looking back on what has been found and proved is always apt to make it all seem so simple."

For a while, they stood in silence, then Giles touched Adam lightly on the arm.

"Forgive me, Adam. I am truly grateful for your help, for I should never have understood any of this without you. As it is, I will be able to tell the deputy lieutenant of the county that we have not only answered the question of how and why Sir Jackman Wennard died, but also cleaned out a nest of highwaymen and sent both killers and robbers to trial. If that doesn't please him, I swear nothing will."

"What will you tell Lord Weybourne and the other executors of Sir Jackman's Will?"

"The plain facts. The rest is up to them and I need have no part in it. If, as I imagine, Robert Wennard is convicted and dies on the gallows, they must find another heir. Yet, now I come to think of it, I may even be able to tell Lord Weybourne another of his mysteries has been solved."

"What is that?" Adam asked.

"Where Sir Jackman Wennard's wife's jewels have gone. I suppose I should now say his second wife, or the wife that never should have been. I heard yesterday that, with Robert Wennard absent and no longer able to prevent them, the executors sent their legal representative and another agent to start upon the valuation of all Sir Jackman Wennard's possessions as required by the process of probate. In particular, they were asked to bring away Lady Wennard's jewels. They had been bequeathed to her daughters when she died. Since they were still but girls, their father undertook to keep them safe until they came of age."

"Did he make those arrangements?"

"He did. He was not all bad, you see. He kept the jewels safe in the strongroom at Upper Cley Hall. As they grew older, his daughters were allowed to wear various items on special occasions. Since they knew the jewels were safe, even when the elder Miss Wennard had her twenty-first birthday, she left her share of the jewels where they were. If was only after she had left the house and married that she sent word to the executors of her father's estate that they should not be included amongst his wealth. They were to take her share from the strongroom and send them to her. She thought her sister's share should also be secured and placed somewhere safe apart from their father's possessions."

"But they could not be found," Adam said.

"Precisely. All that remained in the strongroom were the cases and boxes which had held them. The jewels were gone."

"Brother Robert, of course. How long had he been stealing from his own sisters, I wonder? I expect he had taken the jewellery gradually and pawned it, perhaps even thought he could quickly redeem them so no one would ever know. Thus it is with those who fall victim to gambling. They must ever expect the next wager to recoup all their previous losses. If he had taken them only recently, there would have been no call for him to turn to crime to pay off his debts."

"That must be the way of it. Poor ladies! All their mother left to them stolen. I tell you, brother, spare none of your pity for Robert Wennard. If ever a man deserved to hang, he most surely does. Come, let us make an end of such disagreeable things, sign what I have to sign and join the ladies."

They walked together, side by side, towards the door that opened from the library back into the hall and the parlour beyond. As he took hold of the door handle, Giles had another question.

"Adam," he said. "Will you stay here with us a little longer? You must be as tired as I am—no, more so, for I have remained here and you have covered many miles in the past days. If your patients do not press you too hard to attend to them, why should you not take a little time to recover yourself? Mother will be most happy if you remain, for I believe she wants to ask you to consider the subject of an appropriate marriage."

He grinned, while Adam, like an actor on the stage, clutched his head in a dumb-show of despair.

"Now I have told you that," Giles continued, "I expect you will flee this house as quickly as your chaise can carry you. At least stay another night. I promise to keep her away from the subject for this evening. Instead, you may relate to her and Miss LaSalle the final details of this latest triumph of yours. By the way, that young lady seems most subdued. I would even think she might be trying to avoid you, did I not know this must be purely my imagination. Can you account for her strangeness, all of a sudden?"

"You are a married man, Giles," Adam said. "You of all people must know that the moods and thoughts of women are beyond the understanding of us men."

"So true," his bother replied. "So very true. But will you stay, or must you rush back to Aylsham?"

"I cannot stay, even for one more night," Adam said. "I must go first to Mossterton Hall and then return to my home. Lady Alice Fouchard, Mr Charles Scudamore and his sister will be agog for news. It is almost three days since I was with them last. They have helped me a good deal and deserve to know the outcome."

"Very well, I will let you go. Let us not waste any more of our time together. Amelia will surely be eager to know all is well and this affair ended. A pot of good coffee would also not go amiss."

With that, the two men left the library and closed the door behind them.

A SHORTCUT TO MURDER

Sixteen

Cleaning Up

ADAM WAS IN A SOMBRE MOOD AS WILLIAM TURNED THE CHAISE OFF THE ROADWAY and into the long drive which would take them to Mossterton Hall. All the way from Trundon, the air had been full of the smell of decay and the decline of another year. It had rained in the night too, so now the piles of fallen leaves in the woods and along the roadsides filled the morning air with that characteristic reek of autumn dampness. Ahead lay months of darkness and cold, bitter easterly winds from the German Ocean, driving rain or even snow brought in on westerly gales. He would be snug enough, but the poor must suffer months of misery. Several times last year he'd treated children near crippled by chilblains, their limbs blue and mottled with cold, their faces pinched with hunger. He never charged for what help he could give. Often a few coins accompanied the simple ointments or medicines he gave their mothers. Yet he knew they were little but drops of balm against a vast ocean of pain and hardship.

He felt no sense of triumph at reaching the end of this investigation. Justice was important in a civilised society, but he would never take pleasure in its consequences—the punishment of the guilty was too grim for that. He might have gained a somewhat shamefaced satisfaction at solving the mystery his brother Giles had thrust upon him, but that was all.

What had been the cause of all the misery which had overtaken the Wennard family? The thoughtless arrogance and selfishness so common amongst the rich? The sins of a callous, egotistical father visited on his idle and feckless son? How much was chance, how much cause and effect? He didn't know. He could only hope the other son, conceived through lust but brought up by a loving mother, would prove free of the same taint—a malign inheritance which had infected generations of Wennard squires.

Adam sensed a change in the smells about him. Woodsmoke? Surely there were no charcoal burners in Lady Alice's fine plantations? Woodsmoke it was though and a good deal of it too. Another scent. At first he couldn't make out what it was. Then, as the chaise drew nearer to the cluster of buildings surrounding the great house itself, he was plunged headlong into memories of his childhood. Washing day! That other smell was a combination of lye soap and wet linen and a faint trace of the urine used to help bleach and whiten the cloth.

He had hated washing days—the noisy hustle and bustle, the clouds of steam, the maids running to and fro, bringing more wood to the fires, sorting and piling up the dirty things, wringing out what had been washed and hanging it out to dry on strings, bushes or the branches of any convenient trees.

Still, it wasn't any of these which sent the young Adam running away to hide. It was the two laundresses his mother hired from the local village to supervise the work; two tall, powerful women more muscular than most men. Their vast shaking bosoms, coarse clothes and equally coarse manners appalled the young Adam. One of them, a Mrs Cramshaw, also had a screeching voice enough to frighten anyone. He could see her now. A mountain of a woman with a red and whiskery face framed by tangled, grey hair. Her great arms would be bare, looking more like legs of beef than human limbs. He had nightmares about her for days afterwards.

So it was washing day at Mossterton Hall. As his chaise swung around and drew up outside the grand entrance to the house, he could see plumes of smoke and steam rising up behind the buildings to his left and hear the sharp crackling of the fires. Then he was out and up the steps, to be greeted by a footman and ushered into the relative peace of the entrance hall. Lady Alice must have been watching out for him, for she appeared at once, full of apologies for the noise and confusion behind the house.

"I would generally never countenance receiving visitors on washing day, doctor," she said, "but you know you are welcome here at any time. Besides, my nephew and niece have been driving me insane with their sighs and complaints. If I had made them wait even one more day to hear your latest news, I believe they would have burst. I would rather you had gone home for a few days to rest yourself, but there it is."

"I am a little weary," Adam said, "but you should not blame them. Much has happened, as I am sure you must all have guessed. If I had not been in the midst of it all, I too would have been on tiptoe awaiting developments."

Lady Alice smiled at him. "Is it now over?" she asked. Which was uppermost in her words, pleasure or regret?

"It is," Adam said. "For me, this is the worst time. While I am teasing out the strands of a puzzle I feel as a hound must with the scent of a fox in its nostrils—all eagerness and haste to corner the quarry. Now it is over, all I can feel is sadness for the many who have suffered and a sharp disgust for the actions of the two who caused all that pain."

"You are indeed a sensitive man, doctor," Lady Alice said. "It is ... well ... perhaps one of the most attractive parts of your nature. But are you sure you're ready to face the storm of questions Charles and Ruth will have for you? I can easily find you a place where you can rest for a while and take some refreshment first."

Adam suspected her ladyship was just as eager to know what had been happening as the others. However, she was far more polite and concerned about his welfare than they were. It was easy to forget her ladyship was only a few years older than the Scudamore twins. She so often behaved in a manner befitting a more mature woman. Perhaps that came from having married a man so much older than herself? Now, standing before him, he found her proximity most unsettling. Her hair and complexion retained a youthful bloom undimmed by all she had gone through since her husband's illness turned mortal. Her figure, slim and lithe, and her wonderful beauty had stirred his thoughts—and his loins—in a most embarrassing way several times already. Adam tried to pull himself together. Was it not altogether wrong for him to look upon her ... to yearn to touch her ... in such a way?

He knew he'd been as eager to return to Mossterton Hall that day as he'd ever been when Sir Daniel Fouchard was still alive. What he sought then was fatherly advice—to learn from the wisdom of a man who had long reflected on the ways of the world. What drew him here now was ... well, it was best not to think too much more about that. Sir Daniel had asked him to act as an adviser to his wife, then soon to be a widow, and he had given his solemn promise to do so. Let that be reason enough.

To Adam's great relief, Lady Alice moved a little further from him and turned her head to speak to a waiting footman. "Tell Mr Scudamore and his sister to join us in the study and let coffee be brought there, enough for four."

"At once, m'lady," the footman said and hurried away. The look on his face showed plainly that, despite overtopping the mistress of the house by near a dozen inches, he knew better than to dawdle when she had given him an order.

Then her ladyship turned to Adam again. "I've decided we shall talk in what used to be my husband's study. It will be quiet there, for it lies on the opposite side of the house to the parts where the servants are busy. Follow me, doctor. I'm not sure you've been in this room before. There are so many in this huge place. My husband used to say his study was his haven of peace in a world of haste and turmoil. I have not been in there myself until quite recently. The memories were too painful."

Lady Alice and Adam had hardly seated themselves when Charles and his sister joined them. Miss Charlotte Wennard would not be there. She had gone out riding earlier in the day. Lady Alice suggested it was as much to avoid the sight of the domestic chores as a need for exercise and fresh air. Like many young women amongst the gentry, she recoiled from the all the petty details of running a household. How she imagined she was to be kept supplied with clean sheets and fresh body linens otherwise than through domestic chores, Lady Alice said she could not imagine. Perhaps she thought the fairies brought them in the night.

"The poor young woman is glad enough to be away from Upper Cley Hall," Lady Alice said. "Naturally, she is also concerned what the future may hold for her. Unlike her sister, she is dependent still on her brother. She puts on a brave face, but her anxiety is plain enough."

"At least there should be no doubt she will receive her inheritance from her father in due course," Charles said. "I'm sure what is due to her will have been assigned by name in his Will, so it will not matter whether she is judged legitimate or no. She will probably have a good dowry too. That will go a long way to make most young men overlook any imagined taint of illegitimacy. It is hardly her fault."

"Any man who blamed her for her father's sins would show himself quite unworthy of her affection," Lady Alice declared. There was to be no argument on that point. "Anyway, that is for the future. Miss Charlotte can stay here at Mossterton Hall for as long as she needs. There is ample room and she's proved to be a most amiable guest. Now, doctor. Let us hear what you have to tell us." She turned to her nephew and niece. "Do not interrupt with questions," she told them. "I am sure the poor doctor has had questions enough from others to last him for many weeks. Let him speak without being badgered by your curiosity. There will be time enough to clarify any outstanding matters when he has finished."

The others nodded their heads in submission to this order. Then all three waited for Adam to begin.

This time, he related the complete story of Robert and his father as he understood it. The lessons Sir Jackman had learned from his own father only too well—how to live a life devoted to purely personal pleasures, interspersed with debauchery and seducing respectable women. At least Sir Jackman had some redeeming features. He loved his horses and was plainly a most successful breeder and trainer of the type used for racing. There he exerted himself to great effect. Otherwise, he used people and threw them aside when they ceased to interest him.

His son Robert must have grown up thinking this was the correct way for a son of the household to behave. The difference between him and his father lay mostly in his lack of the capability or willingness to exert himself in any useful pursuits. Instead, he devoted himself to idleness and to wasting his means in gambling.

"It is too often thus with the sons of rich men," Adam said. "They don't realise they're making themselves the perfect victims for those who devote their lives to preying on wealthy, idle young gentlemen like themselves. That sort seek out targets in the clubs and gaming houses of every great city, knowing they will find an ample number who lack the knowledge of the ways of the world to be alert to their trickery. Young fools too much slaves to fashion to find less dangerous forms of excitement.

"Robert was perfect for their needs. I'm sure they let him win at first and win often enough to become convinced of his skill at the tables. Later, little by little, they drained him of every shilling he had. Perhaps his father made good his debts for a while. Many do, recalling their own youthful mistakes. In the end, no more money was provided—or not enough. Either way, Robert began to visit the strongroom in secret to find things he could pawn. His father never checked on the safety of his wife's jewels, while his sisters rarely attended such public events as might encourage them to wear more than a favourite piece or two."

Despite her command for all to stay silent, it was now Lady Alice herself who interrupted with a question.

"Is it sure that he sold all the jewels his sisters inherited from their mother?"

"All or nearly all, I believe. Perhaps he has left a few pieces—the ones they wore most often—to conceal what he had done. My brother said he'd been told by the executors the jewels could not be found. Whether that meant all of them or a majority of pieces they did not make clear."

"Such wickedness!" Lady Alice's voice was sharp.

"Indeed. I imagine at the start he told himself he was just borrowing them to pawn until he could win back the money he had lost. Of course, any sensible person would know that would never happen. The typical way the rogues who prey on such young men work is to let them win fewer and fewer times until they exhaust all their money. If they show any signs of turning away, one or two extra wins will usually hook them again. Once their ready cash is exhausted, other predators move in. These offer them loans to tide them over until their luck changes. Naturally, such loans carry huge rates of interest. That was almost certainly what happened to Robert. In time, he found himself unable to pay back the loans—or even the outstanding interest. Only then did he discover how cruel and ruthless his former friends could be."

They sat in silence for a few moments, their minds busy with thoughts of how young Robert Wennard would have reacted when he discovered his true position. It was plain either his father had refused further help or he had been too frightened to ask him. Then Sir Jackman's death on the hunting field seemed to offer the lifeline Robert needed so badly.

Miss Ruth Scudamore was next to speak.

"So he decided his father had to be killed so he could inherit the estate and pay off his debts? That's monstrous!"

Adam noticed her hands were gripping the folds of her petticoat so tightly they must surely mark the fabric. He hastened to calm her.

"No, Miss Scudamore. That was not quite the way of it. Sir Jackman Wennard's death was unintended, though I agree it came at what appeared at first to be a most opportune time. The certainty a day would come—and now come soon—when Robert would be master of his father's lands and money might well persuade his creditors to wait a little longer. However, the initial plan was to stage a robbery, not commit murder. Robert never intended to kill his father."

Adam explained Robert's plan to lay hold of the money his father had received for the sale of the two racehorses. How the gamekeepers had been bribed to set the trap and act the part of highway robbers. How it all began to go wrong, almost from the start.

"Sir Jackman Wennard didn't come home until the morning. He had spent too long drinking with this Mr Croome. By the time he realised he should have set out long before, it was too dark. Besides, I doubt he could have stayed on the back of his horse. Next morning, he didn't use his expected route. Instead, he went to the inn to check all was prepared for the hunt. He had the money, but now there was nothing to prevent him reaching his home safe and sound and lodging it in the strongbox none could open save himself.

That was but the start of Robert's woes. First, the two rogues he had set to rob his father had become bored, then drunk and finally fallen deeply asleep. When they awoke, it was light and their first thought was to rush to Upper Cley Hall to explain how none of what had happened was their fault. By failing to remove the snare before they left, they brought about Sir Jackman's death barely an hour or so later. No one, son or supposed robbers, had intended to do Sir Jackman real harm; now they had killed him. When Robert Wennard was founded crouched over his father's body telling all around him it was an accident, he was speaking the plain truth. Of course, he could give no reason for his certainty without explaining his failed plot."

Adam rose from his chair and walked over to stand by the hearth, supporting himself by resting one arm on the mantelshelf. This was taking longer than he thought. After all the riding and driving of the past few weeks, he found sitting still in a chair was making him uncomfortably stiff. He turned back to face his audience.

"After that," Adam said, "things went from bad to worse. There had to be an examination of the body by a skilled medical man for the inquest. It revealed Sir Jackman Wennard's death was no simple accident. The inquest jury brought in a verdict of murder. That caused delays in settling the estate. My brother Giles, as magistrate, set up an investigation in the hope of finding the murderer. Questions were asked on all sides. Any sense of urgency in applying for probate slipped away. As a result, Robert's creditors must have become more and more impatient. I expect some demanded partial payment right away as proof of his promise to meet his debts in full as soon as he could. That's when the fool turned to small-scale highway robbery. Not very high returns, of course, but little risk either. He would probably have continued in that activity until he finally obtained his inheritance—as he must—but fate had one final blow in store. His father's first wife appeared out of the blue, claiming to have born Sir Jackman Wennard an elder, legitimate son and threatening to take away all chance of future wealth. If what she said were proved true, Sir Jackman's known marriage was bigamous and his children from it bastards."

"Not just a wife but the only legitimate male heir, if all could be proved," Charles Scudamore said. He was very much the learned attorney now. "Even if Robert contested her claims, victory was far from certain. In fact, I judge Robert would have had a poor chance of winning any action. With his father dead—and assuming the proofs of marriage the woman brought with her were admitted into evidence—the best he could have done was try to persuade the court the marriage was a sham she had engineered to trap a wealthy man; that she, the clergyman and all involved besides Jackman Wennard were playing a part. Maybe that the clergyman was not one after all, but a confederate in the deception and that the proofs were forgeries. None of it would be easy to establish, especially after such a lengthy period had passed.

"He might also seek to contest the paternity of her child. Perhaps he could produce witnesses to say they knew her to have been a woman of loose morals at the time her son was conceived; that she had slept with many men and could not possibly be sure which had fathered a child on her. Such a line might just convince a jury her son could not be proved to be Sir Jackman Wennard's child. Even so, it wouldn't have helped if the claim that the second marriage was bigamous was upheld. If Robert was declared illegitimate, the inheritance and title must still go to the next legitimate male heir—probably a cousin or even someone more distant."

"Indeed," Adam said. "Once the claim by Mrs Sarah Wennard became known, Robert's creditors will have renewed their pressure in full force. It made him so desperate he first tried to obtain a large ransom from the executors by disappearing and pretending he'd been kidnapped. I ruined that plan by advising my brother to tell the executors not to pay. By this time, I was sure in my own mind what was going on. I wanted to make him yet more reckless in seeking a large amount of money. I couldn't set a trap of my own, since I didn't know how or where he would next make an attempt. The best I could do was warn everyone about to be on their guard."

"Will Robert Wennard hang?" Miss Scudamore asked Adam.

"If he does not die from his injuries, I imagine he will be sent to the assizes or the quarter sessions for trial. Then it will be up to the judge and jury to decree his fate. I doubt the evidence against him would support a charge of deliberate murder. Intent to murder perhaps? What do you think, Scudamore?"

"It's of little consequence," Charles said. "He's stolen more than enough as a highway robber to place a noose around his neck. Now nothing is likely to stand in the way of this elder son claiming his inheritance. I imagine he can also assume the baronetcy, despite being a dissenter. A baronet is still a commoner, not a peer of the realm. The honour does not come with a seat in the House of Lords or any other public office, which would be denied to a dissenter under the Test and Corporation Acts. I'm no constitutional lawyer, but I cannot see why the man shouldn't assume the title if he wishes. He might not want it, of course, though it would not prevent him continuing to work as an engineer. The wealth from the estate may do that by rendering the need to pursue a profession superfluous."

Miss Scudamore was still outraged at the way Robert Wennard had stolen from his sisters. "Poor Caroline! Poor Charlotte! Caroline at least has a husband. I wouldn't be surprised if the way her father and brother have treated her doesn't convince Charlotte to avoid men altogether in future. She's lost even the few tangible memorials she had of her beloved mother."

"I would not be so certain of that, niece." Lady Alice had said nothing for some time, but her expression and upright posture in the chair had shown how closely she was attending to Adam's words. "Don't allow your romantic notions to run away with you. Miss Charlotte is what—

eighteen or nineteen years of age? She has plenty of time to get over her sorrow and disgust at her brother's actions. Not all men are like her father—or her brother. I married one who was the soul of kindness and consideration. I know another much the same."

Fortunately for Adam's peace of mind, Charles butted in again. "At least she will suffer no pressure from father or brother to marry someone unsuitable, just to further their own interests. Perhaps their half-brother will come to care for these two ladies. He may even continue to make some provision for Miss Charlotte until she does marry. To my mind, that would be the honourable course. For the rest, one outcome at least must give all of us considerable satisfaction. Those unscrupulous men who tempted Robert Wennard to financial ruin will never see a farthing of what they claim he owes them. It is certain he has nothing. If he's declared illegitimate, as I think is the likely outcome, they'll have no claim against the estate of the late Sir Jackman Wennard either. Robert Wennard will likely end his days at the hands of the common hangman—his proven crimes are more than enough to secure that outcome—and they will lose all the money owed them."

After that, there was little more to say. With great reluctance, Adam declined yet another invitation to stay for dinner. Concern for his much-neglected household and medical practice weighed on him heavily. It was high time to take his leave and turn his mind back to the demands of his life away from puzzles and mysteries.

Lady Alice therefore took her leave of him, once more holding his hand in her own just a moment longer than might be entirely necessary. "I do hope the ending of this investigation does not mean your visits to Mossterton Hall will become sparse again, doctor. I assure you, you are always welcome—most welcome. Please come whenever you can. My nephew and niece are staying here a little longer and I am sure they too will be pleased to see you again."

Adam assured her he would visit her house more often in the future. "Your ladyship," he said, surprising himself greatly by his own words, "I confess I find this house—and even more its mistress—such a source of comfort and pleasure as must draw me back as often as is possible." What in heaven's name had come over him? He had not intended to say any such thing, but there it was. It could not be taken back.

Charles Scudamore had also risen to stand beside him and offer to see him to the door. As the two of them walked across the magnificent hall, Charles had his own news to share.

"My dear doctor, I feel certain we will see a good deal more of one another in the future. I am thinking seriously of setting up my own practice in Norfolk. London holds few attractions for me. It is too noisy, too full of greedy men getting and spending—and far too full of aspiring lawyers of far greater ability and ambition than myself. I've now written to my father on the matter and will begin right away to seek out a suitable place to live and work. I may even become one of your neighbours. I think Ruth will probably stay in Norfolk as well to look after my house— at least until she finds some man fool enough to marry her. In these past few weeks, my sister has become so entirely devoted to Lady Alice I do not think she could bear to be separated from her."

"Will your father assent to this?" Adam asked.

"If Lady Alice chooses to support our wishes, he will," Charles replied with a broad smile. "My father would never dare try to thwart her. It would, I assure you, be more than his life is worth to cross his little sister."

Charles and his sister maybe as neighbours. More frequent visits to Mossterton Hall. It was as if another family had been added to Adam's own. What that might bring about, he could not tell, but it must surely change his future in some ways. Then there was Sophia LaSalle to wonder about and her astonishing display of concern for his welfare. His visits to

London too. Why was it fate would never allow him to look ahead with any certainty about what was to come?

As he settled into his chaise, Adam glanced once more at the house and found Lady Alice watching him from a window to the left of the doorway, her face expressionless. Deny it as much as he could, was she not the greatest source of his uncertainty? What did he feel for her? What, if anything, did she feel for him? He could not bear it if he found she valued him only because of what he had done for her husband. Better to hold back than mistake gratitude for affection. But if her regard should be genuine ...?

As he was driven away, Adam wondered why he had to be cursed with a conscience and emotions that were so easily stirred. Men like Sir Jackman Wennard combined desire for women's bodies with complete indifference to their feelings or welfare. He would never be able to be like them, of course, nor would he want to be. Only ... well, it would be nice to more closely resemble his friend Lassimer. The apothecary seemed to be able to indulge his desires freely without his heart getting in the way— and without his ladies being hurt or upset either. Perhaps he would be willing to share his secrets?

Perhaps he would ask him.

A SHORTCUT TO MURDER

Manufactured by Amazon.ca
Bolton, ON